THE CARY REDMOND SERIES

The Trouble with Black Cats and Demons
The Trouble with Ghouls and Serial Killers
The Trouble with Leopard Queens and Shifter Wars
The Trouble with Baby Gods and Vampires
The Trouble with Magic and Faery Curses
The Trouble with Wizards and Old Enemies
The Trouble with Death and Demon Gods
The Trouble with Shifters and Fae Courts

THE TROUBLE WITH SHIFTERS AND FAE COURTS

CARY REDMOND, BOOK 8

KAT SIMONS

THE TROUBLE WITH
SHIFTERS AND FAE COURTS

First, and always, to my family. You've all been so supportive. I just can't say enough how much I appreciate you. All of you.

And also, to the lovely people who backed this book at Kickstarter! Thank you, everyone, for making my very first Kickstarter so much fun.

1

---

ary's front doorbell rang as she contemplated how best to carry her toiletries because the bag she'd been using going to and from her sister's place in New York was forty-three hundred years old and the silver lining inside it was starting to rip. She wasn't sure if she should take the time to return to the drug store for yet another set of "must have" travel items, or if she should just use a Ziplock bag.

But since this trip involved meeting her mate's *grandmother*, she wasn't sure she wanted to show up with a baggie holding her toothbrush and deodorant.

The struggle was real.

The doorbell was also real. But much more unexpected. And since there wasn't a constant buzz, it couldn't be her former-mentor-now-just-friend-but-apparently-still-a-little-bit-of-a-mentor, Jaxer.

She glanced at her phone where it rested on her bathroom countertop next to the sink. No texts informing her of impending visits. Deacon was at work finalizing things with his sister before taking the month off, and he wasn't due for another hour. Marianne was working. Angie had disappeared with her secret, but now not-so-secret, boyfriend for the last three weeks and hadn't mentioned when she might be back—Cary could hardly blame her but she was a little desperate for the full story to *that* relationship. And Lucy was supposed to be teaching all day today.

Cary didn't get mysterious visitors to her house or surprise drop-ins from people she didn't know. The glamour on her house kept anyone who wasn't invited to her home from finding her home.

She was considering giving permanent permission to her pizza delivery guy because he was here so often, and she was constantly having to give permission for him to find the place. But since she only knew his first name and half his family history, and since he wasn't *always* the delivery guy for her pizza, she'd continued to give and take away permission.

Other than her family, her best friends, her mate, and her mentor—and of course her Faery bosses who'd placed the glamour—she hadn't given anyone permission to find her house today.

Oh, wait, Eriana had permission, too, she realized. But since the Fae healer was also (secretly!) in training to become a Protector mentor, Cary figured she was safe enough.

Even Deacon's family had to give her warning before showing up. And *that* was an issue she had purposefully not thought about too deeply. (Something something, Deacon's mother, the current queen of the leopard shifters, showing up unexpectedly would be bad, something something.)

So it wasn't likely one of the leopards. She could probably afford to give Nicky and Jillian permission to find her home whenever they wanted. And maybe Lucas. Lucas had gone into battle with her and had her back a couple of times now. Including with that whole demon god thing three weeks ago. So…yeah, Cary could trust him. And Nicky and Jillian as well. But…

Well, she was having some trouble (still) adjusting to the fact that one day Deacon would be the king of the leopards. And because she was his mate, that put her, on some level, as a sort of defacto, kind of, maybe like a queen to the leopards. (And yes, she noticed all the prevaricating in that thought because obviously she was *still adjusting*.) Since she wasn't a shifter of any kind, that idea was a little too much for her to take. Which meant giving any of the leopards permanent permission to find her house through the protective glamour felt…like a commitment she wasn't *quite* ready to make yet.

The reminder that she wasn't a shifter, and that was part of the reason she and Deacon were off to Scotland to see his grandmother, followed her to the front door.

Her three dogs, however, did not.

She glanced at them on the way through the living room and grinned. All three were asleep under the bay window that looked out over her small backyard. Pickles, the foo lion turned basset hound, was sprawled half-on, half-off her dog bed, her heavy jowls and long ears flattened on either side of her front paws. Cary's golden Labrador who was also a demon dog (not a hellhound. He didn't like being called a hellhound), Buck, was curled into a fuzzy ball that fit snuggly in his large dog bed.

And Fred, the only mundane dog among them, a terrier-collie cross with the energy of a sugared-up toddler, was sprawled across his bed, on his back, with his hind legs tapping against Buck and his head bouncing against Pickle's side. Fred was obviously deep in a chasing dream, and since Fred was all about the chase, Cary hoped from the bottom of her heart that he never caught whatever it was he was chasing. That would be the best dream for Fred.

None of the dogs popped up to join her at the door. Which was a pretty good indication whoever was on the other side was welcomed and not dangerous. But honestly, someone dangerous couldn't actually *find* her house. That's what the glamour was all about. That was the *reason* for it. And even after she'd passed her Seventh Year test year—early, because of the whole demon god thing—she still kept the glamour because she was still a Protector. A full one now with, apparently, no restrictions on her powers. She could *control* her Protector shield now.

That was new and, so far, untested in a real-life situation because her bosses had agreed to give her some time off. Even though she was newly made a full Protector and technically still should be working. Again, because of the whole demon god thing.

That had been a very very big thing.

And honestly, she still wasn't entirely sure what she'd done to herself in all that. But that was another issue she had chosen not to think about too closely yet because she had to pack for Scotland.

She swung the door open and blinked a few times, more than a little surprised to see her maybe-former-but-still-around-a-lot mentor.

"Jaxer?" She glanced at the doorbell. "You didn't do that irritating thing where you keep your finger on the doorbell. Who's dead?" She was absolutely serious. She couldn't remember Jaxer *ever* not doing that irritating thing where he held the doorbell until she answered the door. There had to be something really wrong.

"No one has died," he said, smiling and shaking his head. "So suspicious. I thought the time off was supposed to relax all that paranoia."

"Right. Like that's going to happen in a mere three weeks." She stepped backward and let him into the house.

He was a ridiculously handsome faery, a member of the High Fae whose most powerful magic was glamour. Which meant he could make anyone see what they wanted to see and experience what he wanted them to experience. Except for little kids, who tended to see through Fae glamour. But he just avoided them.

Turned out the blond-haired, green-blue eyed, sharp-featured gorgeousness that he showed most of the world was actually him tamping down on his real looks, which were so blindingly stunning she still hadn't fully recovered from seeing him that way that one time in Faery. He'd been unreal, a thing of myth and legend in those moments. She preferred him this way. He wasn't *ordinary* looking like this. He was too vain to look ordinary—unlike Eriana who'd perfected looking like an ordinary human in this realm—but like this, he was the kind of gorgeous you might actually encounter in the real world.

There was something soothing and comforting about that.

"So what's wrong that you've changed up the way you ring my doorbell?" she asked.

"That could sound dirty if I were in the right frame of mind," he said, still smiling. But there was tension around his eyes and mouth. The fact that he was letting her see those signs of strain was telling.

"Don't let Deacon hear you say that."

"Deacon and I have a truce now. He won't try to rip my throat out."

She'd noticed the truce, though this was the first time either of them had said anything about it out loud. Still, she wasn't sure Deacon wouldn't try to rip Jaxer's throat out for the flirty comment. Mostly because Deacon's control was...shaky after the demon god thing.

"One day, I'd like one of you to explain this truce to me."

She had a feeling it had to do with Jaxer's ex reentering the picture. Eriana and Jaxer's relationship had gone nova two hundred years ago, but there was still obviously a lot of feeling there between them. And since he was (supposedly secretly) training Eriana to be a mentor for future Protectors, they were spending a lot of time together. Jaxer had been tight-lipped about it all. But that didn't stop Cary from teasing him about it. Eriana was a sensitive spot for him, and Cary got the feeling those two-hundred-year-old feelings had never gone away.

Which was why she suspected Jaxer and Deacon had this truce thing worked out. Jaxer's feeling for Cary weren't so... inconveniently getting in the way anymore.

This made Cary happier, too. She loved Jaxer. Just not in the way he had apparently fallen for her. She'd been pretty devastated to learn this fact since she couldn't return his feelings. They'd weathered that storm, though. And seemed to be back to the usual friendship. Jaxer's feelings still lingered out there as a thing they hadn't settled in words, but it *felt* settled in the rhythms of their interactions now.

She led him to the kitchen and put on some coffee even though he wouldn't drink it. She had a feeling she'd need the shot of caffeine for whatever he was here to discuss. And since she'd already finished her half pot from this morning, a second pot of coffee it was. The rich aroma or percolating deliciousness didn't do anything to calm the nagging worry that had settled into her gut, though. An unfortunately familiar sensation since she'd become a Protector seven years ago.

"Okay," she said, once she had the coffee machine on. "Spill. What's going on? You're smiling, but you're also letting me see your tension. What's the problem?"

"I'm not sure it's *technically* a problem. But...we need to talk about this trip to Scotland."

"For good reasons or bad reasons?"

"Honestly...a little of both. But mostly...bad reasons."

Great. Just what she needed. More trouble.

Oh boy.

2

Cary sighed and pulled down a clean mug from the cabinet as the smell of fresh coffee filled her kitchen and the existential dread of the pending conversation with Jaxer settled into her stomach.

"I'm gonna need coffee before we start."

"Probably." He leaned against the counter and folded his arms across his chest.

She paused mid-way to the coffee pot and blinked at him. Realizing for the first time that he wasn't in his usual linen trousers and silk shirt. In fact, he was wearing…

"Are those jeans? Why the hell are you wearing jeans? And… an ordinary t-shirt?" It was even long-sleeved. Now, to be fair, it did show off his impressive physique still, but these were not *Jaxer* clothes. These were… Well, for him, these were a costume. "What's going on? Why are you dressed like that?"

He glanced down, scowling a bit. "I'm trying something new."

"Why?"

To her amazement and delight, his cheeks actually turned pink.

A blush? Jaxer blushed!? If he was just doing something new, or even doing this for her for some weird Jaxer reason, he wouldn't have blushed. But he did. Which meant this had to do with his ex. Cary would bet her next cup of coffee on it.

She rolled her lips into her mouth to keep from giggling like a child but, yeah, no, she was going to giggle soon. "You're blushing."

"I am not." His complexion returned instantly to its normal pale color but she knew that was his glamour. He'd been caught off guard and forgot to hide the blush earlier. That was even more telling.

"Does Eriana like this look?" she asked casually, her attention on the coffee pot as she poured.

"Cary…" There was warning in his tone.

She blinked innocently at him. "You don't want to talk about your fashion choices, that's fine by me. What's up with my trip to Scotland that you feel the need to give me stomach pains about it?"

To be fair, she was already pretty nervous about this trip, even as she was extremely excited. She was excited for the Scotland part. And getting there by the regular airplane-passport control method rather than the ways she'd gotten to Ireland and London before—by travelling through Faery (did *not* recommend!) and once by dragon-back, which was a more fun but no less terrifying way to travel.

She was much more nervous about meeting Deacon's grandmother, and even more nervous about the *reasons* he felt the need to go now.

"I'm not trying to give you stomach pains," Jaxer said, his voice gentling as he took a deep breath. "Let's sit down and talk."

"That isn't helping my stomach pains."

She added milk and sweetener to her coffee because now

wasn't the time for black coffee eating at her gut, and proceeded Jaxer back into the living room, to her oversized couch facing the fireplace and her small TV. Buck raised his head from his nap finally, giving Jaxer a once over. Then he tucked his nose back into the curve of his body and went back to sleep.

At one point, Buck and Jaxer had had a *thing* of some kind. A lot of staring and, she was certain, some subsonic growling going on that she couldn't hear. Or something. But then, whatever had started Buck's issues with Jaxer had gone away after they'd gotten back from Faery, and Buck had returned to being fine with Cary's mentor ever since. The whole situation had been super weird. And she'd never really gotten a good explanation for it.

Now that her Seventh Year test period was over and the threat of demon gods and death and Oliver Holland were—she hoped—gone, she kind of wanted to dig into that situation and figure out what had happened. Jaxer never told her, and Buck obviously couldn't, but maybe she could nag Jaxer for the story. Or maybe she'd invite Jonathon over and see if he could get the answers from Buck. Jon was a teenager she'd saved from Oliver Holland back at the start of her test year. He could talk to animals, among other things, and Cary's dog pack liked him. Maybe he could ask Buck what the Jaxer thing had been about.

She blinked back to her current predicament. The stuff between Jaxer and Buck would have to wait until after Scotland.

"Spill," she said again, turning on the couch a little to face Jaxer, cradling her mug between her hands. Her first sip filled her with a satisfying warmth, and the hit of caffeine did good things for her brain.

"So… You know how you can officially control your Protector magic now? You can raise or lower the shield whenever you want."

"I'm delighted with that turn of events, by the way."

"I'm delighted for you," he said, and his smile was proud and indulgent, and she was embarrassed that it made her want to preen. Whatever else she and Jaxer were to each other, he was her mentor first and foremost in this whole Protector gig, and when he was proud of her, it made her feel good.

Not that she'd admit that to him, of course.

"The problem is," he said, "we should be taking some time to train that before turning you loose in the real world. You're used to the shield just coming up. It'll take some concentration to raise and lower it now."

"Yeah. I've been a little worried about that. I mean, we could practice now. But I got the impression this wasn't about that."

"It's a part of the whole. You'll be going into Scotland, which is entirely too close to the English and the Irish Fae courts, and while Danu seems to be okay with you, Tatiana is…maybe a little less okay with you. Reluctantly accepts you helped save Faery and maybe she shouldn't kill you or seduce you, but… Well, she's not a predictable queen."

She was a terrifying Fae queen was what she was. So was Danu. But Cary didn't seem to be on Irish queen's shit list the way she was on Tatiana's even though, as Jaxer had pointed out, Cary had quite literally saved Faery from destruction thank you very much. And died doing it, no less! Not for long. But still. *Died.*

Which had, as it happened, come in handy later with the whole demon god thing, but that wasn't the point.

The point was that Tatiana had no reason to resent or be upset with Cary. Even if Jaxer had apparently broken some law or other bringing her into Faery cause at the time Protectors weren't welcome or something. And all the magic she'd pulled in and released into Faery had stopped the rot that was infiltrating the realm. Cary had saved Faery in multiple ways.

The fact that there wouldn't be much of a buffer between her and Tatiana hadn't really occurred to Cary before this moment. Since the Faery incident, Tatiana had only come here that one time and then left Cary alone. She'd seen Danu once more, but that was because Rory the dragon had insisted Cary go to Ireland and help Rory's hero, Joan, to save some kids from the newest—now deceased—goblin king. Which… Well, that's what Cary did. Danu hadn't incinerated her for showing up uninvited, so Cary was pretty sure she and the Irish Fae queen were on a reasonably cordial footing.

Still, being on that side of the world, so close to the two queens that may or may not dislike her probably should have occurred to her before this moment.

And then there was the Scottish Fae court.

She knew a very minimal amount about the Scottish court. It was one of many Fae courts, and she'd never had to deal with them, and Jaxer wasn't linked to them in any way—he was linked to both the Irish and English courts in complicated ways that had to do with his parents—so she hadn't taken the time to learn much about it. Just that it existed, and there were two factions coexisting in the territory. The Seelie court and Unseelie court, ruled by two different queens. That was the extent of her knowledge. To be fair, though, she'd been pretty occupied learning…well, everything else for the last seven years. Some things fell through the cracks.

Lots of knowledge fell through the cracks.

That thought led her to thinking about her bosses, Wisat and Liruk, because Liruk was always the most critical of Cary's inability to know everything about everything instantly. But Cary was trying to cultivate a more charitable attitude toward Liruk these days, after the demon god thing, so she resisted her habitual grumpy thoughts about her boss's judgment. Barely.

"I'll be in Scotland," Cary pointed out, getting back to the issue of Tatiana's potential wrath. "Another court's territory. She won't bother me up there, right?"

"She's only part of the problem. You just mentioned the other. The Scottish court. They're… Well, if it's possible, they're even less open to newcomers than the English court. They've isolated more in recent years. Pulling out of the human realm even more than the other courts. And, honestly, no one's heard much from them in years. The last few decades in particular have been really quiet. I've never even been to the Scottish court, Seelie or Unseelie. And there was a time when I took great pleasure in sneaking into different Fae courts to test my glamour."

Cary didn't doubt that for a minute. "We're just going to visit Deacon's grandmother. We don't have to get involved with the Scottish Fae even a little bit, right?"

"I suspect you won't be able to avoid it. *Because* of Deacon's grandmother."

"What don't I know?"

"Not much more than me. I've only just learned who his grandmother is in relation to the Fae world."

That there was a relationship of some kind between a leopard shifter and the Fae world at all was startling. But since Belle used magic, and Cary and Deacon were taking this trip so Belle could teach him how to use and control *his* magic—which he'd spent all of his soon-to-be fifty-five years avoiding and suppressing—Cary really should have suspected there was more to the story than she knew.

Actually, she did realize there was more to all this than she knew. She just hadn't thought about it too much, assuming Deacon would reveal all on the way, or she'd discover everything when she got there. Deacon was so edgy at the moment she hadn't wanted to push him by digging into his family stuff before he was ready.

But whatever Belle's relationship to Faery was, it was important enough, Jaxer had come over to discuss it with her.

"I'd like to let Deacon tell you everything," Jaxer said. "It's not my place to tell you his family secrets. But you will likely have interactions with the Scottish court. And that will not go unnoticed by the other two queens."

"Well shit."

"Exactly. And I'd say just stay out of trouble, but…" His mouth quirked at one corner and then he chuckled and shook his head. "Yeah, I can't see that happening."

She wanted to scowl. But he was right. Somehow, no matter what, Trouble always found her. She must have done something really rude in a former life.

"So I'll need to be ready to navigate more Fae politics while I'm there," she said. "Great. Love that. Best part of the trip already." Her deadpan tone got another smile from Jaxer.

"With luck, the queens will all pass messages about your presence and the reason your there, and there won't be any need for an audience with either Danu or Tatiana. But I thought you'd better be prewarned that the possibility was out there."

She tapped a finger against her coffee mug, half empty now and starting to cool. "Should I… Should I not go? I mean, I want to. And I got the impression Deacon sort of needs me to. He said he'd handle the training better if I'm there. But maybe that's just the mate thing and him still occasionally having a hard time being away from me. Scotland is a long way and all. But… But if I'm going to complicate things being there, maybe it's better if I don't go."

Jaxer made a face, his mouth pursed as he let out a sigh and stared at the soft tan couch cushion between them. When he met her gaze again, he looked very serious.

"Six months ago, I would have encouraged you to stay here.

To let him do this on his own. For a lot of reasons. Not least because, as you know, I wanted him out of your life."

She opened her mouth to say something but he held up a hand.

"We all know things changed after Faery," he said. "A lot of things. And I suppose I should finally tell you, out loud, that… Well, I still love you." Again, he held up a hand when she opened her mouth. "But…"

He sighed. Shook his head. "Cary, he was going with you. When you died. When we thought you were gone. He was going with you. He would have followed you without any hesitation at all. And I have never seen him that way before. I've known Deacon for years. Longer than either of us will admit out loud. I have never seen him so…" Jaxer let out a huff. "He loves you so much. So much. After watching that, watching him on the verge of willing himself to death, to stay with you, I knew that was not something I could ever get between." He stumbled a little over the last few words, as if he wasn't sure how to express what he was trying to say.

Cary for her part was so stunned, she kept her mouth shut and let Jaxer finish.

"So while I still love you," he went on, "I've accepted that what you and Deacon have is…is it. Is forever. Is that sort of all consuming love the old bards used to write songs about. I wouldn't dare get in the way of that."

Cary swallowed, her throat thick with emotions she wasn't even sure how to name. A surprising amount of gratitude, because she wasn't sure they'd ever get to this point, where she and Jaxer could remain friends and not have his feelings hanging between them.

"I'm sorry," she murmured, "that things have happened in a way that hurt you. But I'm…glad this is where we ended up."

Was she about to cry? Shit. No. She didn't want to cry. She

had a trip to pack for and potential confrontations with Fae queens to worry about. And Deacon's grandmother to face!

Still. She set her mug on the coffee table, closed the space between her and Jaxer, and wrapped him up in a hug. One he returned, his arms tight around her, his face against her shoulder.

"Does this mean we get to stay friends?" she said, her voice watery and a little choked.

"We get to stay friends," he said.

"Oh good. I'd have missed your pain in my ass."

His laughter made her smile.

She sniffled a little as she sat back, patting his shoulders as if she could smooth away some of the moisture that had dripped onto his t-shirt. She still couldn't get over Jaxer in a t-shirt.

"Okay." She nodded. "Okay. So… Back to my questions. Should I go with Deacon to Scotland or not?"

"You should go. He's going to need you."

The words had barely sunk in when her front doorbell rang again.

She didn't even have to wonder who it was this time.

She could always feel when Deacon was close.

3

$\mathcal{C}$ary swung the door open, smiling in greeting, only to find her face between two big, slightly rough palms as Deacon's scent surrounded her. Still feeling a lot of ways after Jaxer's revelation, she stared up at Deacon, her mate, the love of her life, without being able to say anything. She just felt that melting place in her center and everything inside her was all floaty and soft.

"Why are you crying?" he murmured. "What's wrong?" He glanced past her and scowled. "What did you say to her?"

Cary grinned and gripped his wrists, leaning into him. "These are happy tears. Don't worry. Nothing bad. Come on in. We're discussing the upcoming trip."

Deacon stared down at her for a heartbeat, the furrow between his dark brows deep. He was so shockingly handsome she sometimes couldn't quite believe he was real. Dark, nearly black hair he insisted on wearing loose. Tan skin, golden eyes rimmed by dark lashes. A mouth she thought about way too much. The unfair advantage of a Greek god's body. Even after nearly a year, she still sometimes couldn't believe he was hers.

And after what Jaxer had just told her, that feeling mixed with a lot of awe. And love. Lots and lots of love.

Who'd have thought this is where they'd be from where they started.

She rose onto her toes to give him a brief kiss, then pulled him inside. The October air was chilly this week, a nice change from a hotter-than-normal summer. But she didn't have Deacon's leopard shifter metabolism so she felt that cold even if he didn't.

"You want some milk?" she asked him after giving him another hug because of all the sentimental floaty mushy feelings inside her.

"That'd be nice." He was still scowling, glancing between her and Jaxer. But the expression was more confused than angry so she figured she could leave them alone for a few minutes. "I'll be right back." She grabbed her mug and returned to the kitchen for another cup and a glass of milk for Deacon.

The fact that her fully grown adult cat shifter mate drank milk never cease to amuse her.

By the time she came back out again, Jaxer had moved to one of the stuffed chairs that bracketed the coffee table, letting Deacon take his place on the couch. A few months ago, Jaxer wouldn't have done that. He'd have sprawled out on the couch, claiming the space, and daring Deacon to say anything about it.

Things had most definitely changed.

"Do I get to know why you were crying now?" Deacon asked as Cary handed him his glass and sat on the couch next to him, scooching close so she was tucked up against his side.

"We were talking about the trip to Scotland," she said, because that had been how all this started. "About the fact that me being there might cause some issues with the Irish and English Faery courts. Especially with Tatiana since Danu seems to tolerate me in her scary queenly way."

Deacon's gaze jumped to Jaxer, then back to Cary. "Why would we need to worry about Faery courts?"

"Because of the Scottish court and whatever that has to do with your grandmother." She said that casually, like of course he understood so she was just making clear she knew there'd be a thing too.

Except, he continued to look at her like he was baffled. "Why would we have any interaction with the Scottish court? We're going to see my grandmother about my shifter magic. My mother's been trying to get me to her for years to train it. I think she's the only one who can help so I don't—" He cut himself off sharply, but he didn't look away from her.

They both knew what had happened while they'd been facing down a demon god and his unkillable son who just happened to desperately want to kill Cary. After she helped the demon son survive his god father, of course.

Deacon was the first born of two firstborn parents who were also the firstborn of firstborn parents. A pattern that went back seven generations, making Deacon the seventh firstborn of firstborns. Or something. Anyway, there were a lot of sevens involved, which was one of those irritatingly troublesome power numbers, and that meant that while his mother had magic and was extremely powerful, Deacon had magic and was even more powerful. He was like rarely-happens-but-when-it-does-hold-on-to-your-butts-shits-getting-dangerous powerful.

The magic was all shifter magic. Except most shifters didn't have magic. The changing shape thing was biology. A shifter with magical powers was uncommon. A shifter with Deacon's level of power was apparently so unusual, not even his own mother felt comfortable training him.

Which, up till recently, hadn't been an issue because he had spent his entire life suppressing that magic, never using it, and only rarely calling on any of the skills bestowed on him by this whole seventh firstborn of firstborns thing. Some of those skills were super spooky and allowed him to control other leopards so fully, he could take away all their free will and even force them to kill themselves. If he didn't just kill them outright.

Deacon did not like the power he wielded, liked the magic even less, and mostly just used an excessive amount of control whenever he was around other leopards to keep all those dangerous abilities in check. He went so emotionless sometimes around other shifters, she thought of that as his ice man place. She did not like it when he went ice man on her, but she understood it now, accepting the necessity for it when other leopard shifters were around.

But after more than fifty years of refusing to do anything with his magic, he'd finally decided he had to figure out how to control it better, how to deal with it by some other way than just suppressing it under his iron will.

Cary glanced at Jaxer, then back at Deacon. "I…uh. I got the impression your grandmother had…ties to the Fae. In some way. That would force an interaction with the Scottish court?" Her voice trailed off at the end when she realized Deacon still didn't entirely know what she was talking about.

She looked at Jaxer again. "What the hell?"

Jaxer frowned at Deacon. "You don't…know?"

"Know what? What the hell are two talking about?"

"Your grandmother," Cary said slowly, "and her ties to Faery and the Scottish court."

"My grandmother has some inherent magic. That's why she can train me. The same way my mother and I have magic. It has nothing to do with Faery or Fae magic or the Scottish court. Why would it?"

"I don't…" She looked at Jaxer again. "Maybe you're wrong? You said you just learned about the connection. Maybe there isn't really one?" Because if there was, why wouldn't Deacon know about it? Why would his father—his grandmother Belle's son— have kept that from him? Especially with Deacon going all the way to Scotland to train with Belle.

Shouldn't *someone* have mentioned the whole Faery thing?

Jaxer's frown creased his brow but his attention was on Deacon. "I didn't realize they hadn't told you. I don't know much either, only what Eriana has told me. But there is a link between your grandmother and the Scottish court. And I doubt you'll be able to stay there the full month without some curious Fae coming out to meet Cary."

The Fae had come out to help during the demon god thing, and they'd apparently done it for Cary because she'd saved Faery. She had a really complicated relationship with the Fae. And it wasn't actually outside the realms of possibility that some non-queen Fae might come looking to meet her. That was a really weird possibility that she hadn't even considered before this moment. Even if the queens weren't a threat—and of course they always were—the presence of other Fae crawling out of the woodwork— so to speak—to meet her was a thing that could happen.

Deacon's golden eyes widened. "You can't go then," he said. "If it's dangerous for you—"

"Nope," she cut him off before he could go into full blown panic mode. "Still going. Already decided. Even Jaxer thinks I should go."

This had Deacon looking at Jaxer with raised brows. Jaxer didn't respond with so much as a shrug.

"You've said you'll do better at the training with me there,"

Cary continued, pulling Deacon's attention back to her. "I'm going. The Fae don't have any reason to bother me." She hoped. Fae were pretty fucking capricious. And excessively curious. "And even if some of them decide to come out and say Hi, well, we don't have to complicate things there. I'll say Hi and they can go back and report I'm boring and no one needs to worry about me."

Deacon's mouth twitched and she'd swear she heard Jaxer snort. "Boring?" Deacon asked. "You sure about that?"

She waved a hand in the air and rolled her eyes. "I'll be boring to them. You're the one doing all the work while we're there. I'm just going to have your back and eat my weight in shortbread."

That brought a full smile to Deacon's expression and she melted. She really loved his smile. Though the way it made her feel probably wasn't suitable for company. And Jaxer was still sitting right there.

"So, it's decided. I go. No one argues with me about it. We're all good with that decision."

"Okay," Deacon said. "Thank you." He pulled her close and kissed her softly.

Jaxer, always the child, groaned loudly. A reaction that made Cary grin, because now she felt like things with him were finally settled so she could appreciate his childishness instead of worrying about it.

"We do have one more problem to deal with before you leave," Jaxer said, his tone serious. "Beyond the fact that Cary being in Scotland will attract the attention of the English and Irish Fae."

"What else is there?" She wanted to groan herself this time. The potential of pissing off a powerful Fae queen wasn't issue enough?

"You've only just gotten the full use of your Protector

powers," Jaxer reminded her. "You haven't had a chance to practice with them at all, nonetheless to use them in the field. There's every chance you could *forget* to raise the shield."

"And jump into trouble and get hurt," Deacon finished, his attention on Cary again, his expression hard.

She winced. When her shields had been taken away—part of a Seventh Year test—she'd still put herself between bad guys and good guys without thinking about it. And because the test hadn't gone according to the usual plan for reasons that had to do with the demon god, Cary had gotten shot and ended up in hospital and given Deacon and her friend Marianne metaphorical heart attacks. None of which was good. Cary hated getting shot, but getting shot without the shield to slow the bullet was a *lot* worse than getting a little bruise because the bullet was moving so fast her shield couldn't slow it down enough to entirely prevent it from hitting her.

Although, that turned out to be more a problem with the way she channeled the shield because of her own ability to absorb magic. But that was another story.

The problem with Cary was that she would always jump between bad guys and good guys. She was a runner-inner and a freezer once she was there. All super good traits for a Protector. All really stupid deadly traits for someone without a Protector shield.

"So..." She faced Jaxer more fully, but let Deacon keep her close in a hug because that made them both feel better. "So, Wisat and Liruk said the shields will still come up on their own. Did they lie?"

"No. At least not technically. Technically, the shields should still come up automatically when you jump into trouble. They should even protect you better now. You can raise the shields to keep yourself safe, without needing someone to protect."

She loved that part.

"And you can drop them if you need to for…reasons like absorbing magic to use against a bad guy."

She loved that part less.

Even though it could be useful.

But really, she'd had her fill of absorbing magic during the demon god fight—both literally and figuratively. She wasn't quite human anymore, or well, wasn't quite the mundane human she'd been before. A process that had started when she'd become a Protector.

Technically, people like her don't survive their first encounter with strong magic. Thanks to her being recruited as a Protector (she'd given up saying she'd been tricked into the job, but only to herself), she'd had the Protector shields to keep her safe from all the magic thrown at her.

But some of that magic still got through and over the seven years of her jumping in front of magic, she'd been changed. At a cellular level. No one, even Eriana who was a Fae healer and very smart, knew exactly what the consequences of that change were for Cary.

And then to top it off, during the fight with the demon god, she'd had to absorb so much magic, all different kinds of magic, that she was really really not mundane anymore. Since no one knew what that meant, she mostly tried to ignore the implications of it. She still *felt* like herself so that was what counted, right?

Still, having that in the background meant she'd rather not absorb any more magic for a little while. At least not on purpose.

"I won't be doing that in Scotland," she said. "And if the shield still comes up automatically, I should be fine."

"One of my last jobs with you as mentor," Jaxer said, "is to ensure you can raise and lower the shield at will. We don't have the usual time for those lessons, at least not before you leave. But we need to work on the basics before you go."

"Yeah. That sounds like a good idea." Just in case.

Because if something could go wrong with her Protector magic, it did. And if that something was that the shields didn't come up automatically for some reason, and she had to do it herself, if she messed that up…

She could end up dead.

4

The problem with the way Cary's Protector shields had always worked during her seven years of apprenticeship was that she actually had to be protecting someone for them to activate. She had no control over the magic. And if she wasn't protecting anyone, the shields didn't come up.

But when she got between good guys and bad guys… Shields!

Demonstrating the shields before this had meant putting someone at her back that she could protect and then having someone else *try* to hurt that person. This was difficult if the person *trying* to do the hurting was not, in fact, a bad guy and didn't like hurting people.

In her current collection of people to protect and do the *trying*, she had Deacon and Jaxer. Two people who, given the right set of circumstance, were either allies, friends, or rivals, and who, up to a few months ago, probably would have been okay with attempting to hurt the other in the name of science and experimentation.

Which was the reason she'd never put them to that task.

But now that she didn't, strictly speaking, *need* someone to protect, the biggest trick was just trying to get one of the two men to actually attempt to hurt *her*.

And they were both a disaster at it.

She wasn't sure whether to laugh or groan when, once again, Deacon threw the hardback book well to the left, nowhere near her, and so gently it barely even reached her side of the living room.

"This doesn't work if you don't *try*," she reminded him, again, exasperated. They'd been at this for a good half hour. And both Deacon and Jaxer had failed spectacularly at throwing a book at her. She'd never seen anything quite like it. "It's just a book. Even if I don't manage to raise my shield and it hits me, it won't hurt that badly. And I won't blame you for hitting me with a book. I promise."

Deacon scowled and let out a grunt, putting his hands on his hips. "Even my leopard is objecting to this. I can't purposefully *try* to hurt my mate."

"I need to practice raising this shield on purpose. And I won't know if it's up or not if there's nothing for it to stop. I can't throw a book at myself."

"Get Jaxer to try again," Deacon said. There was such a distinct pout to his voice, she almost did laugh.

"Jaxer failed at this, too."

"Tell your mate not to growl at me every time I raise the book and maybe I would have had better aim," Jaxer said. He was sprawled on her couch, looking as exasperated as Cary felt.

She didn't know what he was so annoyed about. His aim had been as bad as Deacon's even before Deacon started growling.

"What kind of friends are you, you can't even throw a book at me?" she said to both of them. "Come *on*. I have to practice this before Scotland, and I still have packing to do."

"Maybe there's someone else we can bring in to help," Jaxer said. "Someone who won't object so much to hurting you."

She smiled. "I do love that neither one of you wants to hurt me, to be clear. But I need someone to at least try it. Who else do we know and trust enough for this?"

Her best girlfriends were all otherwise occupied with work or secret boyfriends. Liruk was the one of her bosses who might definitely throw a book at Cary for training purposes, but her bosses didn't get involved in the training part. Plus, they were pouting a little because she'd left them no choice in her leaving for Scotland for a month. She hadn't even asked in the end. Just told them she was going and they had to deal with it. Given what she'd *just* been through, they hadn't argued with her. But there was a distinct pout about the way they'd given in.

The other leopard shifters in Portland wouldn't throw anything at her because they'd be afraid of Deacon's reaction—even if he told them it was okay. He was their future king and they liked him too, so they didn't do things they knew would piss him off.

Cary's sparring partner at Lucy's gym, the bear shifter Brandon Hawthorn, was currently recovering from injuries he took during the demon god fight. Although, Cary suspected Brandon had completely recovered weeks ago, probably the day after the fight—he was a shifter after all—but since Marianne had been taking care of him and nursing him back to health, he'd been slow to fully recover. But because Brandon threw Cary around during martial arts training—gently so he didn't accidentally kill her; see again *bear shifter*—he'd likely be good at throwing a book at her.

"We could call Brandon," she said aloud. He was one of the few people she knew would understand the need for training and be willing to do what was necessary for that training, while still being gentle about it all. Lucy would probably throw a book at her too, because she was an excellent martial arts teacher and because she had a bit of a vicious streak. But she was still teaching. Brandon was really their best option.

"I'll call him," Deacon said.

While Deacon made the call, Jaxer walked her verbally through the process of raising her own shield on purpose again.

Since she wasn't an innately magical person, the process of *using* magic was not second nature to her. She'd had to do a crash course on how to use it during the demon god thing because using magic that she absorbed was the only way to get it out of her system so she didn't die. Again. And she'd managed in the heat of the moment. But since then, she hadn't purposefully tried to cast spells—she hadn't been in a position to absorb any magic since then either, so she hadn't needed to, and the dragon who was training her to deal with her ability to absorb magic was currently occupied heroing with his hero Joan. She also suspected Rory was giving her a break because of everything she'd been through. He was quite the thoughtful dragon.

Cary's Protector shields were magic. They were Fae magic, given to her by her bosses. She'd always just channeled that magic, never even feeling it when it flowed through her, so finding it to *use* it on purpose was…trickier than she'd hoped.

"You'd think after seven years, I'd know what the Protector magic felt like," she huffed. "At least enough to pull it up when I need it."

"Seven years of habits are hard to change," Jaxer said.

"Then why do you all train people this way? Why not *start* with being able to control the shield. The whole 'start as you mean to go on' philosophy. It's a good one. Works well with the dogs, too."

"That's why they get so many treats? Because you intended to overfeed them from the start?"

"Shut up. They deserve every treat they get." And yes, yes, she was a softy to her dogs and often overindulged them. But it was rude of Jaxer to point it out.

He grinned. "Tell that to Fred's expanding tummy."

Fred, having heard his name, looked up from where he was still sprawled under the bay window. All the dogs had paid so little attention to the shenanigans of the humans, it was funny. Pickles had half looked at them from under her droopy eyelids when they'd stood to start practicing. Buck had watched the two men attempt to throw books at her for a few minutes. Fred had remained blissfully asleep with his legs churning as he chased a squirrel—or whatever he was chasing in his dreams.

Until the mention of his name and treats in the same conversation. That got Fred's attention. He thumped his tail on the edge of his soft bed a few times, then jumped up and sort of angled toward the direction of the kitchen, readying to race there ahead of her when she moved.

"I'm not going into the kitchen, Fred," she told him. "Go back to sleep."

Fred let out one of his yippy barks. Did a little run toward the kitchen, paused to look at her, tail up and wagging, tongue lolling out of his mouth. Pickles cracked an eye open to observe Fred.

"No, Fred. I'm training. I can't get you a treat now. Later. When we're done."

Fred let out another yippy bark, tore across the living room to bounce off her thigh in his enthusiasm, then, after a nice scratch around the head and ears, he went back to his bed, spun in a few circles, settled down, and was back to sleep in an admirably quick moment.

"Oh to be that carefree," she murmured with a fond grin.

Pickles let out a low woof, then resettled herself and went back to sleep too.

Deacon came out of the hallway that led to her bedrooms, tucking his cellphone into the back pocket of his jeans. "Brandon's on his way. Apparently, Marianne called him out yesterday for pretending to be sick longer than he was, so he's back at work today. But he's taking off early to help."

"That was nice of him. He didn't need to do that."

"I get the feeling he's hoping you'll put in a good word with Marianne for him."

"Ha!" She already had.

Marianne was still healing from the breakup of her ten-year relationship, though. After Gina broke her heart, Marianne was not ready to start a new relationship any time soon. She was doing better lately, and that was a huge relief for Cary and the others to see, but still… Ten years was a long time and getting over her ex-girlfriend wasn't something Marianne could do overnight. She said outright she wasn't ready for anything new yet. But the way she was with Brandon also gave Cary hope. There was obviously interest there. Potential. And Brandon was infinitely patient, and kind.

"Does he think Marianne will like him more if he hits you with a book?" Jaxer asked, his brows raised.

"She will if she knows it's for a good cause," Cary said. Marianne loved her and wanted her safe. This was how she stayed safe.

While they waited for Brandon, Jaxer had her practice trying to raise the shield even without the book tossing. The problem was, because she couldn't really feel the Protector magic, she wasn't sure if the shield was up without the book tossing.

"I think I've got it," she said, scowling at the air just in front of her. "But it's so hard to tell." She poked the air but felt nothing. She tried to push her hand against where she thought the shield was, but her hand just continued on. Nothing stopping it. "Is that bad or not?" she asked.

"The shield is supposed to block things from getting at you, not you from getting at things," Jaxer said. "That you could reach through it doesn't mean anything. You could have reached through the shield before, too."

Not that she ever had. Or even attempted to. That would have meant touching a bad guy. Which she tried to avoid. She preferred just standing in their way, safely behind her shield, and watching them get increasingly angry and frustrated.

Speaking of frustrated, though.

"Okay, until Brandon gets here, I'm taking a break. Dogs, treats! Then we'll order some pizzas because I'm gonna need food."

"I'll get the pizzas," Deacon said, already pulling out his phone. He glanced at Jaxer as Cary headed toward the kitchen with all three dogs dancing around her—or at least Fred was dancing, the other two were more amblers. She caught Deacon's scowl as she passed and looked over her shoulder, realizing he was scowling at Jaxer.

Oh oh. What had Jaxer just done?

Deacon's scowl had that more confused than outraged look, though. He tilted his head to one side and said, "Jaxer, what the hell are you wearing?"

Cary chuckled all the way to the mudroom where she stored the dog treats.

5

Brandon showed up minutes after the pizzas, so they all ate and caught up first before getting to the training.

"Usually, I wouldn't recommend training on a full stomach," the huge man said. "But since this training involves standing still and throwing books, I can make an exception."

Not all shifters had a human form that spoke to their animal form. Deacon was quite a bit larger in his human form than he was in his leopard form, though his golden eyes were similar in both. And she'd seen some wolf shifters that were a *lot* bigger in wolf form than they were in human form. But in Brandon Hawthorn's case, he just looked like he should be a bear, even when he was in human form.

A six-foot-nine Black man, wide and thick with muscles, clean shaven to show off his granite jaw, his black hair shaved tight to his head. If he wasn't smiling, his mouth fell naturally into a frown and he looked super intimidating. Then he grinned and all that intimidation fell by the wayside because the kind man inside bloomed out.

He worked as a fundraiser, mostly for non-profits, and he and Deacon had worked together in the past. He'd been a student of Lucy's for a few years now, too. Even without all those character witnesses, though, Cary had liked Brandon right from the start. Better yet, now she knew she could trust him.

And she was trusting him to *try* and bean her with a book.

"Maybe I should go into the other room," Deacon said after they'd cleaned up the cardboard boxes from the pizza—there were no leftovers; between two shifters, a faery, and *her*, the five boxes of pizza hadn't stood a chance—and pushed the furniture aside again to give them room to work.

Deacon eyed Brandon as Brandon bounced the hardback doorstop of a novel in his huge hand, testing its weight—which was insignificant for a bear shifter. "If I watch him trying to hurt you, I might…react."

Brandon raised his brows but didn't scowl. Instead, he grinned. "Understandable. Bears don't do fated mates, but I understand the feelings are complicated."

"Very," Deacon said with a sigh.

Deacon didn't watch her training sessions with Brandon either, though some of that was because Cary didn't want him watching. It was embarrassing the way Brandon and Lucy tossed her around the dojo, especially since Lucy was barely five-foot tall. Cary preferred her mate didn't witness that. And they'd all decided it was better Deacon wasn't there for her training anyway.

For this very reason.

He pulled her into his arms. "I thought I'd be okay, but…yeah, no. I'm going to need to wait in the bedroom. Especially with the first toss. If you don't get hurt, I should be able to come back out again."

Cary rose on her toes to give him a kiss. "I'll be fine," she assured. "It's just a book. But I'll let you know when you can come back out again."

As it turned out, that wasn't for a full half an hour. And Deacon was not going to be happy about the bruises.

"Well, this is frustrating as shit," she said with her hands on her hips. "I thought I was going to love this ability, but not if I can't get it to work!"

"Stop ducking," Jaxer said.

"You stop ducking," Cary snarled. She'd been hit by the big hardback twice before they'd switched to a softer paperback book. After getting hit three more times, she'd just started diving and ducking out of the way when the book came at her and she knew the shield wasn't coming up.

The reason the shield wasn't coming up was because she couldn't bring it up. And neither she nor Jaxer could explain that.

"You channeled demon magic and automatically built a shield with it," Jaxer said. "Shielding and protecting are your natural instinct. Just…channel the magic and raise the shield."

"You've said those exact same words to me forty-three bajillionty times at this point. Give me different instructions because those words are not helping."

"Stop thinking so much?" Brandon suggested. "It's the thing that gets you into trouble during training."

He was right about that. Lucy was always telling her to stop thinking so much. "How do you mean?"

"I mean, this, like the martial arts, probably has to be muscle memory," Brandon said.

"He's right." Jaxer tapped a long finger against his chin. "You've been jumping in front of people to save them for long enough that you do that automatically, even when you didn't have your shield."

"Don't remind me," she muttered.

"It's muscle memory. There's trouble, you jump in."

"And if I do that, my shields will still work. Right? You've said they will." She was starting to wonder. And worry. Because when she hadn't had her shield, she'd jumped into trouble and been shot. That muscle memory would get her killed without the shield to back it up.

"It still comes up automatically," Jaxer assured her. Again. "Here. Let's show you."

He stood just to the Cary's left. "Time to wallop me with the book," he told Brandon.

Brandon grinned. Narrowed his eyes, and arrowed the book right at Jaxer.

Cary blinked, realized she was supposed to keep that book from hitting Jaxer, squeaked, and stepped in the way. But despite seven years of *knowing* this worked, she still raised her hands to protect her face from the book.

When it didn't hit her, when it bounced off her protector shield and thumped against the wall near her hallway, she took a breath.

"See," Jaxer said. "Shield is still there. You're a Protector. And you're still channeling that magic automatically."

Cary let out a long long sigh and nodded. "I just realized that's the first time I've done that since the demon god thing. I haven't..." She blinked hard as the realization sank in. "I haven't used the Protector magic at all since I passed my Seventh Year and got it back. I haven't had to protect anyone. Not since I had to protect people without a shield." And she hadn't realized how much that had affected her trust in her shield. How much it had... shaken her.

Jaxer put his hands on her shoulders and gave them a gentle

squeeze. "I should have thought of that sooner, too. Feel better knowing the shield still works?" he asked quietly.

"Actually, yeah. Yeah, I do. Maybe we should practice with the automatic part for a few more minutes. Let me get reacquainted with the Protector magic."

"Good plan." Jaxer gave her shoulders a pat and moved toward the hallway. "Let me go get Deacon."

She spun around and frowned. "Why?"

"He'd hate to miss out on an opportunity to throw books at me."

CARY WENT THROUGH A FEW ROUNDS OF PROTECTING EACH OF THE men from the others trying to hit him with a book. Sometimes the two book throwers worked together, tossing multiple books at her protectee. Each and every time, the shield worked. No one got hurt. And only her books, and her walls, showed any damage from the training.

"Better now?" Jaxer asked, absently spinning a book around his hand with a twist of magic.

She'd never seen him do that before and it was almost as interesting as the change in outfits. "Better," she said. "Knowing, no matter what, the magic is still flowing and the shield will come up when I need it is a relief."

"Want to try bringing it up on purpose again?"

"I should try."

"You should."

"I don't wanna."

Jaxer grinned. "Ice cream first as a bribe?"

"Good bribe."

THEY SPENT THE NEXT HOUR GOING BACK AND FORTH BETWEEN her protecting someone so the shield would rise and her trying to bring the shield up on her own. After another few wallops from paperbacks, she did finally start to get the hang of it. The process felt awkward, like she was straining to raise and hold the shield. More physical, like when she'd been channeling other people's magic into spells that didn't come naturally to her.

In the fight with Oliver Holland and his demon god daddy, she'd had to hold shields up physically. She had to physically do gestures and say words to cast spells. And in the end, she'd been able to use Holland's magic in a brute force sort of way that was a little too demon-like for her nightmares. But it had worked.

The physical part should have left her exhausted. Channeling Protector magic *and* using other people's magic against them usually wore her out. She'd been forced into more than one lengthy healing sleep over the years. But after facing off against Holland and his dad, she'd felt...fine. Despite all the physical work that had gone into what she'd done.

She was a little worried about that, frankly. Worried about what changes had happened to her at a cellular level that she could channel and throw around that much magic without hitting a wall. But the one positive part was that she hadn't passed out after the confrontation. Even though all that magic had *felt* physical.

Protectoring had never felt physical to her before. The channeling, the shield...all just automatic. And she stood there, being stubborn. Easy peasy. No real physical part to it.

Raising the shield herself felt like work. She had to force it.

And scarily, it was also exhausting. Like an hour-long training session with Lucy and Brandon. Her limbs were starting to tremble and she could feel her mind getting fuzzy from exhaustion.

Was it good or really bad that channeling the magic she was

supposed to be able to channel, doing it on purpose, was tiring, but channeling demon magic had not been?

Yeah, that was probably a *really* bad thing.

Jaxer tried to reassure her. "You're just new to this. It's fine. You've done good. Managed to get the shield up on your own a few times. Now, it's just a matter of practice."

"Practice. Sure." She wasn't so sure, but maybe he was right.

"Look, when you're in Scotland," Jaxer said, "it's entirely possible someone will come after you directly, without meaning any ill harm to someone you're with. In the before times, that could have gotten you killed. Now, you can defend against those attacks. You just need to remember that."

Cary blinked hard a few times as she stared at Jaxer. Shit. He was right. If any of the Fae queens got mad at her, they'd come after her directly. No *also* wanting to hurt someone else like Deacon, giving her a convenient person to protect while scary Fae people tried to kill her. No, they'd just go for her. Because they knew about Protectors. At least some of them knew what a Protector's weaknesses were.

If she didn't have control over her shield now, without someone to Protect, Jaxer was right. She'd be dead. But if she couldn't learn to raise her shield…

"Practice," she muttered to herself. "Just need some more practice."

Jaxer and Deacon exchanged a look. Then Jaxer said, "You're not leaving for another couple of days, right. We'll keep practicing right up until you go. You'll be fine."

She'd have felt better if Jaxer didn't sound so uncertain.

6

The flight to New York, where they'd transfer to a flight to Edinburgh, left early in the morning. Marianne arrived right on time, so Cary wouldn't have to worry about the dogs for even a second. Marianne was going to house and dog sit while Cary was gone, and since the dogs loved her, Cary felt okay about leaving them for a month.

Not great. But okay.

She'd discussed the travel with them already, but she wasn't sure Fred understood. Fortunately, Fred also didn't care because Marianne was there with treats and a new squeaky toy for him.

"You won't mind regular video chats so I can talk to them?" she asked Marianne. Again.

"It's fine," Marianne assured. "You're fine. They'll be fine. I'm fine. We're all going to be just fine."

Cary rolled her eyes. "I'm being ridiculous."

"No, it's natural and normal to miss your pack. They'll miss you, too. But we're going to have fun. Aren't we guys?"

Pickles woofed and nosed Cary's leg, like she was pushing her toward the door. Buck stuck his head under her hand and let her give him a scratch. Fred bounced off her leg once, barked his yippy bark, then settled down with the new toy, the steady squeak squeak sound weirdly reassuring.

"If you have any trouble at all, I'm a phone call away," she told Marianne. "Or if anything weird happens with the house, don't hesitate to call."

Marianne still didn't know about the glamour on the house, but Cary was *this* close to telling her, since she'd be here for a month. After all they'd been through together, Cary really felt strange the girls didn't know.

But the glamour worked best when no one knew about it. Which was why she'd gone so long before even telling Deacon. And she'd only told him because…well, he was her mate and they spent most of their time in Cary's house. And he'd been worrying about her getting killed.

Which, to be fair, was a valid worry.

"We'll all be just fine," Marianne said, but she was frowning a little as she did. "You sure you'll be okay?"

"Sure. Why not? It's Scotland!"

"Last time you were that side of the Pond, you died," Marianne reminded her.

"But not for long," Cary said, trying to joke. Marianne did not look amused. "I promise not to die this time?"

"That's not helping."

"I will be fine," Cary insisted. "I promise. After everything we've just been through… I'll be okay." She didn't mention the possible complications of two Fae queens that may or may not want her on their islands and the possibility of meeting more Fae rulers who might also complicate things. Those were hypotheticals she didn't want to worry Marianne with.

"Good," Marianne said. "Because you need to come back so we can figure out what to do about Lucy."

"Lucy? What's going on with Lucy that I don't know about?"

"I don't know for sure. But I know she's keeping something from us. Even Brandon suspects she's got a secret. And I'm worried about her."

How had Cary missed that? To be fair, she'd had a lot going on the last couple of months, what with the nearly dying and her ability to absorb magic changing her and losing her Protector shield and then the whole demon god and death thing, but still… It didn't sit right with her that she'd missed something as important as one of her best friends keeping secrets. At least Marianne had noticed.

"Does Angie know?"

"What's happening with Lucy? No. That there's something weird going on? I think so. But I need to talk to her more about it after she gets back from her vacation with Sebastian."

"Are we supposed to talk about Angie and Sebastian?" Cary asked. It was out there now. Sebastian had been around for and helped with the demon god stuff. But Angie said they weren't supposed to be together. She'd kept him a secret for *years*. For reasons that weren't clear at all to Cary, discussing that secret out loud now felt…weird. Like they should all still be keeping Angie's secret and not discussing it? She wasn't sure.

"We can ask her when she gets back. If she'll tell us what happened there and why they have had to be secret. She might not want to. You know how she is."

"Yeah."

Angie was extremely cagey about her past and secretive about her connection to the demon hunters—and there was definitely one there. Sebastian was a demon hunter. And Angie could do… something that had to do with demon realms. Cary still wasn't entirely sure what and how she did it, but Angie could open portals into demon realms. And Cary still had a *lot* of questions about all that.

But if Angie didn't want to, or couldn't, tell them everything. Cary would accept that. She respected her best friend's right to her secrets. That didn't stop her from being insanely curious, though.

"Anyway," Marianne said, brushing her fingers through Buck's fur as he sat at her hip. "We can talk about all this when you get back. Don't want you to miss your flight. Glad you're going by conventional methods this trip."

Cary snorted. "Me too. And thanks again for the new rain jacket! According to Deacon, I'm going to need it."

Marianne was a seamstress and made *the* best clothes. Everything she made had pockets. And for Cary, she ensured those pockets had some magic in them. Marianne's ability to weave magic into her clothing was really just the frosting on an already pretty special cake. The things she and her sisters could do together was even more amazing.

Deacon poked his head back in the front door. "All the luggage is in the car. You ready?"

"Almost." She knelt down to give her little pack goodbye hugs and kisses. "I'll be back real soon," she told them. "And in the meantime, Marianne will look after you. But I also want you to take care of each other and look after Marianne, please."

Pickle's let out a deep woof, which Cary took to be agreement. Buck nudged her with his big head so he could get another hug. And Fred sat and did the little prayer thing with his front paws as he kept balance on his butt. Then lunged at her for another hug.

When she stood, she had to brush off a bunch of dog hair before giving Marianne a hug goodbye, too.

By the time she got out of the house, Cary was a bit misty-eyed. She'd never been away from her pack for a month before—at least not on purpose. The time in Faery and then the healing sleep after had sucked more than a month from her life. But, to be fair, she'd been here for the healing sleep, so her pack at least knew where she was. The only other times she went away, it was never more than a couple of weeks.

She watched the house as she and Deacon drove off, Marianne standing in the doorway, surrounded by the dogs, waving them off.

And a pang of melancholy hit. She was going to miss them all.

But when she faced forward again, she remembered she was on her way to Edinburgh. To *Scotland*. And the excitement crept back in again.

Off to see Scotland, see the castle in Edinburgh, walk the hilly streets, meet Deacon's grandmother…

Oh yeah. She was going to meet Deacon's grandmother.

Oh boy.

THE FLIGHTS WERE VERY LONG, AND VERY EXHAUSTING, AND BY the time they landed in Edinburgh, Cary was muzzy and a little delirious from not getting enough sleep. Deacon had splurged on First Class tickets for them—a luxury she was sure had permanently spoiled her on all future coach seats—and that had made sleeping a little easier. But a combination of excitement and just being on an airplane had made sleeping for very long impossible.

By the time they touched down, Cary estimated she'd been mostly awake, outside of a few forty-five-minute naps, for the better part of twenty plus hours.

Which meant getting through passport control and getting their luggage and getting to the car rental—Deacon was driving as he'd at least driven on the wrong side of the road before; and knew how to drive a standard transmission, which Cary did not—was a process Cary did in a fog. She snoozed in the car as they drove into Edinburgh proper, and only caught snatches of the passing countryside and the outer suburbs of Scotland's capital.

According to Deacon, they'd stay in the city for a few days, and then they'd head north to his grandmother's cottage, just outside Stirling.

Cary suspected the few days in Edinburgh—outside of giving them a chance to adjust to the time change—was for her sake, so she could explore.

"I promise to be more awake and excited after I sleep for twelve hours in a bed," she muttered as they hit the winding, narrow, hilly streets of the capital.

Cars whipped past her window, all going the wrong way, which made her grin. Buildings of old gray and brown stone rose up around cobbled streets and butted up against more modern architecture. Crowded sidewalks moved past bustling shops, cafes, and pubs that added pops of color on the ground level under those imposing stone buildings. Some of the stores were familiar staples common even in the US, some of them—like the store selling clan tartans—were uniquely Scottish. The double-decker busses and occasional rail stations reminded her they didn't have to drive everywhere, which she was looking forward to. And while it was too early in the morning for the pubs to be open, she was looking forward to pub food and beer and good tea.

Though right now, she could really use a few gallons of coffee.

As they circled the city center, Cary looked up to the top of a rocky hill, getting her first look at Edinburgh castle. The imposing gray structure, with its parapets and towers and curtain wall was— to her American eye—like something out of a movie. She couldn't wait to get up there and explore. Even if it was mostly just a tourist place now.

Deacon wove them around the castle hill and headed to the south side of the city, toward a residential area where, as it turned out, his family still owned a house. He'd said his grandmother stayed there when she bothered coming into the city. And there were cousins who apparently used the place when they were in town for festivals and business. But mostly the house remained empty, with a housekeeper to ensure it didn't rot—Deacon's words.

The way he talked about the house, she was expecting something old and decrepit, something with walls that let in the cold air and a roof that leaked when it rained. She had no idea why she thought the place would be in bad shape outside of Deacon didn't sound like he liked the house very much.

And once again, she was utterly shocked by one of Deacon's family homes.

"This isn't the relic you said it was," she commented as they pulled around the circular driveway, past a manicured front garden, and parked in front of a charming brown brick, three story house that was probably better described as a small mansion. "Not even a little bit."

Actually, she thought houses like this were called manor houses. Large, but not even half the size of the Jones family place outside of Eugene, Oregon. That place was a real mansion with wings and everything. This place was large, with big bay windows and wrought iron railings around small balconies over the top of… what looked like towers attached to the main building structure. The roof was pitched and there were a bunch of chimneys, which got Cary thinking of cozy fires and big chairs and glasses of brandy. She didn't even like brandy that much, but the image made her grin.

She shivered as she climbed out of the rental car and inspected the neighborhood. Everything smelled fresh, like it had just rained, and the overcast morning sky kept the air chilly. The neighborhood was more lovely compact stone houses and neatly manicured front gardens. There was a small river snaking through the neighborhood, down the block from Deacon's family home. And behind that, an area that looked more like a village than a section of a large city, with cafes and pubs and shops in bright colors surrounded by more elaborate stone architecture. Trees and greenery lined sidewalks and the riverwalk, giving the area a lush feel.

The front door of the house, painted a bright red that really popped in the gray morning light, opened as Deacon was getting into the car trunk—they called it a boot here which made Cary chuckle—for their luggage.

An older white woman, maybe in her mid-sixties, stood in the doorway, her arms crossed against the chill. She wore a long, straight tan skirt and long-sleeved button-down shirt under an apron, flat shoes, and an expression of dubious interest. Her gray hair was cut into short curls, framing a strong face with the sort of bone structure Cary associated with unbreakable women. That jaw line said, "Throw me the worst you've got. I'll just get the kettle on while I wait."

Cary attempted a smile when the woman's gaze swept over her. The smile was received with a sniff.

Okay. Well. Probably good they were only staying here for a couple of days.

"I've gotten ye rooms prepared on the second floor," the woman called. "Kettle's on." She turned back into the house.

Cary rolled her lips into her mouth so she wouldn't say anything about the "kettle's on" part but she really wanted to gloat that she'd seen that coming.

"That's Fiona," Deacon said. "She's looked after the house for forever. As long as I can remember."

"She doesn't look that much older than your technical age." Which was, technically, about to be fifty-five, even though, thanks to being a shifter he was physically more like a human in his mid to late thirties. Shifter aging was a weird and amazing thing. But unless Fiona was a shifter, she'd have had to have been ten when she started here if Deacon remembered her always having been here.

"She's older than she looks," Deacon said, confirming Cary's suspicions.

She glanced around. No one walking past on the sidewalk at the base of the manicured garden. She still lowered her voice. "Is she a leopard?"

If so, that might make Deacon a little tense. He worried about his magic when he was around other leopards. In fact, the only leopard shifter she'd seen him around that he hadn't been uber controlled with was his great grandfather. He even maintained that strict control around his siblings, though they generally got along quite well.

"Not a leopard," Deacon said. "Though she knows what we are. But she was a school friend of my grandmother's, best friends from what I understand. So my grandmother…helped with the aging thing."

"Your grandmother has the kind of magic that can do that for a human?"

Deacon frowned a little. "Honestly, I never thought about it that much. I suppose she must."

"That's not anything you can do." Cary was stating that. If he could slow someone's aging, they'd both be less worried about the fact that Cary's life expectancy wasn't nearly as long as his, since she was a human. Her Protector magic helped—she'd been aging significantly slower since becoming a Protector—and apparently, all the magic she'd been absorbing might affect her aging, too. But whether that was going to increase her life expectancy or cut it short no one knew and Cary wasn't inclined to think about it too closely.

But chances were good she wouldn't live as long as he did—not least because her job tended to put her into the kind of might-well-die situations that had a significant impact on life expectancy —and if he'd thought he could do anything about that, he'd have told her already.

"I never considered it," he said. "There's a lot about my magic I've never thought or asked about."

"Lot about your grandmother's version you don't know either?"

He nodded, his mouth tight, a little crease between his brows.

This was going to be a revelatory trip for both of them.

Cary had worried about packing for a full month, so she might have overpacked a little. Meeting Deacon's grandmother was incredibly intimidating and she didn't want to show up in holey jeans and ripped t-shirts—not that Marianne would allow her clothes to get into that state—so she'd erred on the side of overpacking. But thanks to some packing squares Marianne had loaned her, the excess of clothing all managed to fit into one large wheely suitcase, instead of three. Magical packing cubes were the best.

Still, Deacon grunted when he hauled out the suitcase, which made Cary wince.

He, on the other hand, had one of those rolling bags that was barely larger than a carry-on, and a backpack he'd brought onto the plane that held his laptop. His sister, Caitlin, the sibling most involved with the Portland wing of the family business—which was rescuing animals! Cary had landed in with a family that *rescued animals* as their primary business!—had promised Deacon he could leave the laptop behind and not worry about work. She had it covered. And she did. Most of her part of the job was fundraising and schmoozing with donors. And she was better at that than Deacon anyway. But he hadn't been able to leave work behind completely for a month. He'd lost a lot of the last year thanks to their mate bond, and Cary suspected he was feeling guilty about that, even if he wouldn't admit it out loud because he didn't want Cary to feel bad about it.

She wouldn't have if his job wasn't so important. But his job was *important*, so she did feel a little guilty.

Cary took her own carry-on from him, a backpack as well, but hers mostly had snacks, a change of clothes, and recharging cords for her phone and tablet, which she'd loaded up with books and movies to keep her occupied over the month. She actually didn't have a lot of lazy reading time—for things that didn't involve her work—these days so she was looking forward to sinking into a few novels while she was here.

Even if she'd brought her work with her, her work didn't involve computers or modern technology—except for the research part of things, and she didn't have a travel version of the computer that got her into the parts of the web she needed to go to do her research anyway. If she got called to do Protector things, that would just involve running and jumping in between people. She could do that anywhere.

Well, technically, she might hear about it from one of the Fae queens if she did have to do her job while here. But she'd worry about that problem if it came up. Right now, she was here for Deacon. And to see Scotland.

But, yeah, no, mostly for Deacon.

"We'd better get inside," Deacon said, taking both their suitcases up the stairs as if they didn't weight anything at all.

Which she knew for a fact wasn't true for her bag. "If we let the tea go cold, Fiona will not be pleased."

Cary followed, a little twist in her gut chasing away the exhaustion dragging at her. She wasn't entirely sure why she was nervous. Meeting new people. Staying in someone else's house. A hotel probably would have been easier. But still, she was just here to support Deacon. No need to be nervous about the impression she made on anyone.

Right?

She blinked up at the big house.

Oh boy.

The inside of the house was darker than Cary would have expected given the number of windows on the outside. There were no overhead lights turned on, and the lamp on the side table at the entrance was off as well.

In the dimness, though, the place looked lovely and well kept. Lots of polished wooden floors and elegant rugs and pale wallpapered walls. The entryway had wooden wainscotting, but the sitting room where Fiona had set out a tea service just had walls of pale blue wallpaper and sturdy wooden furniture. Deacon left their suitcases against the wall and sat in a couch with deep blue cushions, pouring tea into sturdy mugs from a delicate tea pot. The contrast of big man and little tea pot and chunky mugs made Cary smile.

"I'm gonna need to sleep soon," she whispered, afraid she'd offend Fiona in some way. "But then I want to see everything. We can do that right?"

"Everything?"

"Okay, the castle and the Royal Mile. I'll be happy if I can see those before we leave Edinburgh."

"Fair enough. Tea. Breakfast. Then sleep. Then we can make a plan."

"Breakfast?" Cary's stomach growled, right on time. She hadn't even realized she was hungry. "An English breakfast?" she asked hopefully.

"Probably. With a side of porridge."

The tea was hot and lovely with milk and some sugar. The breakfast so very satisfying Cary felt like she'd been fed for a week. And the bed in their room was huge. Fiona had even stuck two hot-water bottles under the blankets to ensure the bed was cozy and warm.

After the big meal, Cary barely had the energy to study the room. The warm cozy bed called. She slept for a solid four hours, with Deacon warm at her back.

WHEN CARY AND DEACON FINALLY CRAWLED OUT OF BED AND showered and felt halfway decent, despite the jet lag, Fiona insisted on feeding them again. A basic, hearty, yummy lunch of beef stew and bread. Nothing fancy but lots of it. Which was good for Deacon because he ate lots of it.

Full, showered, and eager to see more of Edinburgh, Cary talked Deacon into taking her to the castle. It was too late in the afternoon to bother with a tour. She wanted a full day for that—a declaration that made Deacon sigh—but she wanted to walk around the area, see the Royal Mile and Princes Street, and maybe stroll through the gardens next to the castle.

Thankfully Deacon was driving, because this wrong side of the road business made Cary's head spin. More so now that she was awake enough to pay attention. Since Deacon hadn't been to Edinburgh in a while, there were also a few moments of arguing with the GPS and nearly turning the wrong way down one-way streets. But they managed to find a parking garage with spaces and within a reasonable walk to Princes Street.

Cary decided, once they hit the main street, with its traffic, and shopping, and huge number of double-decker buses, and the looming view of castle hill, that walking was the absolute best way to see Edinburgh. And so long as she remembered which way to look before crossing a street, it felt a lot safer than driving.

The area in the center of the city was a mixture of wide roads and small, cobblestone streets, all lined with shops and pubs and restaurants. And lots and lots of people. They strolled down Princes Street, in no hurry to get anywhere in particular, and Cary pulled Deacon into a number of Scottish tourist shops that just made him shake his head. She didn't care. She was a tourist here. And if that meant buying silly tartan socks with a sheep on them and a miniature castle statue paperweight because it was cute, then that's what she was going to do.

They passed several men in kilts, which actually surprised her since she hadn't expected to see kilts as casual wear. But she decided Deacon would look extra good in a kilt and started hatching a plan to get him into one. It wasn't much of a plan. She sucked at planning. Mostly, it involved begging and flirting. She suspected she wouldn't have to beg and flirt much because he was being incredibly indulgent with her on this trip. Actually, he was always doing things to make her happy, so really all she'd probably have to do is ask. But the thought of flirting to get her way amused her.

As they exited yet another small shop, the proprietor, a burly Scotsman with a great smile, wished them a fair evening. Cary walked out to the busy street grinning. She couldn't help it. Listening to so many Scottish people talking was a delight.

"I love this accent so much," she gushed quietly to Deacon as they wove through pedestrian traffic toward a crosswalk—or whatever it was they called these here. She was pretty sure it wasn't crosswalk, but not entirely certain.

"Am I going to lose you to a Scotsman?" Deacon asked.

She snorted. "If you haven't lost me to Tom the leprechaun's Irish accent, you won't lose me to a Scottish one." She grinned up at him, chuckling at his snort of amusement.

She liked seeing him this way, without all the growly jealousy that had made the early part of their relationship hard on them both. He hadn't had any control of the jealousy. She'd gotten a taste of that out-of-control chemical response for herself with one of his ex's, so she understood the reaction wasn't something he had a lot of control over.

But she liked this better. This comfort and trust that had developed between them. He was still a little overprotective—which was actually kind of sweet—and he tended to flash intimidating stares at handsome men who looked at her too long. But those reactions were more subconscious, like he wasn't really aware of them. And he relaxed into this kind of joking banter a lot easier now.

She supposed that meant their mate bond was solid enough his leopard was relaxing about it all now, too. A year ago, the thought of being here would have both terrified and amazed her. She hadn't been sure they'd ever get to this place—her being a human had really complicated things and changed the timelines on all the mate bonding stuff—but she was even more surprised to discover how much she enjoyed where they were. Who knew being head-over-heals in love could also be this comfortable.

They wove their way down one of the pedestrian lanes and onto the long strip of road that led up to the castle gates, the Royal Mile. And when Cary spotted a pub with Deacon's name on it, she insisted they went in for a pint.

Two thick stouts and a plate of crunchy, salty "chips" later—

she'd been very American about calling French fries chips—they exited the pub into twilight. Thanks to jet lag, and being in *Scotland*, Cary was still wired. Her feet were going to ensure she knew they were unhappy with her doing all this walking tomorrow. But for the moment, she didn't care. She wasn't ready to go home.

"Let's walk through that garden next to the castle," she said. And added, "Please." When it looked like Deacon might object.

Shaking his head, he grabbed her hand and they made their way through the evening crowds toward the gardens. Cary never worried about walking in places that may or may not be dodgy at night when she was with Deacon. She was a Protector. He was a leopard shifter. And honestly, anyone who tried to mug them was in for a shock. Plus, she had a feeling Deacon put out a sort of "don't mess with me" vibe that the average criminal picked up on well before approaching them. Something about his face when he let his expression go cold and iceman. Objectively, it was a pretty intimidating expression.

So when they reached the entrance to the gardens, where very few people were now that it was dark, it didn't occur to her that maybe they shouldn't have a stroll around the paved paths lined with wooden benches, through manicured lawns and decorative clumps of trees. The surrounding city lights lit up the horizon above the park, which was down in a valley between Princes Street and castle hill. And to Cary, the whole thing was magical.

Dark, but magical. Even the car and tarmac city smell got lost in the loamy green scent of the park. Since it was fall, the temperature had dropped with the sun, making Cary grateful for her leather jacket—her Marianne made jacket she went nowhere without because magical pockets were the best.

Deacon took hold of her hand as they strolled down the winding path, past trees that were bare and some clumps that were still green. The lawn was still green and well-manicured. And a faint mist rolled around the gentle hills inside the garden. Above them, the castle loomed on its rocky base, like a sentinel, casting long shadows over the grounds.

A perfect first day in Scotland, Cary thought.

Or, it would have been if the troll hadn't stepped out into their path.

7

ary automatically stepped in front of Deacon, who automatically let her. For most of their relationship, his best way of protecting her was to let *her* protect *him* so her shields would be up. Now that she could control her shields—sort of—she wondered if that might change. But after a year of this, she supposed his instinct to keep her safe by giving her someone to protect was as strong as her instinct to step between good guys and bad guys.

Though, to be fair, they had no idea if the troll was a bad guy yet. But it never hurt to be cautious. Not in her world anyway.

The troll was one of the huge ones, at least ten feet tall, as wide as three human men standing shoulder to shoulder. It wore a leather kilt around its thick waist, but that was the only nod to clothing over its gray-brown rocky skin. Its body was covered in lumps and bumps that may have been muscles or may just have been the contours of its rocks. A vaguely square shaped, hairless head. And eyes that glowed a sort of purply-green. Like a bruise.

She imagined the troll could inflict some pretty impressive bruises to match its eyes.

"Hello," she said. "What can we do for you?"

The troll just stared. It seemed to have a mouth, but the mouth was a fissure amidst the rocks of its face, and there were a few of those fissures, so she wasn't *entirely* sure which one was the mouth. Or the nose—did trolls have noses? She couldn't remember—but the eyes were obvious. And its stare remained steady on them.

Or, more precisely, on Deacon. Entirely on Deacon. The troll hadn't even glanced down at her when she'd spoken.

A prickly sensation crawled along her neck and down her spine. And she inched a little farther in front of her mate, grateful her shield would have gone up automatically because she was tense in that moment and wasn't sure she had the focus to raise the thing.

Another moment of silence.

Cary's shoulders hunched. She kept waiting for Deacon to growl or something, since he and the troll seemed to be in a staring contest. His leopard rose at challenges like this and that predatory growl slipped out of him almost unconsciously.

Except, she realized, he wasn't growling.

She glanced back, though she was reluctant to take her attention from the troll. She blinked. Deacon was…

Well, he was his usual self, but for a split second, she'd swear he was glowing, a faint golden-purple line around him. She got this weird impression of a cloak draped over him with a Celtic brooch holding the folds together at his shoulder—not unlike the cloak and brooch her bosses had once given him to wear into Faery, a way to safeguard him against the lure of Faery which was as dangerous for a shifter as it was for a human.

The aura of golden-purple around him gave him an

otherworldly, regal sort of air. He was a future king of the leopards, but this was…different. She couldn't say exactly why. But she remembered having that same impression when he'd put on her bosses' cloak and brooch in her house all those months ago. Jaxer had glamoured him up an outfit more in fitting with Faery and with that and the cloak, she'd had this impression that he belonged in the outfit. That he was some sort of ancient king come to life.

Like that moment in her house, this moment ended as fast as it came on, until she was looking at ordinary Deacon again. His eyes were glowing faintly yellow because his leopard was near to the surface. But he was dressed in his usual jeans and t-shirt, with a cream cable-knit sweater over the t-shirt as a nod to the chilly air —an extra layer he didn't need thanks to his shifter metabolism. His black hair was a little messy from the wind. And his jaw was tight because…well, troll. But he looked like his ordinary, dangerous, shifter self.

Okay.

So.

There were some things she'd really really liked to ask his grandmother about this.

But first. The troll.

She faced the creature again, noting it hadn't moved. And hadn't stopped staring at Deacon either.

So she tried again asking a question. "Can we help you with something? Need directions or… Well, I can't help much with that. First time here. But it's great! Beautiful city, isn't it? I might be in love. I mean, I love my home too, but this place. It's got castles. Castles!"

The troll's gaze finally dropped to her, and some of the rocks along its brow moved around. She got the impression of a frown without any of the usual signs of a frown.

She shrugged. "I like castles," she said.

"We are waiting for the queen," the troll finally said.

Which was very useful information. "Ah. Good to know. Thanks. Which one?"

Again that movement of rocks and facial fissures that indicated a frown.

"Which queen?" Cary clarified. "There are an awful lot of them about." Including a human one down south in London. But Cary was pretty sure this didn't have anything to do with her.

This was Faery stuff.

"The queen will be here shortly."

Which was less useful information since it ignored her question.

She hoped shortly meant the same thing to the troll as it did to her. Time in Faery was a very weird thing. She'd been inside Faery for what felt like a few hours and a week of time had passed here in the real world. Shortly for a Fae queen could mean, like, next month.

She was not standing in the cold and dark in the middle of the gardens under Edinburgh castle for a month. She had castles to tour. And shortbread to eat.

Another few moments passed. During which Cary noticed the troll had a sword strapped to its back, the hilt just poking above its massive shoulders on the left. Given the size of the hilt, she was going to guess the sword was one of those long, broadsword type ones that were popular in Scotland, except even bigger to accommodate a troll. The hilt was wrapped in brown leather with silver wires crossing it, colors that blended into the troll's skin, but had a faint purple glow when she looked at it from the corner of her eye, which was the special Fae metal that made up their weapons.

Most Fae were allergic to iron to some degree or other. Some more allergic than others. Jaxer's allergy was so mild, he could go in and out of human buildings comfortably and lean against a wrought iron fence without breaking out in hives, but he avoided getting into cars, and rides in elevators were very uncomfortable for him.

Cary tried to wrack her brain for more information on trolls and their various strengths and weaknesses. She hadn't dealt with many trolls over the years. But there'd been a few living-under-a-bridge sort. High Fae guard trolls were new, however. And she couldn't remember if there were different species of trolls with different levels of allergies.

At any rate, all weapons in Faery were made of special alloy that combined with magic and made the weapons something the Fae could handle. She assumed the troll's sword was that kind of weapon. No less dangerous for lacking traditional steel. Maybe more dangerous because of the magic.

Another moment passed while she went down this mental side road, and when nothing seemed to be happening except for the mist around their ankles getting thicker, Cary considered asking more questions. She was quite good at irritating people into giving her answers. Or at least irritate them into attacking, which at least got things moving. Sometimes, she could irritate a bad guy into leaving—she considered that one of her specialties because the problem with Protector magic was it was strictly defensive so she couldn't do anything offensive about bad guys. So she'd learned to piss them off so much they went away.

She would never admit this out loud, especially to Deacon, but sometimes she really enjoyed doing that.

About to start down that road to irritate answers out of the troll, she opened her mouth, but Deacon laid a hand on her arm, a gentle touch that silenced her. She glanced back at him again. Had to blink hard when she got hit with another of those weird impressions that he was someone else, someone who *belonged* in Faery. When she was looking at her Deacon again, she questioned him with a frown. Without even glancing away from the troll, he nodded down at the mist.

Cary turned her attention down and looked closer at the wisps of fog surrounding them. Not so wispy now, she realized. Now the fog ungulated in the thick waves of white over the ground.

Avoiding the circle of protected grass around her and Deacon.

Her Protector shield was holding back the mist. Which meant it was dangerous. Not normal mist. Something bad enough she could see the outline of her shield's circumference, a shield she couldn't normally see, circling her and Deacon.

"That's bad, huh?" she asked.

She took Deacon's grunt as a yes.

She faced the troll again. "Gonna explain why there's mist that's dangerous to us floating around your ankles, or do I have to wait for answers for that, too?"

"The queen will be here shortly."

"Not an answer." Did it even know any other phrases? The troll had gone back to staring at Deacon, but otherwise hadn't moved a muscle. Or rock. Or whatever. Like it could stand there unmoving for a century and not notice.

Cary didn't have a century. "I'd just like to know which queen we're waiting for," she said with a huff. "Is it Tatiana? Danu? One of the Scottish queens? Someone else I don't know about? The Queen of England? Mary Queen of Scots reincarnated? Who?"

The troll's gaze once again shifted down to her. "The queen," it said. As if that clarified everything.

She rolled her eyes. "Look…" she started, then stopped short.

Around them, the mist started to swirl and churn. Angry waves of movement that rose and fell. A sound like moaning came from inside the thickening white fog. And then it started to shred into strips of white, damp air. As the mist shredded, the grass beneath came into view in increasingly larger swath. Paper tearing away to reveal the present beneath. A scent like pine needles rose up around Cary, pleasant but strong. And under it, she realized she could just get a hint of something sweetly sour. A sort of rotting detritus scent but very faint. The pine smell overpowered it a moment later, until that was all she could smell.

And after another moment, the mist disappeared completely. Leaving behind perfectly ordinary grass in the dim lights filtering down to them from the surrounding city.

The troll remained standing a few feet away. But the mist was officially gone.

Cary looked around, glanced at Deacon with raised brows. He shrugged, but most of his attention was still on the troll.

She glanced back toward their guard just as the air next to him opened up.

And a tall, red-haired woman stepped out.

"Grandma?" Deacon said.

Cary's eyes widened.

Grandma?

8

ary had met Deacon's great grandfather, Keith Ferguson. The man was the spitting image of Deacon, just older. Including Deacon's golden eyes. Deacon's father, Keith's grandson, Evan Jones had the blue eyes that Deacon's twin brother inherited. Until meeting Keith, Cary had assumed the golden eyes came from his mother's side, but there was obviously a lot of his father in Deacon, too.

But given the darker hair, the golden or blue eyes, the overall…look of Deacon, Keith, and Evan, what Cary hadn't been expecting from Belle Ferguson was…curly red hair and bright green eyes.

And given she was a grandmother, the lack of gray threading through her red hair was a testament to both excellent genes and some really great hair dye.

Belle did look older, a woman in her sixties perhaps, who may or may not be a grandmother, but was one of the grandmothers who'd decided not to go with the whole "grandma" look. Her curly red hair was wild and long, tamed only by a few braids at the temple that kept the mass from her face. Her skin was pale and lined, with a scattering of freckles across her cheeks and nose. Her sharp green eyes were circled by pale lashes. And her mouth took up more of her wide face than should have looked good, but somehow it suited the woman.

She was dressed in baggy jeans that hung on a slim frame and a long-sleeved white poet shirt with a purple thistle embroidered on it at around the waist. It was a very sixties or seventies looking outfit for a woman who had become a grandmother in the nineteen sixties. But then, shifters weren't like vampires. They didn't necessarily cleave to the fashions of their youth. Cary wasn't entirely sure when Belle's *youth* had been, and she wasn't going to ask—well, she might ask Deacon later, but she certainly wasn't going to ask his *grandmother* how old she was.

At any rate, it didn't matter because the clothes somehow managed to fit the woman and the woman only looked in her sixties anyway, and if Cary thought about that too long it made her head hurt because Deacon might look like he was in his mid to late thirties, but he was in his mid-fifties and his grandmother had to be a *lot* older than she looked.

All this flew through her mind in the beats between Belle arriving from a split in thin air, and the troll taking a step behind Belle and saying, "My queen," with a slight head bow.

Which was…not at all what Cary had been expecting of this moment.

A troll's queen should have been a Fae queen. Given where they were, that queen should have been one of the queens of the Scottish court—Unseelie or Seelie. Just before leaving, thanks to Jaxer's warning, Cary had quickly reviewed what information she had in her secret attic library on the Scottish queens. Last anyone had recorded, the leader of the Unseelie court was still the witch queen Nicneven. And the Seelie court queen was Elphame.

Not the leopard shifter, and decidedly *not* Fae, Belle Ferguson.

Was this what Jaxer had meant about Belle having links to the Fae court and the queens, because, yeah, this was not what Cary had been expecting and Jaxer really really should have mentioned! Unless he didn't know this part.

Deacon obviously hadn't known. He looked as taken aback as Cary by the troll's honorific, which meant... Well, she wasn't sure. Except that explanations seemed to be in order.

A cold wind swept through the surrounding garden, the twinkling lights from the city the only thing breaking up the dark shadows under the rocky hill and castle. The autumn trees, preparing for winter, shivered their remaining leaves in the breeze. But instead of fresh nature scents or even the scent of the surrounding city, what washed over Cary in that light wind was the strong scent of pine needles. Like someone had just dropped them into the middle of a Christmas tree lot. Except there were not pine trees in the large, manicured city garden.

Underneath the pine tree scent was another something that Cary couldn't put her finger on. Not unpleasant, but a little sharp. Deacon probably knew what that was with his super shifter sense of smell, but it eluded Cary.

Belle took a couple of steps closer to them, her expression softening as she looked at Deacon. "My boy," she murmured, her Scottish accent soft and lilting. "My beautiful grandson. Yer the spitting image of my own dad." She smiled briefly, then her expression cleared and she grew serious. "Taken you long enough to get here. And not a moment too soon, I'd say. Your mum's been in touch. Let me know some of what's going on. Unfortunately, you've come when I'm in the middle of...a bit of a crisis, so we'll have to get going now. I'll let Fiona know I've absconded with ye. Don't worry about your stuff, she'll manage it for ye until I can get you back for it."

"Uh…" Cary said, her gaze jumping between Belle and Deacon. A very uncharitable part of her wanted to whine, *But I'm supposed to tour the castle tomorrow*! Since that didn't seem the best way to introduce herself to Deacon's grandmother, she left her comment at "uh" and hoped Deacon understood her hesitance.

Deacon's frown didn't help the suddenly jumping nerves in Cary's stomach. "What's going on, Nan? What was that mist? And —" he glanced at the troll and raised his brows, "—'my queen'?"

Belle waved a hand in the air, a gesture that drew attention to a big sapphire ring Cary hadn't noticed earlier. The stone winked purple-blue in the shadows, as if casting its own light. "Got lots to explain," she said. "But not here. The Strix is here. I can only dissipate his magic for so long." She shook her head and tsked. "Terrible pain in the arse, I'll tell you." She motioned Cary and Deacon forward. "Let's move. We'll do proper introductions and all when we're safe."

"Uh," Cary said again. "We could technically be safe here, cause, I can, uh, shield us."

"Noticed and glad of that particular skill," Belle said. "Have some questions about you, too, Ms. Cary Redmond of the Dana. But that'll have to wait."

Cary's eyes widened. "Of the Dana?" she squeaked.

Belle motioned them forward again. "Come come. Not enough time to talk here."

Deacon set a hand to Cary's back. They exchanged a long look, then followed Belle to that tear in reality she'd stepped through.

If they were going into Faery, Cary was really not prepared. Faery was scary. And the last time she'd been inside Faery, she'd died. Faery was not a good place for humans. Or shifters.

And the only good thing about it being a scary place for shifters was that she could protect Deacon from the Fae magic and that kept them both mostly safe—including keeping her from absorbing *too* much Fae magic while she was inside a realm literally built of magic. Technically, she supposed she could raise her shield and keep herself safe now even without Deacon, but since she wasn't confident of her ability to do that still—in fact she was very very *not* confident she could do that under stress— she was grateful at least to have Deacon with her.

Still, she really didn't want to go through Faery.

"Uh," she muttered as Belle gestured them through the rip in space.

Beyond the tear, Cary could see a lot of swirling lights dancing around a thick forest of pine and oak trees. A forest so thick, she could only see a few feet into it. Little winking points of white light flickered around the trees like fireflies. But since this was Faery, she was going to assume those lights were dangerous until proven otherwise.

The sky was hidden behind the heavy canopy, but Cary still got the impression of nighttime.

"We're not staying in Faery long, right?" Deacon asked, his gaze on the trees, too. His hand at Cary's back flexing. "I don't want Cary in there long."

Deacon had never really gotten over her dying. She couldn't blame him. She'd be destroyed if he died, too. And even though she hadn't been dead for long, the trauma of that moment still haunted him. She didn't remember it, of course. Cause...you know, dead. Still, neither of them were fans of Faery anymore.

"We won't be. I've promised Danu. Just got to get you to a safer place."

Danu? The Irish queen had been talking to Belle about Cary?

Cary had *so many questions*. And apparently no time to ask. Yet.

Keeping Deacon firmly behind her so her shields could protect them both, she stepped up to the tear in reality. Looked round that rip to the troll behind it who hadn't moved or done…anything but stand there as a silent sentry. She glanced briefly at Belle, who gestured again to the opening.

Okay. Guess they were doing this.

She gave Edinburgh Castle one last look, trying not to sigh in disappointment, then stepped through the rip in reality, into the deep, dark Fae forest beyond.

9

The minute Cary stepped into Faery she felt the pressure of the magic around her. Last time she'd been here, she'd been protecting Jaxer, Eriana, and Deacon—until she hadn't been—and so the ability to absorb magic was mitigated by her shields. Now, she wasn't sure if Deacon was in trouble enough for her shields to come up automatically. She might have to try to raise them herself.

Except…

Usually, when she absorbed magic, she felt a sort of tingling along her skin. Like insects crawling over her, but gently. It didn't hurt. Just a lot of tingles. The more magic she absorbed, though, the more *uncomfortable* things got. And the pressure had, in the past, killed her once and nearly killed her a second time.

Now, as she stood in the darkness under the pine and oak canopy with tiny pinpoint lights dancing around her, with the scent of pine mingling with a loamy freshness and a sort of cinnamon spice undertone, Cary felt the pressure of all the magic around her.

But no tingles.

"I must be protecting you from the place," she murmured to Deacon, out of habit more than to keep the information about her job from Belle.

Technically, most of Deacon's family didn't know what Cary was, outside of his mother, who'd guessed because she was old and smart and had encountered Protectors before. But thanks to Cary's last visit to Faery, everyone here knew what she was. Actually, they'd known before she'd ever entered Faery, or at least suspected, because she was Jaxer's friend, and everyone in the English and Irish courts knew he worked with the North American Fae to create Protectors.

News of the way Cary had unleashed a whole bunch of magic inside Faery and refreshed the entire place had traveled through all parts of the realm at this stage. The flow of magic between Faery and Protectors in North America, plus Cary's unleashing of a *bunch* of magic after it had filtered through her, had pushed back the decay and rot that had been consuming Faery for centuries.

So much so, the other courts were now looking to get Protectors of their own—finally! If the magic in Faery wasn't regularly refreshed with new Fae, new magic, the entire realm started to rot. And as it happened, those renewals weren't happening as much in the centuries since the Fae had stopped the frequent movement between their realm and the human one.

Protectors, and Cary in particular, changed that. It meant the Fae would have to interact with humans more, again, but it also meant their realm would survive. Which was, as it turned out, good for everyone because it meant the Fae didn't invade this realm and destroy it for humans. Win-win.

As Cary took in the massive trees and greenery and sparkling dancing lights, she was glad the Fae realm wouldn't die. For lots of reasons. She still wasn't comfortable standing here in the middle of it. But she was glad it was going to survive.

At any rate, she knew she didn't have to whisper about her shields and such in front of Belle, or the troll who'd followed them through the breach. If Belle was this involved in Faery, could move through the place and had been talking to Danu and apparently had a troll bodyguard, Belle knew what Cary was.

Still, Cary found herself being vague about it all as she spoke with Deacon. "No tingles," she said. "But I can feel the place around me like I couldn't last time."

"We're no' staying long," Belle said before Deacon could speak. "Canna have my grandson here long." She nodded at him and Cary stepped back from his side long enough to take a good look at him.

And gasp.

"Holy shit," she muttered.

Deacon narrowed his eyes at her. "What? What's wrong?"

"Nothing…exactly. But remember last time we were in the Irish court and you were all glowy and sparkly and I said you looked like a king?"

"Vaguely."

"You're doing that again. Only this time without the Nags' cape and brooch. Which means it probably wasn't either of those things doing the king-golden-sparkle-glowy thing."

His mouth twitched into an almost smile at her description, but the amusement dropped as he glanced down at his hands. "I don't see anything."

"You didn't last time either, remember. But from my perspective, you look magnificent. I mean, more than usual. You know the way Eriana and Jaxer look when they drop their glamour? That's what's happening to you. Like, your gorgeousness got dialed up to outrageous levels and now isn't entirely real."

It was, however, overwhelming. She actually had trouble

looking at him. He *looked* Fae, instead of like a shifter. There was an aura around him of faint gold light. His dark hair looked thicker, a little longer, and she'd swear there were braids in his hair that hadn't been there before. He was still just dressed in jeans and his sweater, but the impression of a long tunic, leather trousers, and a cape sort of waivered over the top of that. Like he was *also* wearing the other outfit at the same time, only it was more ephemeral, not quite his reality. But almost.

It was the weirdest thing she'd seen—and she'd seen some pretty weird shit in her years as a Protector. But this...this was more than the purple-gold aura around him right before Belle arrived. He'd still looked like himself then. Now... This was her mate, a man whose face she'd memorized. And in that moment, he didn't look entirely like himself. He looked... Well, like a Fae king.

Which he wasn't.

"Is it because he's going to be the leopard king after his mother?" Cary asked Belle. "Does Faery recognized that and do —" she waved her hand at Deacon, "—this to kings of other species?"

"No," Belle said. "At least not entirely. But this is a story I'll need to discuss with ye when we get to where we're going. No' here where there're too many listening ears."

Deacon frowned at both of them. "Why aren't I seeing any changes?"

"Promise I'll tell you all, love," Belle said to him. "Just no' here."

Cary noticed Belle's accent seemed to be getting stronger since they'd stepped into Faery, though maybe she just hadn't said enough in the human realm for Cary to notice after listening to all sorts of Scottish accents all evening.

They followed Belle along a path through the trees, a path that shouldn't have been wide enough for the troll who walked in front of Belle. Yet somehow the trees made room to accommodate the wide creature and then closed back in around Cary, so that it felt like she barely had room to walk normally.

In the distance, something howled. And the little buzzing lights dancing around them sped up at that sound.

Belle glance in the direction of the howl, scowling, and shook her head. "Och, they couldna just keep quiet for a few minutes," she muttered.

"Something we need to worry about?" Cary said, following Belle's gaze into the trees.

"No' if we get outta the woods before they find us," Belle said, marching ahead faster.

Cary picked up speed to keep up.

She kept Deacon at her back in the hopes of her shields staying up automatically. The pressure of all that Fae magic around her was a constant ticking time bomb in the back of her mind. She might have managed to absorb an absolute shit-ton of magic recently, but too much and she'd be dead. And this was a realm *made* of magic.

She wondered if Deacon was remembering the last time they'd been here together. And the thought that he might be reliving that made her chest tight. She reached back and took his hand, squeezing gently. He held hers tight enough, she almost missed the slight tremor running under his skin. When she looked over her shoulder at him, he still had the kingly regalia superimposed over his real self, but his eyes were now also glowing yellow, a sign that his leopard was close to the surface.

"You okay?" she said. "Not going to run off into the woods, right?"

He grunted something she took as, *Fine.* Which meant he

wasn't. But they'd be out of here soon. She kept his hand in hers as she faced forward again.

The trees cleared ahead of them, opening onto a tall hill. At the top of the hill sat a circle of standing stones, irregular, roughly rectangular shapes like sentries on the hilltop. Small stone steps cut into the hill, leading up the circle. Cary followed Belle up but kept swiveling around to try and see everything around her at once.

The little firefly lights that had been following them through the woods, vanished. And overhead was a black night sky with star constellations Cary didn't recognize. No moon. But the stars were bright enough here to cast plenty of illumination. The scent of cinnamon spice got stronger around the standing stones, a hint of sweetness underneath the pine.

She wondered what Deacon was smelling. The place was sort of designed to lure and then break the minds of humans and shifters alike. What was the realm using to try and lure Deacon into staying?

But she didn't have time to ask. The troll stepped up to the standing stones and, to Cary's amazement, took up a place where a stone had been missing and…sort of shrank down and reformed until it looked just like the other stones.

"Are all the stones trolls?" she asked, her eyebrows raised high.

"They're my guards, aye," Belle said. "They'll keep us safe from aught that might follow."

"Something might try and follow us?" Cary's hand tightened on Deacon's.

"N'er past the trolls," Belle said with a confidence Cary had to appreciate.

To be fair, she wouldn't try to get past guard trolls either. But then, she was just an ordinary human woman, not one of the Fae. Who knew what other Fae species might do.

Belle led them into the center of the stone circle, then raised her hands over her head and chanted something in Gaelic that Cary couldn't catch. Not that her ability to understand Gaelic was any better than her ability to understand most languages. She sucked at languages—much to her bosses' despair.

The air around them shimmered, like waves of heat rising up from the earth. But the air itself was cold. Colder here than it had been back in the human realm. Cary shivered. Deacon stepped closer so that she could feel his heat along her back, even through her jacket. The shimmering turned almost opaque.

And then it faded, dissipating around them.

Cary looked around. They were still standing in the stone circle. At night. On top of a hill. Surrounded by dark forest.

But the scent had changed. Now a more ordinary loamy scent, without the hints of cinnamon or even a very strong pine smell. When she glanced up, the stars looked more familiar. And there was a quarter moon hanging just above the horizon.

"Uhm…" She glanced at Belle as she realized she was no longer feeling the pressure of Fae magic all around her anymore. The air was frosty, little crystals of dew ice covering the standing stones, but no magic lights and no magic pressure.

"We're back in the human realm now, aren't we?" she asked.

Belle grinned. "I knew I'd like ye," she said. "Couldna been just anyone to be my grandson's mate."

"Uh. Thanks?" That hadn't really answered her question, but it was nice to know Belle approved of her. One hurdle down.

"We're near my home," Belle said. She started down the hill. "This way. It's only a short walk. And the kettle's on."

Cary almost laughed. Of course it was.

10

———

*B*elle led them out of the woods, across a paved road and through a small gate in a stacked stone wall that was half overgrown with greenery. The quarter moon hung higher in the sky by the time they left the forest behind, and there was so little light pollution in the area, that sliver of moon gave decent illumination. Not that either Belle or Deacon needed it with their shifter eyesight, but Cary appreciated the extra light.

She picked up a little tingling along her nerves as they passed through the wooden gate, a hint of magic there. But once she'd passed into the front yard, the tingle went away, so she had to assume she wasn't absorbing anymore. The fact that she'd felt the tingling meant they were probably pretty safe here because her shields were obviously no longer up protecting Deacon.

And if all that hadn't given away the fact that they weren't in Faery anymore, the electrical wires strung between wooden poles along the narrow road in front of the house would have confirmed they were back in the human realm.

Comfortable that they were somewhere in Scotland and not in Faery, Cary finally let her shoulders relax. She had no idea where they were, specifically—beyond the fact that it was probably Belle's home—but at least it was somewhere Cary figured must be safe.

The cottage beyond the stone fence was a large two-story building built of dark stone, with a pitched roof and a narrow chimney with smoke gently curling out of the top. The windows were ablaze with light, giving the home a welcoming feel. There was a large glass greenhouse attached to one side of the cottage, which probably looked beautiful in the daylight, and another large glassed-in area covered the front door. The surrounding gardens and lawn were well tended and a bit wild. Cary hoped she'd get a chance to see the area better in the daylight, because in the dark it looked lovely.

A cold breeze whished through the garden as they followed a narrow stone path to the front door. Deacon remained at Cary's back, though now she suspected it was more to do with guarding her back than her protecting him.

The inside of the cottage was as charming as the outside, with white walls and hard wood floors covered in thick rugs and runners. The downstairs was very open, with only a few walls here and there to separate different areas, so despite the size of the place, Cary could still see from almost one side to the other. The opening into the greenhouse was wide and surrounded by more plants. The sitting room on the opposite side of the cottage boasted lots of comfortable, large furniture in an eclectic array of colors, displaying no effort at interior design, and a small stone fireplace with a low fire still flickering on the grate, filling the house with a comforting woodsmoke scent.

Between the sitting room and the staircase that led to the upper floor, was one of the only closed off areas on the floor, but the door was open and through the door Cary spotted shelves filled with books.

The kitchen was on the same side of the house as the greenhouse, open plan with a lot of modern appliances, all shiny silver, and a backsplash behind the sink tiled in thick glassy tiles in blues and greens. True to her word, Belle had an electric kettle on the light gray granite countertop with steam rising from it.

Belle motioned them toward a largish, round wooden table near a bay window next to the greenhouse entrance. "Tea'll do?" she asked as she headed into the kitchen. "We've a lot to talk about. I could put coffee into the French press too, if either of ye would prefer?"

Cary jumped at the offer of coffee and settled at the table, watching quietly as Belle moved around the kitchen getting things ready. Deacon hovered between the kitchen and the table, also watching his grandmother, a frown creasing his brow.

"What's going on, Nan?" he asked. "What was that mist? Why did we have to risk coming here through Faery? What do you have to do with Faery?"

And, Cary thought, why did that troll call you its queen? But she kept her mouth shut on that question. She assumed they'd get to it, and if not, well, then she could ask. But her curiosity made her foot bounce under the table.

"Easy question first," Belle said. "The mist was a magical poison sent from an enemy to take out my grandson as a warning. This enemy didn't anticipate me getting there in time to deal with the poison. And I likely wouldn't have either, if not for whatever shield ye two used to hold it off." She glanced over her shoulder, her arms up as she lifted mugs from a cabinet. "I assume that's yer Protector shield, then is it?" She stared right at Cary.

Cary glanced at Deacon and then nodded.

Belle gave a small, satisfied grunt and turned back to taking the mugs out. They were solid, sturdy ceramic mugs with little stars covering them.

"Your answer is raising more questions," Deacon pointed out. "Enemy? What's going on?"

"I know yer here to learn to control that massive amount of magic in ye, and it's about time. Too long you've gone without training it."

"You sound like my mother," Deacon muttered.

"Aye. She and I agree on this point. You should've been training all along. But I understand yer reluctance, love." She looked up at him while she pushed down the plunger in the French press. "And a bit of what's finally driven you here. We'll need to talk more about that, too."

Deacon's turn to glance briefly at Cary before nodding.

Belle brought a steaming mug of coffee to Cary and a milky cup of tea to Deacon. Her own tea was black and unsweetened. She motioned to the table again and Deacon finally sat. He cradled his mug without drinking—he wasn't a tea drinker or a coffee drinker so Cary wondered why he hadn't protested the tea—his scowl focused on the smooth wooden tabletop.

"This enemy…?" he started. "Since when do you have enemies trying to kill your family members? And why didn't I know about that?"

Belle waved her hand in the air, the sapphire ring winking in the overhead lights. "There's a lot yer father doesn't know, and it's better that way. He'd worry and I'd never hear the end of it. T'was enough getting my own father to retire near to you, so he'd be safe and away from it all."

"Gramps knows about all this?"

"Not all of it. Not any more than yer father knows. Like I said, they'd worry."

"I'm worried. What's going on?"

Belle sat back in the high-backed chair and sighed. "Not really sure where to start," she murmured, half to herself. "And how much you need to know."

"Think I need to know all of it if there's someone out there that's a threat to me and my mate," Deacon said.

And Cary realized his eyes were still glowing faintly yellow, his leopard not too far from the surface. That he was that edgy inside his own grandmother's house was…worrying.

Belle met his gaze. "That part… Aye, you need to know about it. Suppose you could say it all started when I had an affair with Nicneven, the queen of the Unseelie court."

Cary blinked and hid her fascinated surprise in a big gulp of coffee. Belle had history. And while Cary realized she shouldn't be so delighted by the gossip she was about to hear, she was absolutely delighted she was about to hear some really good gossip.

"This was well before I met your grandfather. I was a bit wild in my youth," she said, almost primly, which made Cary's grin grow right along with her admiration for Belle.

"At any rate," Belle said, "in my more wild youth, I spent time among the High Fae. Out of Faery mostly. Didna have a death wish, and even with Nicneven's promises and supposed protection, I didn't trust her not to let Faery lure me to stay. Wild. Not an eejit."

Oh, yeah, Cary really loved Belle at this point.

"Our affair was brief in the grand scheme of things. My parents didna approve, of course, but more because they were certain I'd go into Faery and never come out. Came close to proving them right once. But only because I was tricked and that's where my relationship with Nicneven was supposed to have ended."

Oh, there was a lot more there than Belle was saying out loud,

Cary was sure. But she didn't want to interrupt the story flow, in case Belle stopped talking. But Cary had no doubt that breakup was not as straightforward and simple as Belle was making it sound.

"I thought that was the end of it," Belle said. "But…" She shook her head. "It's impossible to do what I did without consequences. There's no way to interact regularly with the Fae and not be changed by it."

Deacon glanced briefly at Cary, but she only noticed because the statement made her glance at him. Her entire job involved working with Fae, her mentor was Fae, and the magic she channeled was Fae. She *never* went into Faery—except that one time when she died—because she had learned better than that. But still, she was surrounded by Fae in her work life. And that *had* changed her in such fundamental ways, she wasn't entirely an ordinary human anymore.

But she'd assumed that was down to her weird, rare ability to absorb magic. Would she have been changed no matter what, just because she worked with Fae?

When she got a chance to meet more than one other Protector, she thought that might be an important question to ask them. She would ask the one other Protector she did know, right after she got back from Scotland.

Belle watched their silent exchange, and nodded. "Aye, Cary'll have been changed by her job. And by her time in Faery. And I'm afraid, Deacon, you will've too. But that's more to do with yer relationship to me than to the time you spent there for Jaxer."

The fact that Belle knew who Jaxer was probably shouldn't have surprised Cary. Belle obviously knew a *lot* about Faery. More than Deacon had obviously known or suspected. And Jaxer had been both a bane and a darling of both the Irish and English courts. Made sense he'd be known to the Scottish courts even if he never did try to sneak in up here.

Still. Hearing his name from Belle did surprise Cary and left her feeling disoriented, even more so than the trip through Faery to get here had, like two different words were blending together that didn't normal interact.

"After my affair with the queen ended," Belle continued, "I realized some of my previous skills had...changed. Because of my birth order, and the birth order of my parents and theirs before them, I was always a strong leopard. And I had a hint of the magic that yer mother has. Didna pass that down to my own firstborn, which surprised me to be honest. But you got it in spades thanks to yer mother and my contribution. Mostly, my magic let me feel other leopards around me. And if I concentrated, I could shift back into clothes instead of having to get dressed after returning to my human form. That was handy, I must admit."

Cary nodded. She agreed. Not that Deacon hardly ever shifted that way. In hindsight, she knew for a fact he'd returned to his human form naked in front of her on purpose. She didn't mind that even a little bit now. He was magnificent naked. But it had been a thing in the beginning. And knowing he could have shifted back with clothes on and didn't *have* to be naked when he returned to human form had been a thing when she'd discovered the truth.

"Beyond that, though, I didna have the skills someone like yer mother has," Belle said, "at least, not before my time with the Fae." She shook her head. "After, I developed talents that aren't part of normal shifter magic. I could cast spells. And I can see a bit into the future."

"What kind of spells?" Cary asked before she could stop herself. They'd get to the seeing the future part in a bit. She hoped.

"Spells that aren't typical of a leopard," Belle said. She

glanced between Deacon and Cary, then gave a little nod. "One, is the glamour surrounding my home."

"I felt something when I walked through the gate," Cary said, trying not to get too excited at the fact that she'd figured something was up there ahead of time. Her excitement—*hey, I know that, I knew something was there!*—was a little embarrassing.

"How does it work?" Deacon asked. His gaze jumped to Cary, but his eyes were narrowed and there was the speculative crease between his brows he got when he was thinking something serious and important.

"Thanks to the glamour on the wall around my property, if someone is on the outside of that wall, they won't see the house beyond unless I want them to. Anyone not invited in will walk right past my gate without seeing it. If someone looks this way from the road, they see a hillside and some farmland stretching out across the fields. They might see a sheep or two, depending on the day. But they willna see my home."

With each sentence, Cary's eyes got wider and wider. And before she could contain herself, or even think better of it, she said, "I have that on my house, too!" At Belle's silently-questioning raised brows, Cary said, "My bosses, the Fae who make Protectors, they put that on my house as a sort of…perk of the job, I guess. Gives Protectors one place in the world where they don't have to be on guard and can just relax." She winced when she said, "Plus, I don't know about the other Protectors, but I've sort of built up a number of…uh…enemies over the years that are pretty scary and dangerous. It's nice that they can't find me when I'm sleeping or in the shower."

"Certainly it is," Belle said with a nod. "Like it or not, my time with the Fae created a few enemies for me, too. One of which is responsible for that mist that might've killed ye if not for your being a Protector. When I realized I could cast glamour spells, one of the first things I learned to do was to create a safe space for myself."

Something in what Belle had just said struck a memory for Cary. "Your father, he lives in a little piece of peace there in Oregon that he implied was a bit like a bubble realm. He didn't tell me who made that haven for him, but... That was you, wasn't it?"

"Aye. After he lost his mate, my mother, he nearly broke. Was afraid he'd follow her before I was ready to say goodbye to him, so I offered a compromise. He stuck around, I'd give him a peaceful place to live, near his American great-grandchildren, and neither of us would have to say goodbye to the other just yet. He's lived there a lot longer than I'd hoped and I'm grateful for it."

"He's a very nice man, your father," Cary said. "I was honored to meet him."

"He enjoyed meeting you too," Belle said. Cary's turn to ask a silent question with her raised brows. Belle chuckled. "We video chat regularly. Our way of keeping track of each other."

Cary opened her mouth to ask how Belle had survived the loss of her mate, but realized before the words came out that actually, she wasn't sure if Belle's mate was dead. No one had said as much, but also, whenever Deacon talked about his grandmother, it was *only* his grandmother. Not his grandmother and grandfather. The house looked like the home of a person living alone. There wasn't the odd mixing of stuff that two different people accumulated. There hadn't been another set of keys by the front door. And most telling, Deacon hadn't once asked about his grandfather.

All this time, Cary had just assumed Belle's mate had died years ago. But since no one said anything about it, or talked about him in anyway, Cary wondered if there wasn't more of a story there.

And if there was, she'd better check with Deacon before bringing it up. The last thing Cary wanted to do was offend Belle within hours of getting here.

Rather than accidentally putting her foot in her mouth, she instead said, "So you built a safe space for yourself and for your father. What other glamour can you do?"

Glamour was Jaxer's greatest skill, and he could do some spooky things with it, including fooling someone's senses so completely, they'd interact with one of his illusions like it was real. Having seen some of Jaxer's glamour at work, Cary wondered if Belle could do similar, or if her skills were more limited since she wasn't technically a Fae.

"The usual disguising myself if needs be. But whatever I inherited from my time with Nicneven, it's got its limits. I do better anchoring the glamours to things that don't move. Glamouring up a moving thing, like a car, or a person, is harder. Those illusions fail quicker for me."

"Fair. What else? Besides glamour? Any other spells?"

"Some basic spells relating to witchcraft. Nicneven became a sort of patron saint of witches, so apparently, I picked up the ability to cast spells like light fires and, importantly to our conversation, dissipating mist."

"Proper witch level of magic or limits on that too since it's not natural?"

"Limits." Belle narrowed her eyes at Cary and leaned her forearms on the table, the mug of tea still nestled between her hands, though steam no longer rose from the cup. "Your ability to absorb magic… I'd love to know more about how that works."

Oops. Cary forgot there might be a sort of quid pro quo of information exchange. But given the reason Deacon was here, she also figured Belle needed to know in more detail what Cary was capable of. And what she wasn't.

"I've learned to use the magic I absorb. Casting spells to use it up. Even threw some demon fire at a demon once." That had been very satisfying because the demon had been Oliver Holland and it had been his own magic she was throwing back at him. "Using the magic means I don't hold it so I don't die. Which, you know, is useful."

Belle chuckled.

"But once it's used up, it's used up. I don't make my own magic the way a witch or wizard would."

"How much magic can you absorb this way? So long as you use it?"

"Got me," Cary said honestly. "I've absorbed a lot in the last few months. More than in the seven years prior, I think. And it only killed me that one time. So I'm assuming I can absorb a lot—so long as I use it up immediately and don't store it in my cells for too long."

She saw Deacon wince and wondered if it was her bringing up the time she'd died, or if it had to do with her absorbing his magic during the demon god thing. She glanced at him. "Should we tell her now or wait?" she asked him.

Deacon let out a long breath that puffed up some of the hair on his forehead. Which made Cary want to run her fingers through the thick strands and push them off his face. She didn't. Because his *grandmother* was sitting right across the table from them. But she was tempted.

"Nan," he started, "one of the reasons I've finally given in to training my magic is that I shared it with Cary, not long ago. At first on accident. Then on purpose so she'd have it to use in a fight. But... I'm worried I'll share the magic again on accident, and I don't even know what all it can do. So I don't know what it could do to Cary. I can't risk hurting her."

"Of course not," Belle said, nodding. "What did ye do with it when you got it?" she asked Cary.

"I was absorbing a lot of different stuff in that moment," she admitted, "and I ended up doing what I do best. I made a shield." She shrugged.

Her entire life and training in the supernatural and preternatural world involved using shields to protect people, with magic she hadn't even controlled until a few weeks ago. So it made sense that her instinctive use of magic she was finally able to control was just to create a big ass shield from it. She would have been more surprised if she'd done literally anything else with it on instinct.

Inside that thought, she acknowledged that if she could use magic from others that wasn't natural to her to create a shield, raising her Protector shield, with magic she'd been channeling for years, probably should be easier than it had proven to be so far.

"You used up all that magic?" Belle asked. "None of it left now?"

There was a tightness to Belle's shoulders Cary didn't quite understand. After a brief glance at Deacon, she said, "None left. Used it all up. I pretty much have to, though, or I die. And that upsets Deacon, so I don't like to do it if I can avoid it."

Belle rolled her lips into her mouth, then shook her head and softly chuckled. "I'm looking forward to getting to know more of ye, Cary Redmond. I think my grandson has found a very interesting mate."

Cary was well aware that "interesting" could mean many things, and not all of them were complimentary, so she didn't comment.

Belle sighed. "But for the moment, we need to discuss this

enemy of mine. And the reason, all of this is happening now." She rose abruptly and went back into the kitchen, putting the kettle on again.

It struck Cary that Belle didn't move like a woman old enough to be Deacon's grandmother. To be fair, Keith had been pretty spry, too. But Belle moved more like Deacon's mother, like a woman in the prime of her life. Not one who'd moved into her later years. Was that a leopard thing or a had-an-affair-with-a-faery-queen thing?

"The problem, ye see," Belle said from the kitchen, with her back still to them, "is that Nicneven has gotten it into her fool head to live in the human realm for a bit. To play amongst her witches and experience life outside Faery. This left the Unseelie court without their queen. That threw off the delicate balance between the Unseelie and the Seelie courts. That balance is what keeps the Scottish court from bubbling over and causing as much trouble as the English court is want to do. Without it, the Scottish court would descend into warring with itself. That's good for no one in any realm."

"No it is not," Cary agreed with a nod.

Fights in Faery had a way of spilling over into the human realm and causing havoc. That hadn't happened in a very long time because the Fae had retreated so much from the human world. But that didn't mean it *couldn't* happen. And the Fae were so capricious, it wouldn't take much to set off a fight.

"So there's unrest in the Scottish court," Deacon said.

"More than unrest. The Unseelie court needed a queen or Elphame was going to swoop in and take over."

"The Seelie queen?" Cary asked, just to be sure.

"That's the one. As dangerous a queen as any of them, even if she likes to pretend she's all light and air and wouldna say boo to a cat. She's as vicious and greedy as they all are. And she saw an opening to increase her power and rid herself of a rival she'd been forced by circumstances to hold a peace with. She'd have succeeded too, if the Unseelie court hadna found someone to fill in for Nicneven in her absence."

"They got a new queen?" Deacon straightened in his chair, his tea mug forgotten on the table—the tea cold and untouched, which didn't surprise Cary at all. "Who?"

Belle finally faced them, letting out a long sigh. A knot formed in the pit of Cary's stomach. She knew what was coming even before Belle spoke. And still the admission stole her breath.

"I'm afraid," Belle said, "they got me."

11

Belle had placed a second, fresh cup of coffee and two new steaming cups of tea on the table before Cary or Deacon commented on what she had just said. The quiet house settled and ticked around them, those little noises that houses make. The refrigerator turned on. The plastic of the electric kettle made a little crinkling sound. In the distance, Cary would swear she heard sheep bleating. Darkness outside the windows was offset by the low, comfortable light inside. And the fire in the hearth in the sitting room continued to fill the cottage with a lovely woodburning scent.

Everything about the moment felt perfectly ordinary and normal. The house felt like any other house. The sounds and smells cozy and mundane. Yes, Cary recognized that there was a glamour on the stone fence surrounding the property, but she lived in a house with that same sort of glamour on it, so even that felt pretty normal to her.

Hearing Deacon's leopard shifter grandmother was now acting queen of a Faery court was not normal. Not even close to normal.

A shifter. Acting as a Fae queen. Inside Faery.

And not just any Fae court. No. The Unseelie faction of the Scottish court.

With the rival Fae queen of the Seelie court waiting in the wings.

They'd come here to help Deacon learn to control his magic, learn to use it so he didn't have to be afraid of hurting people anymore. Cary had not been expecting to land into a *situation*.

Yes, she'd been worried about Tatiana and Danu making trouble for *her*. And she'd known, thanks to Jaxer, that Deacon's grandmother had some links to Faery that even Deacon didn't know about. But this was…not what she'd anticipated. Something more along the lines of the affair with Nicneven. If that's all the tie to Faery had been, Cary would have understood Jaxer's hesitance and Deacon's ignorance of it—a grandmother is hardly going to tell her grandson about her wild days as a young woman having affairs with faery queens. But Belle *being* a queen…

She glanced at Deacon. Yeah, he looked pretty shocked by the news, too. His face had taken on that iceman look he got when he was carefully controlling all his emotions, when he was afraid of hurting others, so he tamped down all emotion and went into an almost robotic mode that, frankly, Cary hated. But also she understood so she didn't get on him about it. The fact that he felt the need to shut down his emotions this hard here in his grandmother's house was telling.

His eyes glowed yellow, but hadn't gone full-blown-shifter-about-to-break-out-of-his-skin. Yet. So he was in control.

But it looked like that control was thread thin.

Cary cleared her throat. Took a sip of the fresh coffee Belle had poured for her in the middle of the stunned silence. Watched Deacon *very* carefully wrapped his hands around his refreshed mug—Belle had just tossed out the cold, untouched tea that had been in his cup and poured him a new one, without comment. In the part of her brain not occupied with the bombshell news, Cary had to wonder if Belle knew Deacon didn't drink tea and was used to throwing out full mugs of untouched drink, but they went through the process anyway for some reason.

The whole Unseelie queen thing took precedence over asking about the tea thing, though.

She cleared her throat again. Sipped more coffee to wet her throat. Watched Deacon and Belle carefully. Belle was also watching Deacon carefully. She'd set her refreshed mug of tea in front of her at the table but hadn't touched it. She wasn't even holding it. Her hands rested lightly on the table, and her full attention was on her grandson.

Cary blinked when she realized there was no glowing yellow in Belle's eyes at all. No sign of her leopard rising as Deacon's did. She looked attentive and watchful, but not worried. Not nervous. Certainly not scared.

She knew exactly what Deacon could do, and she wasn't worried.

For some reason, that helped Cary relax, her shoulders slumping. And she actually tasted her next sip of coffee. Strong and hot and rich. Good coffee. Better than the instant she'd been expecting. One of these days, she probably should indulge in a French press.

She glanced at Deacon again. His hands had loosened around the mug. The yellow in his eyes had faded a little—though it was still there—and the muscle in his jaw was no longer flexing. All good signs. She wanted to touch him, to give him that mate contact that helped settle him and his leopard. But she didn't want to disrupt his efforts at control until he was ready.

When she saw the subtle signs of his muscles relaxing along his shoulders and neck, she finally put her hand on his forearm.

The rock-hard muscles under her palm flexed and then relaxed fully. And Cary could practically feel the tension whoosh out of the air.

Belle let out a long breath and settled back in her seat in that moment, too. "Aye, it's well past time you came to see me to train all that power. Yer mother, bless her, shouldna have let you get away with not training."

"She had very little say in the matter," Deacon murmured. "Explain how you can be an acting Fae queen. How long? Who knows?"

"No one knows in the shifter family. Not even your mother. I didna want her deciding she had to ride in and help. My son would have been worried and upset. His mate would have tried to fix things for him. And that would have given *me* more headaches than I needed. So no, none of them were keeping secrets from you. They didna know."

Cary felt Deacon's muscles relax further. She squeezed his arm in solidarity and acknowledgment. And didn't release her hold on him.

"How long?" Deacon repeated. There was no growl in his voice, which sort of surprised Cary given how close to the surface his leopard had just risen, but he spoke quietly, barely above a murmur.

"Long, to a human or shifter perspective. Blink of an eye to a Fae."

"How. Long?"

"Forty years, give or take."

Another long silence descended.

So, not all of Deacon's lifetime, but most of it, his grandmother had secretly been an acting Fae queen. And no one had known.

How the hell had she kept that secret? How on earth did none of them know?

"Is that why Deacon looks…kingly whenever we step into Faery?" she asked, glancing between him and his grandmother. "Which, to be fair isn't often." She raised a hand to stave off any comment, though she wasn't sure why. Belle was hardly in a position to give them grief about going *into* Faery, was she? "I promise we don't go into Faery casually. But when we do, like when we were getting here, he gets that gold glow and looks like he belongs there. All regal and majestic in more than his usual ways."

Belle's mouth ticked up in a small smile at that.

"You saw it too, even if he can't. How can he look like he belongs in Faery, as a king," Cary pressed when Belle remained silent, "even though the place is dangerous for him and calls to his leopard? It even tried to lure him into staying that one time he was inside Faery without me—"

Belle raised a hand. "What?"

"Long story to do with a dragon and some goblins in Ireland."

Belle blinked.

"The point is," Cary continued so they didn't get sidetracked, "he looks like a king in Faery. And I thought that was just because he'd be a leopard king one day, when he takes over for his mother, but that wasn't the whole reason, was it? It was because of you and your…I don't know what to call it, status? Your status inside Faery as a Fae queen. Isn't it?"

Belle pulled in a deep breath, let it out slowly, her brows bunched up. She took a strand of her wild red hair, with threads of gray more visible under the indoor lights, and twirled one end around her finger absently. Her sapphire ring winked with the movement.

After a moment, she said, "Aye. My current position in Faery shouldna have affected Deacon that much. But… Given who he is to the leopards, and with my blood in his veins… Aye. His relationship to me is the reason he appears as he does in Faery. Faery recognizes me as a queen, and so recognizes my kin as royalty."

"Faery has decided he's a king so when he's there, he looks like one?" Cary let out a huff and picked up her coffee again. "Makes a weird sort of sense and Faery is nothing if not weird." She gulped down more coffee. She was going to need it before this conversation was done.

"How I look inside Faery isn't really the point here," Deacon said quietly. "The point is my grandmother is trapped as a Fae queen which is *not* a good place for a shifter, and she has an enemy trying to get to her through us." He met his grandmother's gaze steadily. "Where is Nicneven now?"

Belle waved a hand. "Who knows. Out galivanting with fellow witches and having the time of her life, no doubt. She wouldna stayed away so long if she weren't having a time of it. She's always been selfish, they all are, the queens, so it probably hasn't occurred to her that she's left her court in a mess. I'm not even sure if she knows I took over in her absence."

"How do the other queens feel about this? Tatiana and Danu and the Welsh queen?" One of the few inside the islands she hadn't met yet. Well, her and the Seelie court queen. But Cary had a gut-churning feeling she was going to meet Elphame before this trip was over.

Oh good, more Faery queens that didn't like her.

"If they knew, I'm sure they'd be bothered by it," Belle said. "But since the entire Unseelie court has decided we'll all be safer if we keep it secret, no one outside my personal court knows for a certain the 'queen' isn't the one who's supposed to be sitting on the throne. So to speak." She looked at Deacon. "For the record, I don't spend all that much time in Faery. I have loyal Fae that keep track of things for me. I go in when needed. But you'd be surprised how much queening a woman can do from her own home."

Cary pressed her lips together tightly so she didn't laugh. This wasn't a laughing moment. But the thought of Belle running an entire Fae court from her living room was so...modern.

"And the time I have to be inside," Belle continued, "I have a brooch I wear to keep my mind from wandering."

"That must be something like what you wore," Cary said to Deacon. Then to Belle, "The brooch my bosses gave him. It was one of those old-fashioned circular things with the pin across that goes on the shoulder of a cloak. Silver, I think, wasn't it? And with some obvious magic dancing around the Celtic knot design. He said you taught him how to use it."

Belle nodded, giving Deacon a fond glance. "There are a few brooches still around from when our Irish brethren had a closer relationship to the Fae a few millennia ago. Some are almost as ancient as the island itself, from the earliest kings of the Isle. Some are more modern, after the Church came in. I've one that was created for an Irish priest when he thought he might go into Faery and minister to them."

Cary nearly choked on her coffee. "He wanted to...convert faeries to Catholicism? That's..."

"Idiotic? Pig headed? Suicidal?" Belle supplied.

"I was gonna go for bold, but yours work too."

Belle snorted. "The brooch worked well for him, because he was clever enough to have a druid make it, and the druid was on good terms with Danu. The priest's efforts inside Faery didna go as he might have hoped, though." Belle shrugged. "They let him out eventually. And it was the last time the Church bothered with the Fae, so I'd guess it worked out for everyone."

"If they could keep him inside Faery with the brooch, it can't be that powerful," Deacon said. "How is it protecting you?"

"Oh, the brooch was powerful enough. The priest didna lose his mind or die of starvation or dance himself to death or any of the other horrors the Fae can inflict if they're a mind to. But keeping his mind intact and being able to find a way back out of Faery… Those are two different things. The brooch helped him eat while he was there, too, so that was a saving grace."

"Why did he go to a druid and not, I don't know, make one that he blessed or something?" Cary asked, curious even though this wasn't the point of the conversation.

"Another priest had tried that. *He* didna survive the trip. And what the Fae threw back out into the human realm wasn't an end our druid-trusting priest wanted to face. Tried a different strategy, he did. And it worked. More or less. Without all the spreading of Christianity to the Fae, of course."

"Can we get back on topic?" Deacon said, his tone that emotionless one that meant he was still hanging onto his control and his patience by a thread.

"Sorry," Cary muttered. "This is all pretty fascinating stuff."

"If you're not in Faery much, there's time for enemies to band against you, right?" Deacon said. "Who is this enemy we have to deal with?"

The fact that Deacon wasn't even questioning that they had to help Belle deal with her trouble, just wanted to know more about the trouble, made Cary's heart soften a little. She wasn't sure what she would have expected. Deacon was just this kind of man. His grandmother was in danger and he rode in to help. He had as much of a white knight complex as Cary did—Cary had also already been trying to figure out how to take care of this enemy that was a threat to Belle.

He might hate her job because it put her in danger, but the

truth was, he was just as protective as she was, and they made a good team.

She reached over again and squeezed his hand briefly, enough touch to convey they were on the same page and give him a little mate-bond reassurance, not enough to disrupt his carefully held control on his emotions.

"A member of the court that passes between the Unseelie and Seelie worlds," Belle said, answering Deacon's question. "Someone with ambitions of his own. Looking to destroy me in any way he can. With the Unseelie court behind me, and keeping my identity a secret from the rest of Faery, there's not much he can do. Though he's tired a few tricks to get to me. His latest, trying to kill my grandson."

"What was he hoping to get from that?" Cary asked.

"I'd lose my control and do something to endanger Faery in my quest for revenge—which, in honesty, isn't far afield of what might happen—and that would bring the house of cards toppling. He underestimates my network, though. And the information I receive as a queen. Faery itself tells me things he can't possibly imagine. It's how the queens stay in control of so many magical beings."

"Then Elphame must know you're *not* Nicneven," Deacon said.

"I think she suspects. But she's not positive because the court is so loyal to me."

"And this enemy of yours hasn't told her?" Cary asked.

"He's an agenda of his own that involves him gaining power over both courts. He'd hardly bring Elphame into that since he can't control her."

"If you know all this, why wouldn't Elphame?" Deacon asked. "She's been a queen longer, and if Faery speaks to you, it must speak to her."

"Like I said, I think she suspects the truth. But suspicions and having the proof of it are different things. We've spent forty odd years ensuring the court was stable and the powers were in balance. It defies logic to most Fae that a shifter could've done that. I don't think Elphame *wants* her court to know Nicneven isn't the one in charge. Any that've heard the murmurs of another queen… Easy enough to pass me off as just a lacky to the queen herself. One of her consorts. But not the one with the power."

"But Elphame will be working against you, even if she doesn't tell her own court you're the queen," Cary said.

"Aye, she has been. And that's a danger of the job, too. But it's less pressing than the Strix's threat."

"The Strix?" Deacon scowled.

"My enemy that tried to kill ye. He's the real trouble right now. A right pain in me arse, he is. But…" Belle stood and brought her mug back into the kitchen. "For now, we're all safe. He's been thwarted, and he canna find us here. I'll call Fiona in the morning and get her to send your luggage along, so we don't have to risk another transport through Faery with ye. The stone circle is very safe, with the trolls lending their magic to it, but it's not a perfect option. It canna move around much." She grinned at them from over the kitchen countertop.

Cary wanted to ask all the questions about the standing stones and the trolls—troll magic? What?!—but she got the feeling Belle was done answering questions for the night.

"I've got the spare room all made up for ye," Belle continued. "And in the morning, we can start fresh with your leopard magic lessons."

"I have a lot more questions about the fact that you're stuck as a Fae queen," Deacon said.

"Well and that's yer prerogative, isn't it? But for tonight, we're done talking about it."

There was no option for argument in Belle's sentence or in her tone. She met her grandson's still faintly glowing eyes without flinching and waited in silence for him to give in to her timing. She was done talking about this for the night. They'd have to learn more when she was ready.

But whatever else they did while they were in Scotland, Cary was absolutely certain Deacon intended on having it out with the Strix—whatever and whoever he was—to protect his grandmother from the threat.

And Cary would be right there. Standing in front of him to keep everyone safe.

12

The next morning, after an English breakfast so large even Deacon had raised a brow, Belle took them both out into an open field behind the house. It wasn't inside the stone fence infused with the glamour magic, though, so Cary kept a little ahead of Deacon so her shields would work if necessary.

With Deacon here to practice his own magic, Cary thought she should probably be practicing raising and lowering her shield at the same time. But since she couldn't feel it and wasn't sure if it was up or not without someone throwing something at her, she wasn't sure *how* to practice. Maybe she could get Belle to throw some harmless magic at her. And if she absorbed some of it, well, she could just light a few candles with her finger—the first spell she'd learned and could consistently do to, literally, burn off magic.

Her own practice came second to Deacon's though. And Cary was not so secretly fascinated by what that practice would entail.

Once out in the middle of a hill, surrounded by soft grass and a few patches of heather, Belle stopped. Cary glanced around. They were far enough from the house it looked smaller, but not so far the shifters couldn't reach it in seconds at a run. The sky was gray that morning, the air cool and crisp. A light breeze made things chillier, making Cary grateful for her leather jacket, but it brought the scents of grass and heather with it, so Cary didn't mind. On the next hill over, a handful of sheep quietly grazed, looking like little cotton puffballs against the dark green grass.

"Now," Belle said, clapping her hands together. "Leopard magic." She waved at her grandson. "Shift."

He did in a blink. Without question.

So fast that, for a moment, Cary worried the shift hadn't been voluntary and Belle had somehow forced it on him. But Belle had said she couldn't do the same things Deacon and his mother could do, and Cary assumed that meant she couldn't force another leopard to do things the way Deacon could. Still. Cary watched the proceedings warily. Just in case.

"When you shift back, bring your clothes with ye," Belle said.

Cary started and looked around. Yup, no shredded clothes. He'd shifted without tearing his clothes apart. And done it so fast, she hadn't noticed.

Deacon returned to his human form as fast as he'd dropped into his leopard form, and fully dressed in the jeans and long-sleeved t-shirt he'd worn from the house that morning. Not even a tiny rip in the cotton to show for the transition.

Belle nodded. "Strong," she muttered under her breath. "Okay, back to the leopard. Ye'll train that way at first as it's the more instinctive part of you."

Wordlessly, Deacon shifted again. Another blink and the black leopard with glowing golden eyes stared up at Belle.

In his leopard form, Deacon was also pretty magnificent. The animal was all sinewy muscle and slick black fur. The hint of his leopard spots very faint, but there. His eyes were so golden yellow, they almost looked like they existed on their own. Especially in the dark. In the gray morning, the effect wasn't so prominent, but still pretty intimidating.

Or it would be intimidating if he wasn't her mate.

"Now," Belle said, "the leopard's magic is all about control and emotion. Your anger feeds it."

"Oh, not to interrupt, but yes! That's what I felt when he accidentally fed me some of his magic. I was mad anyway because of the whole having to protect an enemy thing, but what I felt when he shared his magic was *way* beyond my usual rage. And my body wanted to do things like sprout claws to rip out the throat of my enemy. Which, obviously, I can't do." She frowned. "I can't, right? Even with Deacon's magic in me?"

Because that would probably be bad since she wasn't a shifter. Though, claws might be handy in some circumstances… But, no, no. She didn't have claws. Sprouting them suddenly would definitely be bad.

"Yer not a shifter," Belle said. "No claws."

Cary was not disappointed. Nope. Not disappointed at all.

"But the rage was part of the magic," Belle continued. "And to control that magic, the rage has to also be controlled."

"Well, he's nothing if not controlled," Cary said, exchanging a look with Deacon.

He hadn't been for a while there, after they'd met. And he still had his moments. But around other shifters, he was the very definition of control. Imposed so strictly on himself, he shut off all emotions. Not just his rage.

"The trick," Belle said, "is to feel it. Not cut it off."

Cary got the strange sensation that Belle had just read her

thoughts. Was that possible or were their thoughts just on the same path?

She nodded at her grandson. "I know that's how ye've been dealing with it for all these years, cutting off most all emotion around other leopards. But that's only going to help you so much. Because it leaves you vulnerable to your rage. You're a lot more dangerous then, when the rage takes over, than you'd be if ye understood your rage and could work with it."

The leopard didn't flinch, but Cary still got the impression of Deacon wincing. He *was* dangerous when his rage got beyond his control. She'd watched him nearly kill his ex-girlfriend in his rage —and to be fair, the ex had kidnapped Cary so he sort of had cause. Still, he would have been devastated to have done something like that once he came back to himself. His rage had definitely been in the driver's seat then, not his own control.

"So we'll make ye mad," Belle said, "and then we'll work with that anger."

Deacon shifted instantly back to his human form, clothes and all, and said, "I don't want to hurt you, Nan. Maybe we'd better start with something smaller."

Belle waved that away. "All of the 'smaller' things will be for naught if we canna get you to a place where you can feel rage and control what happens in those moments."

Deacon frowned, his hands on his hips as he stared down at his grandmother, worry clearly etched in the bunching lines on his brow. "I don't know," he murmured.

"I understand yer worry, love," Belle said, gripping his arms, waiting for him to meet her gaze. "But I willna let you hurt anyone, including me. Were you younger, we could maybe start with the smaller magics and build up. But you've spent more than fifty years honing that rage. Suppressing it. It's the thing we canna ignore now. We start with it."

A muscle in his jaw popped as he ground his teeth together. Cary watched silently, afraid to comment at all and disrupt the process.

Deacon glanced at her, though, and said, "Will you get between us if something goes wrong, please. Protect my grandmother from me if I can't…" He swallowed and let the rest of his sentence trail off.

But he didn't need to say more. She got it. She'd seen him in that place. "I will, don't worry. I won't let anyone get hurt. Not you or her. Promise."

"Or you," he said.

"Or me," she said. Though he wouldn't hurt her, even at his most enraged.

His mother had commented once that it was probably a blessing his mate wasn't a leopard. At the time, Cary hadn't understood that as well as she did now. She'd just worried that because she wasn't a shifter, that somehow she'd made things worse for him in the beginning. In hindsight, someone like Deacon having a mate that *wasn't* a leopard really had been a good thing for him.

Belle watched the exchange. "You won't be able to hurt me," Belle told Deacon. "But if it'll make ye feel better and trust the process, will I stand behind yer mate?"

"Please," Deacon said solemnly. "Please."

Belle patted his arms, then motioned Cary between them. "Didna think you'd be put to work during all this, did ye?" Belle asked her with a chuckle.

"I don't mind. I'm happy to help." And honestly, it sort of went with the territory. Even when she went on rare vacations, she still somehow ended up working. There were always people in trouble that needed protecting in this world.

Once Cary was firmly in front of Belle, ready to protect at the first sign of trouble, Deacon dropped back into his leopard form. Again, so fast it happened in a blink. Again, no shredded clothing. He'd mentioned moving between forms that way easier since the fight with the demon, that he was doing that without thinking about it now and that was one of the things that scared him. Cary was starting to understand. Watching him use that particular skill so casually, when he'd deliberately *never* used it before, was disconcerting.

"Now," Belle said, "I need ye to access all that rage you keep locked up. Let it flow."

The leopard growled a little, his eyes glowing. But Cary couldn't tell if that was his rage or not. She'd seen Deacon in a rage. Seen his leopard in a rage. This looked more…annoyed.

"Don't waste my time pretending," Belle snapped. "Grab hold of the anger."

The leopard stared at them for a moment. Then sat down. And Cary would swear she heard a harrumph. Which would have been hilarious if it wasn't so ill-timed.

"Yer resisting it. Blocking it." Belle harrumphed, too. "Fine. We'll have to make you mad. What pisses him off most?" This last to Cary.

She raised her brows, staring down at Deacon. "I suppose you could think about the time when Oliver Holland was throwing all that demon magic at me and trying to kill me? That pissed us both off a lot. Actually, that happened a couple of times, so any of those times might work. Or you can think about Sheldon trying to kill you to steal your body? Although he's doing his penance with your mom now, so maybe that's not as rage inducing as it used to be. If that old wizard wasn't dead, you could think about him trying to kill me all the time. Oh oh! The thing with your ex-girlfriend kidnapping me! That's a good memory for rage, right?"

Belle made a little noise that had Cary glancing back at her. Belle was looking at Cary in a way that was difficult to read.

"What?" Cary asked.

Belle's mouth ticked at one corner. But if it was a smile or a frown, Cary couldn't tell. "Lot of people have tried to kill you."

Cary shrugged. "Part of the job."

Belle glanced at Deacon again. He was back on his feet, but otherwise there were no signs of his rage. The leopard wasn't even growling.

Cary frowned at him. "Nothing yet, huh?"

"He's resisting," Belle said. "Years of control. Won't let go of that so easily."

The leopard did make a sort of growling whine, but that wasn't his rage either.

Belle tapped her nose. "I can tell what you're feeling." She glanced back at Cary. "But there were a few spikes. You dinna liked to see your mate in danger." This last was a quiet murmur to Deacon.

"See," Cary said to him. "Just focus on those times. There were plenty to choose from. What about that time I had to fall onto a guy trying to blow up the restaurant? Remember that… Oh wait, that's probably more scary than rage-inducing. You could think about the threat the Master Vampire of Portland is to me. We still don't know what he's up to."

James was tentatively a sort-of-kind-of ally but sort of not. And since she had no idea where to put James in the good guy-bad guy balance of things, she mostly kept him over in the bad guy side to be safe. Even if she did kind of like him.

Mentioning James made Deacon growl. That was good.

"Ye've had an interesting life," Belle said, her tone neutral.

"'Interesting' again, huh? That doesn't sound like a compliment."

"Maybe I consider interesting good."

"Since you're trapped as a surrogate Fae queen, I'm gonna say, no."

Belle shrugged but her attention was on Deacon. Cary opened her mouth to mention more potentially rage-inducing memories for Deacon, but never got so much as a squeak out…

Before Belle grabbed her and threw her across the field.

13

Cary landed hard in the grassy field, half on her side, the air knocked out of her. Wheezing as she tried to drag in a breath, one whole side of her body aching and sure to bruise. She'd barely rolled into a seated position when another bolt of… something slammed into her chest.

The second blow stole whatever breath she'd managed to recover. And hurt!

But, she realized as she tried to breath, not as much as all that.

Deacon was beside her before she could reach up and rub her chest. "Cary!"

"Fine," she wheezed. "Fine. I'll be fine." She blinked up at him, in his human form. But with only jeans now. No t-shirt. "Where's your shirt?" Despite the fact that she was still catching her breath, having Deacon crouching over her without his shirt on was…distracting.

He glanced down, frowning. "Forgot to shift with it. Are you hurt? Anything broken?"

"Nothing broken." She adjusted herself until she was sitting easier. Deacon helped her, practically wrapping around her as he checked her for injuries. "Nothing that won't heal," she reassured him, getting even more distracted by the warmth of him.

This is not the time, hormones!

But her hormones were suckers for his warm, bare chest and all his caring concern.

"I'm fine," she reassured, patting his chest. Which was a mistake. Because taking her hand away was not actually something she wanted to do. "You, uh, you should probably get a shirt back on." She patted him again. "With your grandmother over there and all."

His grandmother who'd just tossed Cary across a field and then hit her with…something. "What did she hit me with?"

Cary glanced down at her own chest. No gaping wound. But when she lifted her hand, she realized it was glowing. Her eyes went wide. Faint purplish-white light danced over her fingers and palm, like she was wearing a glove made of light. She tilted her hand to one side, then the other…

"Okay. That's weird."

"Magic," Deacon said. "You need to use it. Get rid of it." There was an edge of panic under his voice, carefully controlled, but there.

"Got any handy candles laying around I can light," she said with a snort, watching the light dance over her skin. It didn't hurt. Even the tingles weren't very bad. None of the insects crawling over her skin sensation. But she could feel the magic like a faint tickle and pressure.

"Angie taught you other spells," Deacon said. "Use one of those."

"Which one? The one that blocks a demon or the one that helped me ricochet power back at another demon? Cause your grandmother might have tossed me across a field, but I doubt you want me throwing magic bolts back at her."

She scowled past Deacon to where Belle stood a hundred yards away, frowning at them both. "Why the hell did you throw me?"

Although, she had a pretty good idea without an explanation. Belle had been trying to trigger Deacon's rage. Her bad luck he was more worried now than angry.

"You shouldn't have hit her with magic," Deacon said, without looking at his grandmother. To Cary, "Maybe you can toss it into the ground or something?"

"I don't know how to do that."

She considered the light, and then the surrounding field. A few rocky clumps in the grass not too far away—good thing she hadn't landed there!—and a sheep standing a few feet away, staring at them. She blinked at the sheep. The sheep let out a loud bleating sound, then turned around and ran away.

"Why does it have that pink stuff on its back?" Cary asked as she watched the mostly white fluff ball disappear over a hill.

"Don't remember," Deacon said. "Something to do with breeding, I think."

"Huh. Live and learn." When she'd been training to be a vet tech, she had specialized in smaller domestic animals like dogs and cats, rather than farm animals. She didn't really know that much about sheep.

She faced Deacon again, momentarily caught by the fact that he was still shirtless and leaning over her all warm and yummy smelling and strong and hers. She couldn't even feel her bruises anymore. They'd likely healed already—benefits of being a Protector—and without the pain to offset her hormones, her hormones tried to take over the situation.

Still not the time, hormones! Not with his *grandmother* standing right there.

Deacon leaned in closer, his nostrils flaring, and he brushed a kiss across her temple. Which, honestly, didn't help with the hormone situation but did make her melt.

She blinked back to the present. She still had some magic to get rid of. "I suppose I could do that lighting my own fingers trick Rory taught me." Of course a dragon had taught her how to use up the magic by creating fire. She'd been amused by that at the time. But as she looked at the light skimming over her hand, almost liquid in its flow across her skin, she was grateful for those lessons. Candles were easier, but she didn't *have* to use one.

Before she could start, though, Belle shouted. "Ye two are impossible! Deacon, I wanted rage, not worry and lust."

Cary's cheeks heated. Belle had scented that from so far away? That was embarrassing.

"I am angry," Deacon said. "You didn't have to do that, Nan."

Belle huffed. "You are still not allowing yer rage out. Control is one thing. This is something else. You have to let go." She looked at Cary, her eyes narrowed. "This isn't working with ye here," Belle said. "He's distracted."

"Cary can keep me from hurting you," Deacon pointed out. "She should stay."

"No, it's okay. I can just go back to the house if I'm too much of a distraction." Cary stood with Deacon's help, though she wasn't hurting anymore. "It'll give me a chance to light some candles, or my fingers or whatever, and get rid of the magic." She wanted to pat his chest again, but the liquid light covering her hand made her pause.

"If I lose control without you here," he murmured, "I might hurt her."

"Obviously not," I said. "She just tossed me across a field to trigger your rage, and instead of hurting her, you came charging over to help me. And didn't let go of your control." She glanced at Belle. "I'm not happy about getting tossed around, by the way." Then back to Deacon, "But you didn't hurt her. You'll be fine."

She smiled up at him, wanting to touch him more but still a little worried about the fact that her hands were glowing with magic. Instead, she set her forehead against his when he leaned in closed. "I'm proud of you for not hurting your grandmother," she murmured.

Which made him shake his head and let out a sigh that was almost a chuckle.

"This willna do at all," Belle said. "What are ye two like?"

Cary leaned away from Deacon and sighed. "I'll head back to the house."

She started toward the house, but Belle shook her head.

"No," she said. "This willna work. We need to try something else."

Cary opened her mouth to ask what. Once again, she didn't get a chance to finish the thought.

Belle made a few gestures with her hands. Cary frowned. Then a cold brush of air at her back. She looked over her shoulder to see a split in reality, opening onto a forest. She barely had a chance to register, only just turned back to frown at Belle, when Belle hissed a few words and threw her hands forward.

Hitting Cary in the chest with another bolt of magic that shoved her hard backward.

Through the split in reality.

Cary landed on her ass again and cursed as a rock bit into her hand when she hit the ground. What the actual fuck? She started to rise, spotted Deacon reaching for her through the rip in reality.

And then the opening snapped shut. Cutting Cary off from Deacon and stranding her…

Where?

She snarled and climbed to her feet, looking around as she rubbed the spot on her chest where Belle had hit her with more magic. She stood in the middle of massive trees, stretching branches from thick trunks covering the sky overhead. But some light filtered into the forest through leaves that were…not green.

She blinked. The leaves throughout the canopy were a multicolored rainbow of light. Blues and purples and reds and oranges. And not the changing colors of the fall. No. These leaves lit like actual lights and flickered in bright, florescent colors that had nothing to do with real trees.

A sweet cinnamon scent and the smell of pines. A breeze that was almost cold. Little flickering gold flakes fell from the sky like snow. As they touched the ground, tiny red flowers sprouted, grew, and died in a few short moments. The remains of those dead flowers littered the forest floor in a carpet of red that looked a little too much like blood.

The reality of her surroundings only sank in though, when she realized her skin was tingling. Badly. And the pressure of all the magic around her pressed down hard.

Oh no.

She was in Faery.

With no one to protect.

14

Panic rushed through Cary's blood stream, making her both dizzy and hyper aware of every detail of her surroundings. Her breath came in pants that were going to make her hyperventilate if she wasn't careful. But she couldn't control the panic.

She was in Faery.

A realm made of magic.

And her body was absorbing it as she stood in the middle of the weird forest with its red carpet of dead flowers that looked like blood.

She looked down at her hands. The glowing liquid light that had already been crawling over her skin seemed thicker and more luminous now. Cary could feel the magic rushing into her. And it reminded her so much of the last time, when she had purposefully absorbed all that magic to save the realm, that she almost couldn't think.

She'd died that last time. She'd died because she'd dropped her Protector shield and absorbed the magic on purpose.

There was no effort this time. But without her shield, the magic still flowed into her. Without anything to check it, to stop it, she'd fill up. She could die again.

And this time, there was no convenient Fae healer on hand to bring her back.

Her breath coming in harsh, gasping pants, a whimper escaping her, she tried to force her brain to work.

Okay. She couldn't use up all this magic because it would just be continually replaced. She'd literally have to light the forest on fire, and even that wouldn't completely drain what she'd absorbed because she'd just keep absorbing more. This wasn't a limited amount of power tossed at her. This wasn't like the fight with Ho'Lud and Oliver Holland. She'd absorbed a *lot* then and survived. But it hadn't been a constant flow from the very air itself. She'd had time to send back out everything that came in.

Her only hope inside Faery was a shield to block the magic.

"Okay, okay. You can do this." Her voice sounded funny to her, like there was an echo at the end of it. She ignored the weirdness because speaking out loud calmed her panic. Sort of. "Just need to raise my shield. That's it. I practiced this. I can protect myself now. I'm allowed. I can do this."

She focused on the power flowing into her, looking for the Protector magic. It was also of Faery, through her bosses. So she could use what was coming from Faery here too. Just needed to raise the shield.

Sweat broke out on her forehead as she concentrated. The drips of golden light and dying red flowers around her broke her concentration and let panic in, so—somewhat stupidly given she had no idea what else was around that might attack her—she closed her eyes to focus.

In her mind's eye, she pictured her Protector shield coming up, surrounding her the way it always did, keeping her in a little bubble of safety where even the scariest of scary beings couldn't touch her. She'd faced a lot of very scary bad guys over the years. And she'd survived them all behind this shield. She could survive Faery behind the shield, too.

The pressure around her started to ease, lifting until she only just barely felt it. The tingling on her skin calmed from a waterfall of insects crawling over her, so intense it was pain, to something more like butterflies tickling her. And then, even that was gone.

She blinked her eyes open. A faint glow in her peripheral vision startled her. She never saw her shield. But she was seeing it now. Not directly in front of her. Only out the corner of her eye. But still. She could see it.

The flow of magic had stopped. When she looked down at her hands, they no longer glowed. She wasn't sure how that had happened. Was the magic still in her? She didn't use magic to raise her Protector shield, technically. Not her own anyway. And even when she'd been practicing with Jaxer, she hadn't absorbed any outside magic so it was just the flow of her Protector magic she'd had to call on. Using the shield didn't use up the outside magic she absorbed. Usually.

Had she built a different kind of shield?

She blinked. She'd automatically used the magic thrown at her during the demon fight to build a shield of magic, when she hadn't had her Protector powers to rely on. Had she…had she done that this time, too? Even though she had access to the Protector shield again?

She reached out a finger to poke at the protective barrier in front of her, where she knew it was, and her finger created a little ripple in the otherwise invisible bubble, creating a prism of colors through the tiny wave before settling back into translucence.

"This is so weird," she murmured.

But at least she was safe from all the magic around her now. She hoped.

Carefully, she turned to take in more of the forest. Where was she inside Faery? And did that even matter when this was Faery, and time and space and reality weren't what she knew to be time and space and reality. Everything worked differently here. Weirdly.

And nothing could be trusted.

When no beautiful monsters came charging out of the forest behind her, and none of the dying flowers tried to eat her—she'd encountered some roses in Faery that were carnivorous so she didn't take anything for granted—she faced the spot where Belle had shoved her through a rip in her own reality. Then closed off that escape route. How the hell was she going to get back?

Oh shit. What was happening with Deacon? He'd be in a panic. Would that trigger his rage or just make him nonsensical with fear? She'd be pretty nonsensical if their positions were reversed. In fact, now that she had a shield blocking all this magic, she was more worried about him. And Belle—even though Belle had shoved her here in the first place; and weren't they going to have words about *that* when Cary got back, no matter who the woman was to Deacon, or this realm. Deacon was terrifying in his rage. And while Cary knew that was the point, still…

She needed to get back out of Faery.

But how?

"I might be able to help," a voice said, its high, tinkling tone grating across Cary's nerves like nails on paper. "For a price."

Cary turned slowly, her gut tight, a resigned sigh escaping. She'd only been in Scotland for what? Two days? She'd sort of hoped to get a full week in before this confrontation.

"Tatiana," she said, dipping her head in a faint bow because, after all, this was a queen.

The first time she'd met Tatiana, the queen had glowed so brightly, Cary hadn't even been able to see her until she'd lowered the glow to something less blinding. Even then, she'd seemed to be made up of white light and sparkles. This time, she'd forgone the blinding light, but she was still haloed in a white glow and sparkles. She wore a translucent gown of blue shimmering material covered in glitter, skimming over a willow body and hiding none of it. A high collar rose behind her head, framing her sharp-featured face. She had her blond hair piled atop her head in spiraling curls that also sparkled with tiny, winking jewels. She wore a small diadem tucked into the curls and low on her forehead, another piece made up of light and sparkling gems, mostly in shades of green and blue. Even her pale skin sparkled.

She was a magnificent vision, the very definition of a High Fae. And even without her scepter, and only a small diadem instead of a full crown, she was very obviously a queen.

Cary wanted to scowl but knew that wouldn't get her anywhere. Instead, she kept her expression as neutral as possible when she said, "What are you doing here?"

"You've entered my realm. Without permission. Where else would I be?"

"Not voluntarily," she muttered. "And maybe not even your realm… This is part of the Scottish court's territory."

Actually, she wasn't entirely sure about that, but it was a good guess given Belle had sent her here. Cary would even go so far as to assume she was in the Unseelie faction's part of the Scottish territory. But she wasn't absolutely certain, so she didn't push that part. It might give too much away to Tatiana anyway. About Belle and the trouble in the Unseelie court.

"You've still entered Faery. Without permission." The queen's tinkling, high voice deepened and strengthened until Cary could practically feel the power of it hitting against her shield like rocks. "You've been warned not to do that."

"Yes, but I'm not here on purpose. I promise. If you'll just open a door and let me back out, I'll be gone."

Tatiana tilted her head to one side. "There is a price on my clemency. A price for your release."

Cary sighed. Of course there was. "I'm not making a deal with you." That way lay madness and probably all kinds of trouble. No deals with faeries. Jaxer was the only exception to that rule, and even then, she didn't make proper, official deals with him.

"I'm the only one who can release you," Tatiana said, her voice light and sparkling again, almost like a laugh. The English court's queen was notoriously mercurial, her moods swinging from joy to anger to offense to pleasure to rage in an eye blink.

Since Cary couldn't predict her moods and since it wouldn't really matter what she said to affect Tatiana's moods, Cary didn't bother trying to be diplomatic. She sucked at diplomacy anyway.

"No," she said. And left it at that.

"Ah, then maybe I will keep you. Danu thinks she can steal you from me. Like she stole Jaxer. But I don't think that's fair. You should be mine."

Cary blinked. "You… You don't like me."

"You're wrong. You saved my realm. I love you."

Cary just only barely stopped from snorting, but a weird choked sound managed to escape. "I'm gonna say no to that too." To all of it.

"No one says no to me," Tatiana said.

More people should, Cary thought, but didn't say aloud because…well, mercurial Fae queen. "Where is Danu, by the way? Thought she might have words about me being here, too." And also since Danu had apparently claimed her, she'd be a good distraction for Tatiana.

Not that that situation would be any better for Cary. Two unhappy queens wasn't better than one unhappy queen, but at least in the case of two, they'd be unhappy with each other and not her.

"This isn't Danu's realm. She understands the rules."

Oh, that was a leading taunt. And Cary nearly fell for it. They'd already established this wasn't Tatiana's realm either. Instead of getting sucked into a cyclical argument, Cary changed tack. "I haven't met Elphame or Nicneven yet. They around here somewhere? That'd be interesting. How do you three get along?"

Cary was betting they didn't but only because none of the High Fae seemed to get along, even with their own courts.

"The Scottish court is not our concern," Tatiana said.

And Cary couldn't tell if she'd switched to the royal "we" with that "our" or if she meant Cary. "Kind of is my concern, given I'm in *Scotland* now." Or…well, sort of.

"Why don't you want to play with me?" Tatiana said, switching moods again, adopting a beautiful pout that probably would have worked better if Cary weren't safely behind a shield.

"I just want to get back to where I was," Cary said.

"How far back?" Tatiana said, her eyes narrowing as a rather evil grin spread over her sharp face.

Fucking Fae, always twisting words. Couldn't say a damned thing without it being taken in twelve different ways you didn't intend.

"Not… Never mind. I'll figure it out. You don't have to hang around anymore. You can go. Nothing to see here."

"I don't trust you in my realm," Tatiana said, returning to the haughty queen.

Cary's head was spinning with these mood switches. They were giving her a headache. Or maybe that was just being in Faery.

Wait…she wasn't absorbing more magic, right?

She did a quick body scan. No tingles. Nothing that spoke to more magic flowing into her. She studied her hands. No glowing liquid light flowing over them.

Okay. No need to panic. She was fine. Just that Tatiana was a literal headache. That's what Excedrin was for.

If she could just get back to her own world.

"There will be a fight for you, Cary Redmond," Tatiana said, pulling Cary's full attention back to her. "You have made a name for yourself in this realm. That is…unusual for a human."

"Great. Love it. Always wanted to be famous."

Tatiana erupted into a tinkling laughter that actually made Cary's ears hurt. So much she winced and was milliseconds away from covering her ears before she realized that would probably trigger the queen. Maybe. She might also be laughing like that on purpose.

Jesus, Cary hated dealing with Fae queens.

"This is why we fight for you," Tatiana said. "I will have you."

"No," Cary said again.

Tatiana lifted a hand and the dead flowers started to swirl around her. For an instant, Cary thought perhaps the queen was sending her back to her realm—though there was no telling where she'd turn up, and her without her passport—but there was something aggressive about the swirling dead flowers.

The air filled with the musty scent of them. And something just under that that was entirely too close to the smell of blood.

Cary braced, ensuring she could still see her shield in her peripheral vision, and held the queen's electric green-eyed gaze.

As a split in space-time opened to her left.

And something very large moved through…

15

Cary blinked a few times before recognition hit. The large figure moving into Faery wasn't some new and scary monster. It was a beloved and scary man.

"Deacon!"

She rushed to him without thought. Without fear. Even though she knew he had to be in a panic and his leopard was probably right at the surface. He was in human form, but that didn't mean much when he went into a rage with worry for her.

He scanned his surroundings briefly before his gaze settled on her and he caught her easily when she threw herself into his arms.

"Fucking hell," he muttered into her hair. "You're okay? Alive…"

The little choking sound in his voice twisted her heart. "I'm fine." She hugged him close, until his trembling body stopped trembling. "I'm okay. Promise." She leaned back to take his face in her hands. His eyes were glowing yellow. And he had that sparkling thing that happened in Faery. "You didn't hurt your grandmother, did you?"

"No. But she got her wish."

Which meant this had triggered his rage.

"We can talk about it once we leave," he murmured, glancing behind her.

She looked over her shoulder. Tatiana was staring at them, her eyes narrowed, an inscrutable expression on her sharp little face.

The whirling dead flowers were no longer spinning up into a cyclone. Everything had settled in the colorful forest. Even the dripping golden light that gave birth to the flowers when it hit the ground had stopped falling—weirdest rain ever!—and the air had stilled completely. No more cinnamon and pine scent either. Something more sickly sweet, like rotting detritus filled the clearing.

The stillness made Cary's skin crawl.

Tatiana dipped her head at Deacon, without smiling. "Majesty," she greeted.

Cary blinked and looked back at Deacon. Yeah, that sparkling golden thing was happening to him still, but…

"Wait. Why are you wearing a kilt?"

She looked him over. The kilt wasn't a typical tartan but was instead a more solid tan color, with very faint hints of purple and silver lines running through it, but so pale they were hard to see. He had a cream-colored shirt with laces across the chest to keep it closed, the sleeves rolled up to display his extremely impressive forearms. And over his equally impressive shoulder hung a length of the tan wool that made up his kilt. That bit of wool had more purple in it than the rest of the kilt. He had a leather sporran hanging in front of the kilt, held in place by a leather belt and silver chain. Cary scanned down to see he was even wearing thick, soft leather boots that ended just at the hem of the kilt.

She blinked a few times. He looked…magnificent. Like… Really, really… Wow.

"Uhm," she said dumbly as every girly part of her melted and heated and she forgot her own name. She'd been pretty sure she'd enjoy seeing Deacon in a kilt, but this was…

Wow.

He frowned down at the outfit. "I have no idea why I'm wearing this. I shifted just before stepping through the portal, but I thought I'd shifted back to my own clothes."

He fingered the length of wool over his shoulder, the purple threads catching the weird filtered light dropping through the overhead canopy. There was a brooch at his shoulder, pinning the wool material to his shirt. Another circular Celtic brooch with elaborate knots and whorls, brightly silver, with animal heads at the curved opening that looked suspiciously like leopards.

Cary tapped his chest gently with her palms, trying to ensure herself he was real while her brain sort of collapsed in lust. "This is… I don't know where it came from or why you're wearing it, but, uh, do you think you can keep it? For…later."

His mouth ticked up at one side as he stared down at her. The yellow glow of his leopard faded to leave just his normal golden eyes, boring into her with a kind of knowing smugness she couldn't even be mad about. Her heartbeat had started to pound a little harder and she was definitely breathing heavier and the fact that they were standing in Faery, in front of a Fae queen, who'd just called Deacon "majesty" wasn't enough to calm Cary's rising hormones.

This was the joy and problem with being mate bonded to a leopard shifter. The lust was always right there, ready to pounce at the most inopportune moments.

Deacon glanced away from her and pulled her closer suddenly. She wasn't going to object to being held against his big warm body, but his scowl got her attention. She glanced over her shoulder. Tatiana had moved closer, was standing only a foot away now.

Her eyes were entirely focused on Deacon.

Well, shit.

But, Cary realized, her Protector shield was working. Now it would be working automatically to keep Deacon safe. Cary didn't even have to do anything anymore or worry. She knew for certain the shield would protect them both now.

The relief that washed through her made her realize just how tense she'd been about the shield she'd raised to protect herself failing. She hadn't trusted it the way she trusted her shield now.

"What are you doing?" Cary asked the queen, who never looked away from Deacon.

"Seducing your mate," Tatiana said in a sing-songy voice that probably did seduce most beings. "A magnificent king to add to our realm."

"Yeah, no, that's not happening," Cary said with a snort. "Any of it." She made a shooing gesture at Tatiana. "Mine. Go away."

Deacon's arms tightened around her and she could swear she heard him chuckle. The sound tickled over her skin and lit her on fire. Speaking of seduction with just a voice…

"We would make beautiful babies to refresh Faery, majesty," Tatiana said to Deacon, ignoring Cary.

"Ew," Cary said. "He's not a brood mare. Or…stud." She winced and glanced up at him. "Sorry."

"Don't be. I'm not either of those things and I appreciate you saying so." He kissed the top of her head.

She grinned.

"Would you prefer I bred with you, Protector?"

Cary's eyes widened. "Since when did we start taking about breeding? No. Besides that wouldn't work." At least, she didn't think so. Faery was weird. Maybe it would. But the answer was still, "No."

"Would you prefer Oberon?" There was an edge to the queen's voice, sharp enough to cut, even though she'd maintained that high, soft, sweet quality. "I'm sure he'd be happy to get you with child. He has…mentioned you. A child of a Protector would add great magic to our realm."

Cary's eyes widened more as Deacon's arms flexed around her.

"No!" she said at the same time Deacon growled, "No."

And the two of their voices blended together so seamlessly, so perfectly, they almost sounded like a single voice. So singular and aligned Tatiana blinked and drew back, as if someone had shoved her.

Cary blinked too. She and Deacon had been on the same page before, and even said the same thing in unison before, but they'd never sounded like the same voice before. A voice that was different to each of their individual voices but both of them at once.

Weird. Must be a Faery thing.

She gave her head a little shake and said, "Stop talking about breeding to distract us. What is wrong with you?" Well, that was actually a can of worms she didn't want to get into. So she hurried past the questions. "We're going now. Thanks for the weird and threatening hospitality. Go away now. Bye."

Facing Deacon, she murmured, "How do we get out of here, by the way? How did you get in?" She lowered her voice more, "Did Belle finally…?" Talking in front of the queen without giving anything away about Belle was inconveniently difficult.

He scowled at Tatiana, before dropping his gaze and murmuring, "The…training I'm doing? Turns out one of the skills buried in my unique blend of magic is…" He made a small hand gesture to fill in the blank, but Cary already got the idea.

"Oh shit." He'd been the one to open the portal into Faery. He could open portals into *Faery*? A leopard shifter? That was some weird shit they were going to have to talk about soon when there wasn't an even weirder Fae queen watching them.

And Tatiana was still there watching them. Cary could *feel* the queen's gaze on the back of her head. It was *not* a comfortable feeling. Probably would have actually hurt if it weren't for Cary's shield.

"So can you…now?" Cary murmured, though she was sure Tatiana could still hear them. "I mean, you're not in a rage or anything. Or well, maybe you are after all that breeding talk." She glanced back. "Which was a super super weird non sequitur," she said to Tatiana, who was watching them with that inscrutable expression of hers that Cary couldn't read but which usually meant trouble.

"One way or another, Cary Redmond," Tatiana sang in her high, soft voice, "you will be mine. I will have you in my court. Forever."

Cary shivered. Again, Ew. When Tatiana did that singing thing, it made Cary's teeth hurt.

"I need to get you out of here," Deacon said.

"Ready to leave when you are."

Against her ear, he said, "I'm not sure I can do this again."

She gave his waist a squeeze. "You can," she said. "And if you can't, Belle will figure it out soon enough and open the portal again for us." The one thing she was *pretty* sure about was that Belle wouldn't leave her grandson here. Maybe Cary. And that begged a conversation. But not Deacon.

Deacon's grip around her flexed again, flattening her to his chest. He glanced over her head to Tatiana, growling softly under his breath. Cary wasn't sure he even knew he was doing that. But it was probably good. Rage, right? They needed his rage. Or something… Actually, she wanted to know more about all this when they got back. Just had to get out of Faery first.

Still growling softly, his lip lifting in a snarl, he half closed his eyes. From the slit left open, Cary saw the glowing yellow of his leopard rising. His muscles tensed. Another growl rumbled through his chest, too low for her to hear, but she felt it vibrating through her own body. Then a silence and stillness that worried her for reasons she couldn't quite name.

And behind him, a line wobbled in the air, a thin, narrow span that flickered in and out. Tatiana laughed, but Cary squeezed Deacon tighter, hoping he wouldn't be distracted by the sound.

Or maybe it helped? The line in the air solidified. It was strange looking, like a wrinkle in reality, the trees behind it bent and folded to look thinner. And then with a grunt from Deacon, the opening spread wide enough to form a narrow rip between realms. Not very big, but if they turned sideways, they could squeeze out. That was all Cary needed. She'd squeeze through an opening the size of a quarter if she had to to get out of Faery.

Deacon back toward the exit, his gaze on Tatiana, keeping Cary close but between him and the queen so Cary's shield worked without her having to concentrate on it. Cary stumbled over a root on the ground. Looked down to see another flower shiver and die as they passed over it. She glanced back then too. The clearing around Tatiana was filled with living flowers now, growing up long vines and tangling in the air around the queen. The flowers pulsed, which was creepy, and…something dripped from the petals. Something red.

That was as much as Cary wanted to see. She faced the narrow opening back to her realm.

"We'll meet again soon, Cary Redmond," Tatiana called, her voice still that creepy sing-songy tone. "I'll look forward to it."

Deacon stepped backward through the rip, which distorted to let him pass. Same with Cary as he pulled her out of Faery, back into their real world. Cary turned in time to see Tatiana heading for the tear.

And then the portal closed with a snap that sounded suspiciously like a leopard hiss.

16

Back in the open field behind Belle's cottage, Cary took a deep breath of regular air. Air with the scent of grass and dirt and sheep and, because he was still holding her closer, Deacon. No cinnamon and pine. No weird Fae perfumes. The light was normal sunshine behind ordinary gray rain clouds. There was a sheep a few yards away who bawwed at them and then wandered farther up the hill. The trees at the edge of the field had ordinary green leaves and pine needles.

And best of all, there was no magic.

At least not the kind that she would absorb.

She let out along, deep breath and rested her head against Deacon's shoulder. "Well. That wasn't fun at all."

"No," he agreed, cupping the back of her head in his big hand as he hugged her. "I'm sorry my grandmother did that to you. I… I don't think she realized… With the magic."

That was possible, that Belle hadn't realized how dangerous being in Faery would be in the short term for Cary. It was always a dangerous place for humans. But maybe since it was her section of the realm, Belle assumed Cary would be able to wait there without harm while Deacon got angry enough to rescue her.

Possible. But given Belle *knew* Cary absorbed magic and Faery was made of magic… Cary was betting Belle had multiple reasons for picking Faery as a place to send her. Maybe a test, to see how much magic Cary could absorb now? Maybe some other reason?

Something Cary intended on asking Belle.

But speaking of. She looked up and around. Deacon's grandmother stood a few yards behind them, her head tilted to one side, looking speculatively at them.

"Not. Fun." Cary repeated but louder for the woman. Not that she needed to be loud since Belle had shifter hearing.

"Tatiana came here to see you," Belle murmured. Didn't ask. She'd probably seen the queen through the opening between the two realms. "Strange…"

"Why strange? She hates me. I think. Or something. Anyway, she's a threat to me. She'd hardly let me traipse through Faery without investigating." The fact that Danu hadn't crossed into another court's territory but Tatiana had was…weird, too.

Belle blinked and met Cary's gaze. "We've a lot to talk about." She turned back toward the cottage without another word.

"That's…" Cary let out a frustrated growl. "This trip is not turning out how I imagined. And we've only been here two days. I just wanted to see some castles."

Deacon pulled her close again, into another hug. "I'm sorry."

"Nothing to do with you," she said. "Don't apologize. I wouldn't be anywhere else. But I did imagine things going…differently."

"Less terror and trouble filled?"

"Yeah." She frowned. "And with Belle's enemy who tried to

kill us, and now Tatiana in the wings, I think we're due a lot more trouble.

Which just really…

Well, honestly, it was so normal to her life, she wasn't sure what she'd expected. Of *course* there was trouble.

And of course she was right smack in the middle of it.

"Let's get back to the cottage," Deacon said. He pulled back and took her hand.

Cary glanced down and raised her eyebrows. "You're still wearing the kilt. I sort of half expected it to vanish and return to your own clothes when we got back to this reality. Like a Faery glamour the realm itself dressed you up in." She fingered the brooch on his shoulder. Something about it looked very familiar. It wasn't exactly like the one the Nags had given him—and she should probably stop calling her bosses that nickname now that they nagged her so much less, but years of calling them that had turned the nickname into a habit—but the brooch was still…familiar.

Weird.

This whole trip had been weird so far. And she wasn't even through the jetlag phase yet.

Deacon looked down at his outfit too. "I can change it. I'm pretty sure. But I got the impression you liked it."

She grinned. "What gave you that idea? The fact that I said so out loud, or the fact that I was ready to crawl up you and wrap my legs around your waist despite the audience of a Faery queen?"

His sexy smile made her toes curl. "Both, actually. Though I suspect our…mutual interest was probably what got the queen talking about breeding."

Cary shuddered. "Don't remind me. That was creepy as fuck."

"Yes," Deacon said dryly. "It did cut through the lust, didn't it?"

"It surely did," Cary said. Then she looked at him again, taking in the way he filled out his mysteriously made outfit. "But I think I can come back around to the lust again." She waggled her eyebrows at him to make him laugh.

It worked and she grinned at the sound. She loved his laugh. That sound was a relief. Whatever else had just happened, at least the lesson his grandmother had been trying to teach him hadn't done him any damage.

By the time they reached the cottage, Belle already had the kettle on and was pulling mugs out of the cabinet.

"So," Cary said as she took a seat at the table, "I'm pretty sure you weren't trying to kill me. But for the record, Faery and I are not a good mix and I can't be there like that. Remember, the magic absorbing thing."

"Ye survived, didn't you?" Belle said with her back to them.

"Not for lack of Faery trying."

She glanced at her hands. None of that glow still. But she had no idea how much magic she'd absorbed, how much she'd used, and how much she was still storing in her cells. And what any of that was doing to her. She didn't have Eriana around to tell her now either. Honestly, Cary had been hoping to go longer without absorbing any more magic, since she was worried about the multitude of changes all the magic from the demon fight had made on her poor body.

To be safe, she needed to do the candle lighting trick soon. Or at least see if she *could* do it. Maybe even do the thing with her fingertips that Rory had taught her. She'd know the magic was used up when the flames went out then.

But that was for later.

Belle faced them finally, her brows lowered. "No other queen should have entered the Unseelie territory."

"It wasn't Tatiana that was the threat," Cary emphasized. "Or, well, no she was a threat. Obviously. But she wasn't the *first* threat."

"The Strix wouldna come after you when I was so close either."

"No. No. I mean the way I absorb magic." Belle *had* to know that was the problem. They'd *explained* the problem to her. But she seemed to be glossing over it as the main threat to Cary in Faery. "You saw it when you threw magic at me. When I pull it in, I need to use it up or die. And in Faery, I can't use all the magic pouring into me up because there's just more magic behind that. I would literally have to destroy Faery. And, you know, that would be bad."

Plus, she was pretty sure she couldn't do that. She was one lone human with only so much capacity and Faery was a ginormous realm. She'd explode before she churned through a tiny section of the realm. That's how she died last time.

Deacon took hold her of her hand and squeezed. Something in her scent must have given away her thoughts. Or at least the emotions—the fear and anger—underlying her thoughts.

Belle stare at her from the kitchen, letting out a deep breath, almost a sigh. "I was not thinking about that part as much as I was trying to force my grandson's hand, and I dinna think you would be in there long enough to matter."

"It doesn't take long," Cary said. "It happens instantly. And fast. And in Faery…very fast."

She flicked a glance at Deacon. They didn't tell people how her Protector powers worked, specifically. Safer that way. And she wasn't entirely sure whether to trust Belle or not because of what had just happened. She *understood* why Belle had done it. But it hadn't engendered much trust on Cary's part. And if Belle needed to, Cary had very little doubt she'd use whatever she could to get what she wanted or needed.

It occurred to Cary that Belle had been a *Fae queen* for forty years. That wasn't something that could leave her untouched. Unaffected. And Fae queens were manipulative and mercurial and dangerous.

Because this was Deacon's grandmother, and up to now, she'd been kind and friendly, Cary had forgotten that. While Belle might have been a leopard shifter first, she was *also* a Fae queen.

So, yeah, no… Telling Belle in detail how Protector powers worked was a bad idea. Very bad. Instead, she said, "I have trouble building shields to keep myself safe in Faery if I'm not prepared ahead of time. I need a heads-up. You didn't give me that, and I had to take precious moments to separate myself from the magic. I absorbed a bunch of it. I'll need to get rid of it soon." Maybe. "So, if you wouldn't mind, don't do that to me again."

Belle raised her brows. Maybe it was Cary's tone. Or the direct eye contact. A faint yellow glow rose in Belle's eyes, her leopard actually rising. It wasn't something Belle had shown Cary before. And again, Cary reminded herself the woman had been acting as a queen in Faery for decades. Cary couldn't afford to take what Belle showed her at face value. There would be meaning and manipulation behind it all.

The meeting with Tatiana had reminded Cary sharply what it meant to be a queen in the world of the Fae. Belle wouldn't still be alive if she hadn't adapted to that. There was still a lot about what this had done to her that she hadn't explained either, as far as the magic was concerned. So, yeah, this supposed rising of her leopard, as if Cary was challenging her, was probably designed to manipulate.

But why? And to what end?

Didn't matter to the way Cary reacted, but she was curious what game Belle was playing out.

Cary held Belle's gaze even as the faint yellow glow

intensified. Even as Deacon squeezed her hand tighter. She stared the older shifter down and waited for whatever Belle had to say.

When Belle finally blinked, Cary felt like some sort of taunt line had been cut and all the tension went out of the interaction. Belle made a little "huh" sound under her breath and turned back to making tea.

"Let's settle on the couch," she said, with her back to them, "instead of sitting at the table. I'm tired after everything that's happened. My bones need a rest."

Cary raised her brows but let Deacon help her to her feet and didn't argue about sitting in front of the fireplace. Which was cold and bare as they settled on the oversized, deep cushioned couch.

But as Belle joined them, she made a little hand gesture and a pile of wood appeared on the hearth. "Light it," Belle said. "That'll take some of the magic? Ye said something about candles."

"Uh." Well, honestly, Cary had never tried to light a fire in a fireplace this way before. Was it different?

As Belle set steaming mugs of Earl Gray onto the thick oak coffee table, Cary moved around to the fireplace and crouched down by the wood. She piked a small stick from the pile and held it in one had while she touched the tip of it with her other fingers. Remembering what her dragon mentor had taught her, she visualized her fingers lighting, the flames rising, the magic flowing into the flames.

It took a moment. She hadn't done this in a while and had only just been learning it when the fight when the demon god happened, so she wasn't well practiced. She also wasn't entirely sure how much magic she had left to use up.

But then the flames rose, a flash of them at first, strong enough to catch her entire hand on fire. Oops. The flames didn't burn her so long as she concentrated, but the sight of her hand on fire was…disconcerting. She focused on bringing the flames under control, arrowing them into flames just on her fingertips.

The little stick in her hand had caught the instant her hand when up, so she set it at the bottom of the pile of wood, and then put her still lit finger to more of the kindling under the pile, lighting little fires in several places. When the flame continued to burn, she set her finger against some of the thicker logs. Pine scent filled the cottage, a nice pleasant campfire smell that eased some of Cary's worries.

It took her a good five minutes before the flames coming out of her fingers finally started to die down of their own accord. She sat back on her haunches, the fire on the hearth warm and crackling in front of her as she watched the last flame on one fingertip waiver and finally die.

The flames from her finger weren't, like, normal fire. This was magic fire. When practicing with her dragon mentor, she'd started a few little fires in her backyard grass and Rory had had to put them out. He'd warned her the magic flames could spread easily if not controlled. So she watched the fire in the fireplace for a long moment to make sure it was contained.

It was churning through the kindling and logs. Would it go out without help, when the fuel was used up? She had no real idea and wasn't sure if she should ask.

A problem for an hour from now. She'd keep an eye on the fireplace in the meantime. And at the very least, she'd drained the excess Fae magic from her system. No exploding today.

At least not in the next few minutes.

She settled beside Deacon on the couch and his arm went immediately around her, but he was staring at the fireplace. After a moment of silence, he murmured, "That was no small amount of magic left."

"No," she agreed. "But it could have been worse." She

suspected what she'd brought from Faery wasn't any more than she'd carried before. She hadn't noticed it at all or felt that sense of…fullness that could happen when she absorbed lots and lots of magic. But it was better to have it gone.

In case someone decided to throw more magic at her.

Deacon's arm tightened on her shoulder. She leaned into him, letting the feel of his heat and strength settle her jangled nerves. She often did that for him and his leopard, as part of the mate bond, but it never ceased to amaze her that the physical contact worked to settle *her* as well.

Another few minutes passed with all three of them silent, just watching the crackling fire and sipping tea. Or well, Cary and Belle sipped their tea. Deacon left his mug sitting on the coffee table.

Finally, Belle cleared her throat. "Ye'll make a fine leopard queen," she said. "When Deacon takes over for his mother. Not backing down, even to a more dominant shifter is important."

Cary glanced sharply at Belle. "That was a test."

"Not at first," Belle admitted. "To be honest with ye, I've more dealings with faeries these days than shifters. On purpose. Wasna expecting my leopard to raise her head in challenge. But it's good to know you'll be able to stand yer own beside my grandson."

Cary wasn't sure that's what she'd been doing, and she really really didn't want to think about one day being a queen or queen consort or whatever to a leopard king. Mostly, she ignored her part in that future. She'd be with Deacon of course—at least she hoped she would. The mate thing was a pretty permanent bond, so she was pretty sure this was it for both of them, together from now on —but she ignored the fact that as his mate, she'd be looked to as something of a leader to the shifters as well. She liked to pretend that part wasn't going to happen even if she couldn't quite figure out how that was possible.

A problem for another time. A future time she hoped was a long long way off. Since she was looking at Deacon's grandmother, had met his great-grandfather, and both were pretty spry and active still, Cary assumed Deacon's mother wouldn't be going anywhere soon. Cary would likely have decades or more to get used to this idea of being mated to a leopard king.

She silently wished good health and long life onto Deacon's mother as she took another sip of tea. Then said, "Accidental leopard challenges aside, how did thing go once you'd pushed me into Faery?" She glanced at Deacon. "I figured you'd panic because I would have."

His hand tightened on her shoulder again, his nod so faint it was almost imperceptible.

"And obviously you hit the critical mass in rage that let you use some of your magic," Cary continued. "But…what happened?"

Deacon glanced at his grandmother. She gave him a raised brow that probably conveyed a lot that Cary couldn't interpret. There was probably even more information exchanged between the two in their scents, something the leopards did without thought but that Cary couldn't even begin to pick up on being a not-a-shifter.

"My rage came out," Deacon said after a moment. "Nearly got the better of me."

Cary felt the tension in his arm across her shoulders, saw the very subtle wince. "What happened?"

"I… I might have attacked her," he muttered.

"Nothing I coudna handle and wasna prepared for," Belle assured him. "I knew what I was doing."

"Doesn't make me feel better," he said, so quietly it was barely a sound over the fire. "But…I got hold of the rage when she told me I could open a portal to get you out. Felt…weird."

"An understatement?" Cary tried a little smile.

His tension eased a fraction, but his muscles were still tight and flexed where they were leaning into each other. "Understatement," he agreed. "The shifting to clothes, the sensing my kind… That all feels natural. Too natural. Even after the years of pushing it down. But doing more…"

"Is him being able to open that portal into Faery a him-thing, as the seventh firstborn of seven generations of firstborns, or is that a having-your-Fae-connection thing?" Cary asked Belle.

"Both," Belle said. "Why do ye think his mother sent him here to train? We've never known exactly how his birth order magic and my genetic contribution would manifest in his magic. I was already changed by my affair with Nicneven when Deacon's father was born. But as my own son didn't develop any dangerous magic, I thought…" She let out a sharp sigh, her nostrils constricting and then flaring. "Well, anyway, it is what it is."

"If you weren't sure he could open a portal to Faery," I said, "why tell him that? Why push me *there* of all places?"

"There, because I could easily get you there and get you out again. It's as much my domain now as this house. I told him he could to see if he could. His rage needed a focus that wasna trying to make my head explode. And I wanted to see what he could do."

The comment about making her head explode made Deacon wince again, more obviously this time. Cary scowled at Belle. "If he'd hurt you, he'd never be able to forgive himself. Don't do that to him again."

Belle raised her brows. "You're more upset about how that affected him than ye are about what risk I put you at?"

"I'm upset about both things equally," she said.

"Aye, but it worked. My plan. And we now know he's got access to even more magic than he thought. The kind his mother and I have both feared."

That didn't sound good. Cary knew Deacon's mother wanted him to train the magic and worried that he hadn't. She wouldn't have attempted to recruit Cary into trying to talk Deacon into training that magic if she weren't worried. But Cary had had no idea how deep that fear went, *why* it went so deep.

Deacon had been able to rip open a hole into Faery this entire time.

And he'd had no idea.

17

The fire crackled in the fireplace, giving Cary something to focus on as this new realization sank in. The pine smoke scent and warm smell of the cooling Earl Gray tea in her mug swirled around her in such a soothing combination it was hard to reconcile with the edge of fear tightening in her gut.

Fear for what could have happened, might have happened before this moment, because they hadn't actually *known* what Deacon was capable of.

He hadn't known.

"Your mother should have mentioned," Cary muttered.

"She didn't know," he said. "Not…this. Not for sure."

"She was afraid ye'd retreat farther from your magic," Belle said, "if you knew the truth. Afraid, ye'd refuse to ever train and then get yerself killed because you dinna understand your power. She thought, if you *only* knew the dangers from the leopard magic, that would be enough to finally push you forward." Belle shrugged. "Maybe she was wrong. Maybe we both were."

"You weren't," Deacon said. "I would have shut down even more. Cut off more of myself before letting that loose."

"And ye would have been even more dangerous that way. When you met yer mate, you lost control for a time? Like we all do."

Deacon nodded briefly.

Cary made an effort not to flinch, but she did internally. He hadn't just "lost control for a time." Because she was human and not a leopard shifter, Deacon's control had taken a lot longer to come back than it might have otherwise. The pros of her being human, and therefore not someone he could kill with his power over other leopards, also had the cons of leaving him less in control of that power for a lot longer than if she'd been a shifter.

"You should have trained well before that," Belle said. "It was a dangerous thing, letting you go through that without any idea what could have happened. A testament to your control you both survived."

Cary blinked at that. So much of this last year, what they'd been through, what could have happened… Shit. That was going to add to her nightmares.

She leaned deeper into Deacon's embrace, pressing herself hard against his side in an attempt to remind herself they were both safe and everything was okay, and this would all work out fine.

"How the hell did we get through a fight with Oliver Holland and his dad, twice, without you unleashing any of this?" she wondered aloud, looking up at him.

"Never had a reason to rip into Faery during those fights," he said. "You weren't trapped there. You were in danger here." He shrugged. "And during that last fight, I did send a lot of… whatever I have into you."

"Which I used up in the fight. Don't worry. What magic I got from you was no worse for me, and probably a lot better for me, than what I got from the various demons."

Cary caught Belle's slight headshake and glanced at her in time to see her eyes closed. "Yer life," she muttered.

"Tell me about it," Cary said. "But this is about Deacon. So, the only reason he hasn't done something to get into Faery before now was just...he didn't want to? No reason to so it didn't come up?"

Belle shrugged. "Likely."

"What do we do about this?" Deacon asked. "I have no interest in Fae magic or using any of this. I want control over it so I don't hurt anyone. Especially Cary. That's it."

"Control requires ye know how to use what you've got. Magic doesn't...atrophy from lack of use. It's not a muscle in that way. Magic gets wilder and more dangerous without use. We'll have to find ye ways to attend to all aspect of your powers to keep them controlled."

Deacon's turn to close his eyes and shake his head. "Jaxer is going to have a field day with this."

The accuracy of that statement made Cary chuckle. But also, "He'll be as worried about you as I am."

"What do I need to do, Nan?" Deacon asked. "That doesn't involve Cary ever *ever* being sent into Faery again."

His muscles tensed as he said this, coiled and ready to pounce. The intensity and meaning in his words would have been hard for a human to miss. Cary was pretty sure his scent made his meaning impossible for Belle to miss.

"No more sending Cary into the Fae world. Between Tatiana and the Strix, it's safer for us all to avoid the realm anyway. As much as possible." She glanced away as she said the last, her gaze going to the fire.

Not hard to get her meaning either. She couldn't avoid Faery completely.

"But I think we've done enough training for the morning," Belle said, standing. "I'll get some lunch going." She took Deacon's untouched tea cup with her as she went back to the kitchen, leaving Cary and Deacon staring at the fire Cary had started with the residual Fae magic she'd absorbed.

"Looks like we'll both be training while we're here," she murmured.

"What?" Deacon turned a little to face her without releasing his hold on her shoulders.

"I built a shield in Faery to cut off the magic, but, honestly, I have no idea if I built it from magic I was absorbing, like I did in the demon god fight, or if I was raising my Protector shield. I couldn't tell. I could *see* the one I put into place before you arrived, though. Which worries me. Like you, I need to figure out what I'm doing so I don't do things on accident. Relying on a shield I construct from magic and spells rather than raising the Protector powers... That could have unforeseen consequences. The two shields could work differently, and if I think I have one instead of the other..."

She trailed off because they both knew the dangers. The Protector shield was almost impenetrable. It stood against all comers and kept Cary and her charges safe from all directions. And she didn't have to think about it, or concentrate on it. She didn't have to physically hold up a "shield," the way she'd had to when she built one from other people's magic.

And those other types of shields tended to be directional. Not all encompassing. If she thought she was safely in a Protector bubble and wasn't, someone could just...sneak up on her. Which they couldn't when she was protecting someone.

This new element, of being able to keep herself safe, of control of the magic, was great. But thanks to her weird, rare ability, it was also a lot more complicated.

She reminded herself most Protectors had to deal with their own skills around learning to do the job. Most Protectors had some sort of magic, or power, of their own that they worked with around channeling this Protector power. Cary had just been so—supposedly—ordinary when she'd been tri— Dammit. Didn't have that excuse anymore. When she'd been recruited to this job, she hadn't had to worry about integrating different skills.

Now she did. And she had no idea how to do it.

"It would be bad to have Jaxer here, wouldn't it?" she asked.

"Why Jaxer?"

"He's my mentor…sort of still. He's trained other Protectors with multiple skills. I could use his help working on this."

"He won't be able to be here without it attracting more attention from Tatiana," Deacon said quietly. Then, even more quietly, "Do you… Do you want to go back home? I'll stay here to—"

She cut him off with a sharp hand gesture. "No. I'm here with you, for you. This is important, and I'm not leaving you to go through this alone."

That might not even work since their bond meant he needed to be around her a lot. They'd been able to remain apart more lately, but he still got itchy and restless and had a hard time of it. She did not want him trying to learn how to use and control something this big without having her around to keep him steady. One less thing he'd have to worry about.

"I'll figure something out," she said. "I'll practice when you do. Without absorbing any more magic to add to the mix, I can work on raising the Protector shield until it comes more naturally, instinctively. If I have control of it, and can raise it consciously as easily as it goes up when I have someone to keep safe, then it'll be what I turn to when I need it. I just have to…make it into a habit. Easy." She grinned, but he didn't smile back. "Look, we've got time here, right? Enough time to form a habit. It'll be fine. And since I'm technically not working here, that means I won't have to worry about doing anything *but* getting this stuff down. It works out for both of us."

He didn't comment, but he did lean back into the couch, pulling her with him. They stayed that way, staring at the fire as the cottage filled with the lovely scent of whatever it was Belle was cooking—something with meat in it, smelled like, but Cary wasn't sure—and both tried not to worry.

The next few weeks were going to be…interesting.

18

By night four, Deacon was exhausted and sick to death of all of this. He'd never wanted this magic shit and he certainly didn't want to use it regularly. Learning how to use it, after all these years of mostly shutting it down, felt like trying to wrench a torn muscle that hadn't finished healing into use. It hurt like hell, was awkward and exhausting, and he really just wanted to sweep Cary back off to Edinburgh where he could watch her discovering the city and enjoy some much needed quiet time with his mate.

Not that the time here wasn't technically quiet.

Belle's cottage was in the middle of nowhere, surrounded by fields and farms and sheep and cows. Watching Cary's first in-person introduction to a Highland cow had been one of the more entertaining events of the last few days, her charming delight and the cow's willingness to accept her scratching it around its head and horns, had been a moment of lightness and fun.

But most of the last week had been work. And resistance to that work. At least on his part.

"That's yer problem," Belle snapped. "You're resisting. And the more ye resist, the harder it is to do what I'm trying to teach you."

They'd moved on past trying to bring out his rage, though Belle still insisted he access it sometimes. Not having to regularly try accessing rage that was dangerous around his grandmother and his mate was a relief, though. No one had been sent to, or opened a portal to, or disappeared into Faery again after that first day either, so that was a relief.

But he was still having trouble figuring out all the things he could do with what he'd inherited—from his mother, his grandmother, and his birth order.

Today, in leopard form, he was practicing the short distance porting his grandmother was trying to teach him. It wasn't something he could do over long distances. It wasn't even technically teleporting. It worked more like speed, but it was a speed other leopards, other shifters, didn't have access to.

Deacon could, essentially, move from one position to another by folding the space in between. There were no portals to move through. Just…one moment he could be in one place, and the next he'd be in another without exerting the usual burst of speed to do it. In the usual way, he could move so fast he blurred to human vision, and could move from one place to another fast enough that it happened in a blink. For a human.

This was even faster. Almost instantaneous. Even beings that functioned at speeds faster than humans, like other shifters and vampires, wouldn't be able to see him move when he used the magic. This was one of the few things he was learning he really wanted to get down pat because he could see all sorts of uses for this skill.

Especially in circumstances where he might need to save his mate. Because those circumstances came up a little too often.

He focused on getting from his position at the top of the hill behind Belle's house, to a position right next to her. The trick was not overshooting, undershooting, or disrupting the space of those standing next to the spot you were aiming for.

That was the tricky part. Not inadvertently tossing someone a great distance because he'd bunched up the actual space around them and that space gave them a mighty shove when it straightened out.

He'd accidentally sent his grandmother flying exactly once. And he'd been upset enough over that that he'd been pulling his distance ever since, landing yards away from her instead of right next to her. Even when he was trying to get next to her.

"I'm no' gonna break, Deacon," his grandmother said with a huff when he appeared ten feet away from her. "You'll notice how I'm back on my feet this whole time? If it was so easy to hurt me, I wouldna still be alive."

She was right. She was right. She'd changed to her leopard form in mid-air and landed on her feet. Not even taking a bruise. She wasn't a delicate old lady who might break a hip. She wasn't even his great-grandfather, who was getting old enough that Deacon felt justified in worrying over him. Belle, for all her age, was still agile and strong.

His mother would be annoyed by him being too delicate with Belle, too.

He let out a rumbling hiss and jumped back to where he'd been. Porting this direction, he landed exactly on the spot he'd been aiming for. He knew he could do this. One more time and they could call it a night and he could go hug his mate.

Cary had taken herself off to a different field to practice with her shield. And being that far away from her, in a strange—to her —country left him itchy and restless. After the first day, Belle had thrown up her hands and asked Cary if she could send her troll guard—who went by the name Wee Doug—to guard her back so Deacon could concentrate.

After Cary had finished chuckling over "Wee Doug," she'd agreed, much to his relief. He'd been able to concentrate a lot better knowing someone had her back, just in case one of the Fae queens showed up again. At the very least, Wee Doug was someone Cary could protect and that meant her shield came up automatically and that kept her safe.

He did have to wonder how a troll would feel about a human protecting him. That'd be something to see.

Deacon shook off thoughts of his mate—still a distraction even knowing she was (probably) safe—and focused on one last port. He stared at the spot a foot away from his grandmother, concentrated on the space between him and that location folding over on itself, bending like a piece of paper so he could simply jump from where he was to that spot a foot from Belle. A little leap to cover more than two hundred yards, a distance close to the length of two American football fields.

He let the magic he was learning to feel trickle out until his fur bristled. Twitched the tip of his long, thick tail. His lip lifted in an unconscious snarl. He blinked once.

And leapt.

Landing two feet away from his grandmother instead of one.

But he hadn't knocked her over and that was closer than he'd gotten in the last three hours. He'd take it.

He shifted back to his human form, jeans and t-shirt coming with him, and gave his grandmother a shrug. "Best I can do for today."

She grunted, but gave a chin jut of acceptance and they walked back down to the cottage. "That last was better," she acknowledged. "Ye'll get there, love. I know you will."

He hoped she was right. He didn't have any choice now,

anyway. The fight with the demon god, feeding Cary magic he'd barely tapped himself, letting some of it leak into her when he hadn't even realized he was doing it... That had changed something for him, pushed him over some tipping point. He couldn't allow himself to feed her magic on accident again. But his control over that magic had...broken. It wouldn't go back down into the box he'd kept it in his entire life. He had to learn to use it or risk hurting people.

He'd done that once, when he was young, without meaning too. He'd nearly killed a young leopard who'd bullied Deacon's twin sister and brother. His mother had intervened, but still. Deacon had only been seven at the time. The bully was barely twenty—only a teenager in leopard years. And if not for his mother's help, Deacon would have murdered the boy.

This wasn't the kind of power he wanted over anyone, but he especially didn't want to hurt any of his people. And he'd die before he hurt his mate.

Thinking of Cary had him moving a little faster toward the cottage. He couldn't sense her the way he could his grandmother, the way he could other leopards when he tried. Most leopards couldn't sense their own kind this way, so this wasn't a difference other leopards would notice with a human mate—his youngest brother certainly didn't with his human mate—but Deacon did. And it made him itchy to get back to her. To find out if she'd returned from her own training yet.

If she hadn't, he'd go find her, walk home with her so she had more company than a taciturn troll.

He wasn't sure whether he was disappointed, worried, or content to discover Cary wasn't home yet. Only content because he liked the idea of walking back to the cottage with her through the quiet countryside. She was such a city girl. He delighted in her delight of their surroundings.

And frankly, he could use some alone time with her. They hadn't really had that since arriving, with his grandmother around most of the time. Cary was…sensitive to the fact that shifters had excellent hearing. All his assurances that Belle would respect their privacy hadn't swayed Cary. So having her out in the middle of nowhere, where she'd be comfortable felt like taking a weight off his shoulders.

His grandmother's only comment to him announcing he was going to find Cary was a grunt and an absent hand wave as she put on the kettle and started puttering around the kitchen to get dinner ready—she'd refused both Cary and Deacon's attempts to take over some of the cooking and since neither of them were great cooks, they hadn't argued too much. Deacon's dad loved to cook, like mother like son, but he hadn't passed that love down to Deacon.

The countryside was quiet and dark once he moved past the few road lights that marked the area outside his grandmother's cottage. The road that ran past her place led, after a few miles, to a small village and from there wound through farmland to a motorway that branched off southeast toward Edinburgh in one direction and southwest toward Glasgow in the other.

When he'd come here as a kid, there hadn't even been the street lights outside his nan's cottage, and the electricity wires had only been installed a few years before he was born. There was still very little light pollution, with Belle's nearest neighbors three miles away, their farmhouse behind several hills and a thicket of woods. Overhead the stars popped out bright against the black sky. A few gray whisps of clouds scuttled past, but mostly the night was bright and sharp and cold.

The cold air felt glorious after the day spent trying to master his magic, and a deep part of him wanted to shift and just run. As far and as fast as he could.

But a larger part of him wanted to see his mate.

He found her walking back toward the cottage along the empty road, Wee Doug a huge hulk of moving rocks behind her. Before he was close enough for her to see, her voice carried to him, asking Wee Doug if he ever wore moss to symbolize his position with Belle or if he just stuck to lichen. Deacon chuckled quietly. He loved that woman so damned much it took his breath away.

She looked up and spotted him a few minutes later, and her smile was like the sun rising. How could he have lived this long without her? Without the very sun? Seemed impossible. He couldn't even quite remember life before Cary. His brain kept trying to insert her into parts of his past where he knew she hadn't been, as if she'd been there all along.

His leopard rumbled contentedly in his head when her scent reached him, and he felt what was left of the day's tension drain out of him. No one else in his entire life had been able to do that to him. For him. He'd only noticed the underlying level of tension he carried at all times when he'd met Cary and that tension had vanished in her presence. This kind of peace… He'd gotten a form of it with his great-grandfather, at the bubble of peace Belle had created for him in Oregon. There, Deacon could relax too, the terrible tension losing its hold.

But outside of that one place, the tension clung to him. The need to hold himself rigid and controlled ever present.

Until Cary.

Her job might scare the shit out of him. Her noble soul and determination to save people no matter what might put her regularly in harm's way. But she was the one person in the world he could truly relax and be himself with. And he was grateful every day that she'd been the one to show up at that kid wizard's apartment to rescue him.

She trotted into his open arms for a hug without him having to say a word. For a long moment, they just stood that way, in the road, wrapped together in their own little bubble of peace.

When she did finally pull back, she looked up at him with narrowed eyes. "How did things go today?"

"Okay. I only tossed my grandmother across the field once."

"So. Progress."

He chuckled and turned her back toward the road, settling his arm around her shoulders. She leaned into him easily. None of the worry or fear that had been there early in their relationship was there now, in her spicy sweet scent, that hint of vanilla at the edges that he loved. She was still worried, but it was *for* him now, not *about* him. He could handle that.

He'd never expected to have anything like this. This settled, peaceful feeling with one person. Because of his birth order, his magic, his future leading his people, he'd honestly expected to be more...constrained with his mate. He'd expected to have to control himself, his magic, his emotions around his mate even *more* than he did around other leopards. Because he'd expected to find a mate among the leopards, not a human.

And, if he were being honest with himself, now, looking back, he'd dreaded the moment he'd find his mate. Dreaded what that would do to him. To those around him.

To her.

Knowing what his twin sister was going through right now wouldn't have assuaged those fears either. But Cary had turned all that worry on its ear. Giving him new and different fears, to be sure, but also giving him this. This peace. This ability to relax and just walk along a quiet road at night, with the stars stretched bright overhead, talking quietly about his attempts to rein in the skills he'd been ignoring all his life.

Wee Doug plodded along behind them until they were level with the path in the woods that led back to the standing stones.

"Heading back," the troll said, his deep voice a rocky rumble in the dark.

"Thanks again," Cary said to him. "Tomorrow? Same time?"

Wee Doug grunted and ambled into the trees, his passage made the underbrush shiver.

"He's awfully chatty, isn't he?" Cary said, looking up at Deacon with a deadpan expression that made him want to laugh.

"Mmm," he said. Which made *her* laugh, as he'd hoped.

He glanced across the street to his grandmother's house and sighed. He didn't want to go in yet. He was tired. And he wanted to be alone with Cary. "She's still cooking. Want to walk a little more?"

"Yes," she said without hesitance.

He glanced at her as they continued down the road past the cottage. "Is this bothering you? Being here. With her. Especially after…"

She waved that off. "She did what she did because she thought it would work. It did. She didn't fully understand what it would mean. And she hasn't sent me back into Faery since, so I'm fine."

"The years of being a Fae queen… She's not quite the grandmother I remember as a kid."

"Well, you were a kid. Of course she's not the same. Your memories are colored by childhood and innocence and all that."

"My great-grandfather is the same person," Deacon said quietly. "But Belle is…harder than I remember. There's a sharpness and a cunningness that wasn't there before. Even when I was a teenager and she was teaching me all that old-fashioned stuff like how to fight with a sword and how to use a Celtic brooch or wear a kilt properly. I was old enough then, to remember her clearly. And, if she's right about the forty years, she'd started as a stand in for Nicneven by then. No. This is different."

Cary frowned up at him. "Are you worried? Should we…leave

earlier than we intended? Your mom thought this was a good idea, but maybe it's...not?"

He let out a long sigh. "I don't think we need to leave. Things are working out. It hasn't even been a week. The training is happening, if not always going well. And outside of tossing you into Faery and hitting you in the chest with magic to try and piss me off, she hasn't done anything to warrant my worry." He ran his free hand up through his hair and sighed. "Maybe I'm just uncomfortable with what I'm trying to do here and looking for excuses to worry about something else."

"Learning your grandmother isn't entirely who you thought she was has to have been a blow, too. You're probably still adjusting to that."

He nodded, squeezing Cary a little closer. He'd never realized how isolated he'd been until he had her in his life and could talk to her about this kind of thing, with this level of honesty. He'd have never talked to anyone else in his life like this. Not even his mother. And she was the one person in his life who understood the weight of his responsibilities. But with Cary, he didn't have to check or analyze what he was saying. He could just...spill his guts and she accepted him. Just as he was.

What the hell had he been before her?

They walked in silence a little more, her scent wrapping around him, sneaking in past all his worries. Realized he'd missed her quite a lot during the day.

Realized they were alone on this road with the lights of the cottage far behind them now.

He glanced down at the top of her head. Her scent had that extra flavor weaving through it now. That sharp, edgy, lusty flavor that made his heart start to thump harder and his breathing deepen. He might love that scent most of all.

Inside his head, his leopard growled quietly, a rumble of approval. Of need.

When he started to draw circles against her shoulder, through the barrier of her leather jacket, her desire edged up.

He glanced at her again from the corner of his eye as she pushed harder against his side and a little sigh escaped her, a restless sound he'd come to know very well.

The memory of that moment in Faery when she'd noticed he was wearing a kilt came back to him. She *had* mentioned wanting him to wear that again, hadn't she. And he was supposed to be learning to harness and use his magic.

He concentrated for a few moments. He hadn't tried this before. He could make his clothes appear and disappear when he shifted, but this…

Letting his gaze lower, he visualized what he wanted to happen, the way he did when he shifted. And he let the magic he'd been slowly opening to the last week spin around that image. Giving it weight and reality. The change felt strange, the material sliding around his skin making his nerves feel more sensitive than they'd already felt. Heightening every sensation, including his desire for his mate.

When he opened his eyes full, he glanced down. Smiled.

And wondered how long it would take her to notice.

19

———————

 $\mathcal{E}$ xactly one minute. That's how long it took Cary to realize Deacon was no longer wearing his usual jeans, t-shirt, and the sweater he put on for show, not because he was cold, despite the night temperature dropping. But in that moment of realization… Actually, in the moments leading up to that moment, she wasn't feeling the cold much either anymore.

Deacon's heat and scent had woven around her until her mind had wandered off into significantly warmer thoughts.

When she glanced down and realized Deacon's clothes had changed, those warmer thoughts turned hot. Scorching. And maybe even a little shocked.

"The kilt?" she said, her voice breathy and deep. "Didn't know you could change your clothes like that without shifting in between."

"New trick. What do you think?"

"I approve. Also, now I want you out of that kilt."

His rumbling chuckle of agreement made her thighs clench.

His voice… She would never get over the way his voice could make her feel.

The lusty need she'd been suppressing for the last few days, because it felt very weird to have fun sexy times in his *grandmother's* cottage when the cottage wasn't all that big and shifters had scary good hearing, came roaring to life then.

They were alone now. Yes, it was dark and cold and they were in the middle of a road next to woods and farmland and stone fences. But they were alone. No grandmothers. No trolls. No random humans or Fae queens. (She hoped on that last one. It was hard to tell sometimes with Fae queens.)

All alone with her gorgeous mate. Who'd purposefully replaced his ordinary clothes with a kilt because he knew it turned her on.

Well. That wasn't a set of circumstances she wanted to let slip through her fingers.

She paused in the middle of the road and turned into him. Her body grew restless the instant he wrapped his arms around her, flattening her against his big body. His eyes were glowing faintly in the starlight. Not the leopard glow. Just his usual Deacon-ness, his golden eyes glinting with intent. An intent that made her body hum and melt and maybe beg a little.

Or a lot. Definitely a lot of her girly parts now begging for some attention. Without conscious thought, she rubbed against him, trying to relieve some of the growing tension. His low growl only spiraled that tension higher.

Even after a year, this need, the desire to push him against the nearest solid surface and wrap herself around him, lose herself in his touch, his mouth, none of this had eased even a little. Changed, yes. She knew him now. Knew what made him groan, what made him lose his mind completely. But the intensity of sex with Deacon hadn't eased at all.

She only realized how much she'd been holding herself back on this trip when she finally felt free to let go.

Middle of the road in mid-autumn when it was downright cold? Well, what the hell. There was no traffic out here. And she was pretty sure all the sheep and cows were asleep. And she wasn't feeling the cold at all as she let Deacon's heat seep into her skin.

He jerked her hips closer to his, to the hard line of his erection through the rough wool material of the kilt and she groaned. Buried her face against his neck. The way he smelled just wrapped around her, made her stomach dance and tighten. She could live right there with her face pressed into his skin as he nuzzled her temple, her cheek.

Then his lips found hers and "thinking" became this abstract concept, this thing that other people did.

Thinking? What did that even mean?

Deacon lifted her off her feet and she wrapped her legs around his waist as he carried her—with shocking ease!—backward, deeper into the cover of the woods. She expected him to lean her against a tree, which she would have been fine with because desperation made her impervious to shame and tree bark. But he continued to walk her deeper into the darkness, kissing her mouth, her neck, his hands flexing on her ass.

When the darkness broke, light from the star-filled sky spilling down over them, she lifted from his mouth long enough to look around. They were at the edge of a small clearing, the ground covered in thick, course grass and the air scented with heather from a small, hearty patch of the purple-pink flower at the edge of the clearing, still in bloom despite the lateness of the season. The clearing felt isolated and private, only a few ambitious night birds and bugs making any noise. No breeze reached them over the trees, but it was still a cold night.

And yet, Cary, who was not a fan of fucking in the cold, couldn't feel anything but desperate to get under Deacon's kilt.

She locked her legs around his waist as he lowered them both to the grass. His strength never ceased to amaze her, and that only heightened her restless need, lust coiling low in her gut. Her leather jacket and jeans protected her skin from the rough grass, though she could feel it through her hair. Mostly, though, she was too obsessed with getting her hands on Deacon's skin to notice any discomfort.

And wasn't the kilt just an absolute delight for this desire because it took no effort at all to run her hands up under the long wool material and get her fingers onto Deacon's thick thighs and around his hips, up to his ass.

She grinned against his mouth. "Did bother with underwear, huh?"

"Seemed like a good idea."

"Very good idea," she said with a nod. "Very very very good idea."

His rumbling chuckle vibrated through her and made her nerves sing.

Getting her jeans out of the way was a lot more complicated than the kilt and it made her appreciate the traditional Scottish garb even more. She didn't wear skirts or dresses very often, not for lack of desire but mostly out of laziness and the fact that her job involved jumping and running a lot—to get in between bad guys and good guys—and unless she was wearing one of Marianne's magical skirts that didn't fly up, she'd end up flashing way too many bad guys her underwear. Which, she didn't want to do. But in that moment, when she just wanted Deacon's hands on her skin, between her legs, she regretted the jeans.

Deacon, on the other hand, didn't seemed bothered with the time it took. He unwrapped the material over his shoulder—which she realized wasn't actually part of the kilt only then, silly her—and settled it underneath her. Then he stripped off his shirt, which made her head spin and angels sing. The man was the embodiment of a statue of a Greek god. Just...magnificent. His tawny skin, lit only by star-light, gleamed. Muscles bunched. The light coat of hair across his chest and arrowing downward impossible for her not to touch. Once he had his shirt under her as well, he finally went to work on her boots.

Somehow, with a lot of giggling and groaning, they got her shoes off, her jeans and underwear off, and her arms out of her jacket—which she left under her as more cushion. By the time she had enough clothes out of the way to be satisfied with her state of being, she was on fire, one big ball of anticipation and need.

Deacon scooted down her body, kissing his way over her stomach, settling his mouth between her legs. Cary arched up against him, one hand in his hair as everything in her tightened. She'd gone too many days without his mouth on her. She lasted exactly two minutes. And then his clever tongue pushed her over the edge. She came so hard she screamed.

That shut up the ambitious night birds and bugs, she thought with a breathless amusement. She was entirely too overwhelmed to say that out loud, though. She didn't have the breath for it. And by the time she'd settled enough to open her eyes, Deacon was there, over her, his golden eyes twinkling. She couldn't even begrudge him his smugness after he made her come that hard. In fact, she kind of liked it.

She pulled his face down to hers, kissing him hard as he surged into her, the feel of him thick and hard and so fucking satisfying she moaned. Nothing had ever felt so perfectly perfect. Even with the rough grass under her, the hard ground, that fucking rock too near her hip. All of it was perfect because this was Deacon. And he was all hers.

The fact that she came again before he finally let go did not dampen her own smugness even a little bit. In fact, from his sexy smile, he kind of liked it.

With a little maneuvering, he settled on the ground on top of their bunched up pile of clothing and pulled her over the top of him, taking her weight easily and cushioning her. She settled her chin on his chest and toyed gentle with is chest hair as she stared up at him.

"Missed this," she murmured.

"Me too," he rumbled back.

His eyelids were heavy, and she felt like she could sleep in that moment too, easily. But the heat of him under her wasn't *quite* enough to ignore the cold air brushing over her naked ass. He could shift and sleep here in a fur coat, but she needed to get back inside before she collapsed.

And there was also Belle…who was cooking for them. Damn, she'd forgotten all about that. No naps for her yet. Her grumbling stomach didn't mind the delay, though.

"We should get back, huh." She sighed and burrowed deeper into his heat, his arms snug bands around her back.

"We should. But in a minute. She'll understand why we needed some time. She had a mate too."

Which brought up the question Cary had been desperately curious about but hadn't wanted to ask. Since he'd brought it up… "What happened to your grandfather? You never talk about him. It's always your grandmother. No one mentions Belle's mate."

Deacon's deep sigh lifted and lowered Cary's head. "He died. Years ago. I never even knew him. He was alive when I was born. I'm told I met him a couple of times. But I was…two, I think, when he passed so I don't have any memories of him."

"So Michael and Jocelyn wouldn't either?" They were Deacon's twin brother and sister, who were technically younger.

Was just Deacon's (bad?) luck to be born the first of the three and inherit all that came with that birth order.

"Not that they've ever mentioned. I doubt it, though." He shook his head. "I don't remember how she survived the loss, but I get the impression from my father, and sometimes from her father, that it was a close thing. A dark time she won't talk about. But it's why she created that farm and the peace she made for my Gramps in Oregon. She understood how he was feeling when he lost his own mate."

"How did he die?" Since Belle's own mother had lived longer than her mate, it struck Cary that Belle's mate, Deacon's grandfather, must have died pretty young for a leopard shifter. Not as young as Deacon, but given how long they lived… It wasn't likely a natural death.

"I was told he was killed in an accident. They'd been living in Wales at the time—she only came back to Scotland after his death —and there was an accident at one of the coal mines not far from where they lived. He had a lot of human friends who were miners, so he raced in to help. Apparently, he saved a bunch of men before the tunnel collapse that killed him."

Deacon recited the story quietly, a little by rote, with a note of melancholy for the grandfather he'd never gotten to know.

"I'm sorry you never got to know him."

Deacon nodded. "Me too. I have some vague memories of the house in Wales. She stayed there for a few years after his death. But by the time I was…nine, ten, she was back up here. With her kids grown and her mate gone, I guess she didn't see any reason to remain in Wales."

Cary tried not to think too hard about a time when Deacon would die. She hoped (fingers crossed and lots of knocking on wood) that would be many many decades into the future. But given her job, his position among the leopards… Well, that's why she tried not to think about it. He'd had to watch her die once. In the fight with the demon god, he'd promised to follow her if she died again, and wow, had she not wanted him to die. She hated even a hint of the thought of him not being in this world anymore. So she mostly blocked the very real inevitability of it.

Which she had to do again in that moment or risk crying all over him for reasons she'd have a hard time explaining. Then again, he knew what this mate business meant more than she did. He'd probably understand.

She snuggled against him for a bit longer, letting the cold air wash over them, letting the quiet night sounds bring her back to that moment of contentedness. They were both alive. They were warm and breathing in this moment. And she'd take that.

"I love you," she murmured into his skin.

He nuzzled her hair. "Love you, too." His voice was deep and rumbly and the sound made her heart squeeze tight.

Getting redressed was as much of an adventure as stripping off had been, and sparked enough giggling for Cary to release the melancholy of Deacon's story about his grandfather. By the time she had her jeans and boots back on, and Deacon had pulled his shirt over his head, she was back to being happy and content. She was starving now, though, her need to nap well outweighed by her need to eat.

Deacon kept a hand at the small of her back as they made their way through the trees to the road. By the time they reached the cottage, he'd done that magical clothes thing and was back to the jeans, t-shirt, and sweater he'd had on earlier. She missed the kilt. But also, it was probably better he wasn't wearing it when they stepped into the cottage and faced his grandmother again.

Deacon in jeans was distraction enough.

20

The blissfully uneventful-but-for-training week came to an abrupt end when Wee Doug showed up at the cottage unexpectedly two days later.

He moved deep into the garden with Belle and they muttered together for a few minutes, and then Wee Doug moved off toward the woods across the road and Belle came back into the house looking disturbed and irritated.

"I have to leave for… It'll probably be a few days here. Hard to tell." She waved a hand vaguely. "Time in Faery."

"Something we can help with?" Deacon said, but his gaze cut to Cary, and Cary knew he didn't want to take her into Faery again.

Since she didn't want him in Faery either, there was some mutual gaze exchanges. But also, she wanted to go and help Belle because it's what she did and she was the one with the Protector shield, which she had gotten a *lot* better at raising on her own in the last week. Wee Doug didn't have any hesitation about hitting her with rocks. That had been very motivating to get the shield up to block those rocks. Because Wee Doug did not always remember to throw *small* rocks.

Belle considered them both for a long moment. "Better not," she said with a chin jut. "Tatiana will feel Cary there. And I canna have her sticking her nose in where it does not belong."

"This to do with the Strix?" Cary asked.

"Court business," Belle said, her expression closing up. "I'll handle it. Back in a few days. Help yerselves to anything from the kitchen. My car is yours to use, too. Shouldna be too long. You've both earned the days off anyway."

There was no smile at that last, and Belle was already moving toward her bedroom, twisting the sapphire ring on her finger, before the sound of the words died down. None of which struck Cary as a particularly good sign.

"What do we do?" she whispered to Deacon, though with Belle's hearing that was probably pointless.

"What she's asked us to," he said, even though his eyes were glowing faintly yellow. Then against her ear, "Unless she's gone longer than two days. Then we go in and make sure she's okay."

She nodded. Two days was a long time to wait. But since it wasn't that long in Faery, hopefully they'd get there before anything terrible happened.

To anyone.

Two days did prove a long time to wait. Especially because they didn't have a lot to distract their attention and worry after Belle marched out of the house wearing a purple cloak over her shoulders and a never-before-this-moment-seen sword strapped to her hip. Her clothing and hair had all flowed into something a little different by the time she'd closed the door, too. Her hair longer, redder, and decorated with little sparkling jewels that winked like stars in the house lights. Her usual casual jeans and vaguely hippy-like shirt had transformed into a flowing tan dress accented with velvets and more gold and jewels. The vaguely lined pattern on the material matched the pattern that had been on Deacon's kilt, though it was a much more pronounced purple color for Belle's dress. And the sapphire ring Belle always wore looked somehow larger.

Just as the door closed, Cary spotted the diadem low on Belle's forehead. She was going into Faery as the queen. In full regalia. How that worked, how that fooled anyone outside the Unseelie Court, Cary had no idea. But in the regalia, she could understand completely why the Unseelie Fae took Belle seriously as their queen.

By the time Cary had reached a window by the door, Belle was gone. Not walking across the street. Just gone. No doubt stepping into Faery without wasting time returning to the stone circle and her troll guards.

Did that mean she entered Faery without the guards? Or had Wee Doug been waiting for her just inside Faery?

So many questions unanswered. Which always irritated Cary, even though she tried to keep her curiosity and frustration to herself for Deacon's sake. In this case. Usually, she wasn't so reserved with expressing her irritation.

The next day, they took advantage of Belle's car and drove into Stirling. But the questions about Belle and her safety nagged at Cary the whole time, so her enjoyment of the castle was dampened a little. She still delighted in the magnificent beast of a structure and the tour around the place. The view out over the countryside from the Queen Anne Garden and the cemetery beside the castle's parking lot were all equally beautiful. But in the back of her head had been the nagging countdown. The worry that they needed to get to Belle sooner rather than later for reasons she couldn't entirely put her finger on.

Probably to do with Faery being a terrible place full of danger and scary things.

Deacon had to remind her over their late lunch in a pub that his grandmother had, apparently, been functioning quite well inside Faery for forty years as an acting queen. She was more capable of maneuvering through the realm's machinations and dangers than either he or Cary.

Which Cary knew on a *logical* level. But she'd been a Protector for almost seven full years now and her instincts were well honed. So well honed, she'd gotten herself into trouble trying to protect someone when she didn't have a shield. And her Protector instincts were nagging her. Not pushing her to run out and save someone that very instant. That was a different sensation and usually meant someone right around the corner was in need of her particular brand of help. But there was a low level of anxiety in her gut that she couldn't shake, despite her excitement at seeing Stirling.

They finished their rich meal of sliced beef roast, roasted potatoes and veg, and she got a bunch of scones from the bakery next door to the pub to take back for breakfast. And all the while, though she tried to ignore the nagging sense of unease, that unease swirled through her. A constant reminder that there was a clock ticking.

She was half hoping Belle would be back already by the time they returned from Stirling, a few extra groceries loaded into the boot—she loved calling the trunk the boot even though Deacon teased her about it—to replace all the food Belle had been feeding them. But when they walked through the door, the cottage was quiet. The fireplace cold. And the kettle off.

"I'm going to make some tea," Cary announced after they'd

unloaded the groceries and put everything away. "You want milk?"

"Thank you," Deacon said with feeling.

She managed a real chuckle at that. He'd been accepting and ignoring cups of tea all week. The habit of putting a cup into his hands seemed ingrained in Belle, so Deacon didn't argue. Cary found it sweet, even if it did mean throwing out a lot of cold tea.

A quiet evening in front of the fire with them both trying *not* to glance at the front door every few minutes bled into another restless day where the best they could muster was a long drive so Cary could admire the countryside. Deacon had asked if she wanted to go back down to Edinburgh—which wasn't too far away driving—to tour that castle, but she was too antsy and was afraid she wouldn't enjoy it. So they drove aimlessly through the countryside, stopping to talk to the occasional Highland cow. Had lunch at a country pub. Cary drank a pint of beer to try and get into the spirit of things.

None of it settled her anxiety.

The weather cooperated both days, remaining dry and beautiful, if increasingly colder. Which for some reason made Cary even more restless. It should be raining or something, shouldn't it? Stormy? Like the sense of impending doom she was trying to ignore. But no, lots of bright, sharp sunshine and blue skies and magnificent green fields surrounded by stone walls interspersed with dark rocky hills.

The storm hit the second night, crashing over the fields with such a torrential downpouring of rain, Cary worried about flooding. And a little about the roof collapsing.

She paced around the open sitting room and dining room areas, a circuit that took her from Belle's big kitchen table to the fireplace and its quietly crackling fire, back to the table. Outside, the night sky was an extra level of darkness, no hint of the stars getting through the clouds. The rain bucketed down, sliding across the windows in sheets.

"We should go check on your grandmother," she said, for the fifty-hundredth time as she circled past the fireplace again. Deacon was sitting on the couch in front of the fire, but he was leaning forward, his forearms on his thighs, his gaze jumping between Cary and the ceiling.

She paused long enough in her circuit to face him. "We need to go check on your grandmother."

"So you've said." He held up a hand when she opened her mouth. "And I agree." His gaze flicked to the window and the sheets of rain. "But getting to the standing stones through this is going to be tough."

He didn't look at her when he said that, but she knew he was talking specifically about getting her there. She couldn't shift and run through the rain and then shift back and put on dry clothing once they got into Faery. Where hopefully it wasn't raining.

Or maybe it was? Maybe that was why the skies had opened up in this realm? She wasn't even sure how rain worked in Faery, or if it did rain. Given some of the flowers could be carnivorous, she was a little afraid of experiencing Faery rain.

"I don't mind getting wet," she said. "Grew up in the Pacific North West. Getting rained on is not a new experience. And since I'm not made of sugar, I won't melt."

That last comment was designed to get a hint of humor from him. The effort worked, though his bark of amusement was short and dropped away quickly when his gaze returned to the window and the storm beyond.

"We can't go from inside the house," he said. "The portals are in fixed places. I can't just randomly open one. They're like doors. The closest we might be able to get is walking through one of the portals in a tree in her garden. We'd still get wet, but we wouldn't be in the downpour for long."

"There are umbrellas for that," Cary pointed out, though she hadn't actually seen any umbrellas around Belle's house, which suddenly struck her as odd.

"Outside of opening the portal to come get you, I haven't done it again," Deacon said quietly. "I'm not sure if I can without getting to the standing stones. That will…amplify the effort."

"And there are the trolls there who might help," Cary added. "As well as ensuring we don't end up in the wrong part of Faery."

"A very real danger."

She put her hands on her hips and finally stopped pacing long enough to stare out the same window Deacon was. It usually revealed the lush garden in front of Belle's cottage. At that moment, all she could see was darkness and the lash of rain against the double-paned glass.

"It's almost like the storm is trying to keep us inside," she muttered. A flash of lightning and the following clap of thunder made her jump. "Did the storm just agree with me? Cause, you know, that would be weird." And terrifying.

That was also the first thunder or lightning that had come with the rain.

"The storm is getting worse." Deacon didn't comment on whether or not the storm had actively answered Cary with a clap of thunder. "If we go, we'll need to go soon."

A harsh wind slammed against the side of the house, rattling the windows. Cary really couldn't escape the feeling the damned storm was trying to keep them inside.

"I don't think I can do Protector shields against rain," she said, at least she'd never been able to keep rain off before since it wasn't a threat to anyone usually. Getting drenched did not qualify as danger to the Protector magic. "But I can keep us from getting struck by lightning." No one could argue that was dangerous.

Deacon stood, coming up beside her as they both stared at the window. Another flash of lightning revealed the storm swept gardens. The bushes were blown near sideways and the trees were bending ominously under the guts. The rain seemed to be slashing sideways across the view. A view that only lasted a second before darkness descended again. This time, the clap of thunder didn't make Cary jump. But only barely.

"I'll carry you so we can run," Deacon said.

She didn't argue. They both knew this was going to be both miserable and dangerous. The faster they got to the standing stones, the better.

Once there… Well, she hoped Deacon could get them into Faery or that the troll guards would let them in. But that was a worry she'd deal with when they reached the stones. First, they had to get there.

Cary grabbed her leather jacket and slipped it on, considered the inner pocket, and then went upstairs to the bedroom and stuffed a change of clothes for her and Deacon into the pocket. Thanks to the magic Marianne had imbued her pockets with, they carried a lot more than they looked like they should, and didn't even leave an unsightly bulge. Truly amazing pockets. she also grabbed the raincoat Marianne had made for her and slipped it over her leather jacket. It wouldn't keep all of her from getting wet, but it would help.

When she returned to Deacon, he was already by the front door, his hand on the knob, his eyes glowing faintly yellow. He'd put out the fire on the hearth and turned off most of the house lights, leaving only the one in the kitchen on. Without a word, he opened the door, the rain tearing inside across the hardwood floor. She jumped up into his arms, wrapping her arms around his neck.

They stepped out under the portico, which did nothing to protect them from the weather, and got drenched in the seconds it took Deacon to close the cottage door. He looked at her, waiting for her nod.

The instant she did, he took off. Racing the rain drops as they flashed into the woods. Moving at Deacon's top shifter speed to get to the standing stones.

And whatever danger Faery had in store for them.

21

Speed and tree cover helped keep Cary and Deacon from getting completely soaked. Until Deacon stopped running at the edge of the woods to look up at the hill with the stones. At that point, Cary finally felt the rain, drops of it trickling down her neck. She sighed. She'd known they'd get wet, but still, the cold water sliding down her neck was not pleasant. The only consolation was the Marianne-made raincoat prevented the water from dripping under her jacket.

The woods smelled wonderfully of rain and pine and damp earth, but it was too damned cold for Cary to really appreciate. The area under the trees was pitch black, and with no city close enough to matter, the cloud cover was dark and ominous. No light leaking through or reflected back to give the clearing illumination. The standing stone circle at the top of the hill was just a darker shadow against a dark sky.

Deacon set her onto her feet and they stared up at the stones. Stones that were trolls. Cary would never guess that just looking at them now. Never would have believed the idea if she hadn't watched Wee Doug turn into one before her very eyes.

The stone that was Wee Doug wasn't there, however. Which… probably wasn't good.

"Will any of the others even talk to us?" she asked, not bothering to be quiet because the sound of the rain in the trees was too loud. Deacon probably could have heard her whispering even with that noise, but why bother? She *wanted* to wake up one of the trolls.

Probably.

Deacon shrugged. "We'll find out." He grabbed her hand, though his attention was still on the stone circle, and they walked up the gentle slope together.

The grass was slick and slippery, but Deacon didn't seem to notice and his solid grip kept Cary from sliding down the hill. An aid for which she was grateful. The hill wasn't particularly tall, the angle of the slope gentle and easy in ordinary weather. But her hiking boots, despite good traction, kept slipping on the wet grass.

It only occurred to her when they reached the standing stones that there might be some magic involved. She wasn't feeling any tingling along her skin—no threat and no absorbing magic going on that she was aware of—but that didn't mean there wasn't some sort of spell that made the wet grass harder to navigate.

Another flash of lightning flickered above the treeline, temporarily lighting up the dark sky. A count of three before the thunder crashed. Close but not on top of them. For the moment.

Deacon went directly into the center of the standing stones and released her hand to turn in a circle. None of the stones moved, or acknowledged their presence. Cary walked up close to one and gave it a gentle tap in an area she thought might be an arm. At least…she hoped so.

Nothing.

"Not sure they're going to acknowledge us," she murmured, rubbing a hand over her face in an attempt to get rid of some of the rain water. "We're not their queen."

"I am their queen's grandson," Deacon said.

Cary started. His voice had a deep rumbling quality that hadn't been there before. She turned to look at him. His eyes were glowing yellow in the darkness. And another flash of lightning cut across his features, making a dangerous mosaic of shadow and light. But there was also a sort of…glow around him that hadn't been there in the woods. That golden light that happened when he was *in* Faery.

They weren't technically supposed to be in Faery yet. Were they?

"We haven't… We're not in Faery already, are we?" she asked, glancing around the circle.

It was still freezing and wet and the lightning in the distance was not so distant anymore. This still *felt* like her realm. She wasn't soaking up magic. Maybe she was protecting Deacon from Faery already? She couldn't be certain. But if she was, would he look quite so…feral?

When he didn't answer, she moved closer to him, ignoring the rain dripping through her hair now. She set a hand to his arm, a gesture that brought his gaze down to her. He didn't have his iceman expression on, he wasn't shutting down his emotions even a little. In fact, he looked dangerous and deadly in a way that wasn't quite controlled.

This couldn't be good.

"You okay?" she said, shouting above another clap of thunder.

"Why is your scent full of fear?" he asked, his head tilting as he studied her.

For the briefest instant, it was like being stared at by a stranger. He didn't *look* like her Deacon in that split second. He looked like someone else. Someone magnificent and terrifying. Someone with the curious distain she associated with the High Fae.

"You look strange and you're freaking me out," she said bluntly. "Like you're turning into one of the Fae right before my eyes. That didn't happen the last time we were in Faery. Even with the overlay and all the glowing and shit. When you looked at me, you still looked at me through Deacon's eyes. You...aren't now."

He blinked and frowned down at her and suddenly he was hers again. The man she knew so well and loved so much. The golden, sparkly light still surrounded him. His eyes were still glowing shifter yellow. But the man looking at her was familiar. No longer the stranger that had been staring at her a heartbeat before.

"What are you talking about?" he asked.

"Faery is doing some freaky shit on you and we need to be careful." She held his gaze as he blinked again a few times and gave his head a little shake.

"We're not even inside Faery yet," he said, sounding so confused, she moved closer to wrap her arms around his waist.

"Something to do with the space inside the stone circle," she said. "Not sure. But I've got you. You'll be fine." Even as she said that, the golden halo around him dimmed. The image of him as some sort of Fae king faded back to that weird overlay that she could still see Deacon through. And the yellow glow in his eyes eased, his leopard stepping back.

Deacon nodded as he wrapped his arms around her. "We'd better do this fast. I hate this shit. And I hate Faery."

She snorted. "No arguments from me."

She turned to face the stones again, but stayed in front of Deacon now, with her hands behind her, gripping his arms. Putting herself into the position that clearly meant she was keeping him safe. She knew already her Protector shields had come up, when she got Deacon back through that terrifying glimpse of him as a Fae king. But she wanted to make it abundantly clear to both herself and to Faery that he was under her protection now.

A voice that sounded suspiciously like Jaxer's and Liruk's blended together in her head and reminded her that she could *consciously* raise her shields now so she didn't have to worry about whether they were raised or not.

But she was still defaulting automatically to what she knew. Even after a week of working on that habit with Wee Doug.

Who would be very handy to have around now. But his position in the circle was a very obviously empty space.

Did that leave a leak? She rubbed a hand over her head, slicking her soaked hair back from her face. Did a missing troll mean some of Faery...slipped into this realm?

Couldn't be that easy or there'd be a lot more Faery here. But maybe the other trolls kept the leak contained?

Questions she'd have to ask later. Because if Faery leaked through when Wee Doug wasn't at his station, she wasn't sure it was such a great idea her taking him out of his station just to train with her. She could find someone else willing to throw rocks at her, she was sure. Maybe she could get one of the cows riled up and have them charge her?

She shook off the thoughts and said to Deacon, "Okay, I've got you. And it doesn't look like the other trolls are going to bother acknowledging us. So we're going to need you to get us into Faery. Think you can?"

She looked over her shoulder at him, hoping he heard the full sentence: *Do you think you can without going weirdly Fae king on me again*?

He grunted and glanced around. "Not sure I can do whatever it was Belle did. But maybe..."

Running his hands through his wet hair and then down over

his face, he pulled in a deep breath and focused on a spot on the ground at the center of the hill, dead center in the middle of the standing stones. A few moments passed, the rain water washing thickly over Cary as she waited, her skin so cold now she was starting to go numb. More lightning brightened the clearing and the clap of thunder was right on top of it this time.

She was about to open her mouth and ask questions, when a section of the ground sort of faded back, revealing a stone stairway leading down into the hill.

"Whoa." She'd seen Jaxer do that to get into Faery. She'd gone into Faery through one of these stairways with Jaxer and the leprechauns. But having Deacon open the passage was…

Well, it was what they'd been trying to do. Still, it was a little terrifying to watch him *actually* do it.

He met her gaze, his jaw tight as he took her hand. "You ready?"

"Ha!" She shook her head. "No."

Then she led the way down the stone steps, Deacon's hand firmly in hers, stepping into golden, sparkling light as another thunder clap and lightning burst broke open the sky overhead.

22

No rain from the human realm fell through the hole above them as Cary and Deacon descended the stone stairs into the realm of the Fae. The transition was shocking enough to make Cary squint. The light inside Faery was bright, mid-day sunshine. Glowing with little sparkles and that falling gold that turned to red flowers when it hit the soil below them. Flowers ran along the steps, blooming and fading and reblooming as they passed. The ground at the base of the stairs was littered with the dying blooms, their deeper red color creating a path that looked like bricks leading through green grass and streaming vines of bright, colorful wildflowers.

The light *felt* thicker here, though Cary would be hard-pressed to explain what that meant. But it felt thicker than regular air and light, and yet not as thick as water. The temperature was mild and spring-like, which helped warm her freezing skin somewhat, but did nothing for the bone deep chill that had set in. And the scent of pine and a warm fire with that hint of cinnamon got stronger the farther down the stairs they went.

There was something else, too, though. That weirdly metallic undertone that was a little like blood and a little like something burning and a lot unpleasant when mixed with the more pleasant smells.

"You picking that up?" she asked Deacon as she reached the bottom step.

"The smell?" He nodded.

"Is it blood?"

"Not...quite."

"Helpful," she muttered, looking up at the passage they'd come through. She could still see the rain, but it was like it was dropping on a weird skylight or something. None of it came down the stairs. None of the darkness penetrated the bright air here either. She saw one more flash of lightning above her. Thought she saw some large dark shadow move close to the edge of the opening. A shadow that vaguely reminded her of Wee Doug's shape, maybe another of the trolls? But before she could get a clear look, the hole whirled closed.

Cutting them off from their realm.

Leaving them smack in the middle of Faery.

"Boy, I sure hope you can get us back out again," she said quietly.

"Me too." Deacon nodded down the path made of dead flowers that looked like bricks. "That way?"

She shrugged. "That way."

Cary stepped onto the path reluctantly, a part of her afraid the dead flowers would magically rebloom and then surround her and...she wasn't sure. This was Faery. Maybe try to eat her?

But when she stepped onto the edge of the flowers, holding her breath and waiting, nothing happened. She released her held breath and started down the path.

"Was worried too," Deacon said, squeezing her hand.

Good to know she wasn't the only one who thought everything inside Faery might eat them. Technically, that was probably the safest default position.

"How are you doing?" she asked, glancing back.

Still had the golden halo. His clothes hadn't changed, though, which was probably a good sign. And his eyes were no longer glowing. His leopard had settled completely. She hoped that was a good sign.

"I'm okay," he said, grunting a little. "Not feeling the usual call to go charging off and chasing things here. Your shield is working."

She released some of the tension in her shoulders. She was still tense and anxious, but it was good to have one less thing to worry about.

So long as she kept protecting him.

The feel of wet jeans rubbing and her hair dripping cold water down her neck didn't do much for her mood. She gripped her ponytail and tried to squeeze out some of the excess water. She felt bedraggled and waterlogged. Not a great way to face a Fae court, most of which went in for glowing glitter and extravagance. Waterlogged human in jeans was not the look.

She did have the spare change of clothes still in her magic pockets, but now that she was here, she was feeling too vulnerable to stop and strip. Something about being caught out naked, midway through changing clothes, by some horrible Fae monster. She'd rather be wet and bedraggled.

She glanced back at Deacon. Despite also being soaked to the skin, he still somehow managed to look good with his dark hair slicked back off his face, his features cut sharp with his scowl. His wet t-shirt just looked impressive—he'd left his sweater at home on the grounds that wet wool would be worse than wet cotton, and she felt like he was right about that, but Deacon in a wet t-shirt was...distracting.

No time for that now.

It was sort of unfair, though, that even drenched, he still looked like he could walk into a Fae court and belong, with no one scowling at how underdressed and rough he looked, while she on the other hand...

Sigh.

She turned back to concentrate on the path. Now that they'd followed it for a distance—a distance that was impossible to judge because magical realm and weird sensory perceptions—she worried about losing the trail. She had no idea where they were going and the path seemed like their best, and maybe only, way to reach the Unseelie court without getting lost.

They'd had a faery escort the last time they'd had to go any distance in this realm. She missed that teeny, tiny bit of security. Jaxer had even been able to glamour them up some appropriate attire so she didn't have to worry about being an insult to anyone—because the High Fae were *very* sensitive to insults. Having Jaxer here would have been convenient for the glamour and the not-getting-lost part of this. But given his history, it was better he wasn't here. Last thing they needed was to call more attention from the Irish and English queens.

Whatever was happening in the Unseelie court, Belle wanted it kept quiet, and Cary figured that was a pretty wise idea.

The path of flowers that looked more and more like red bricks the farther into Faery they got led through a forest not unlike the one Belle had sent her into, but the trees here didn't have the plethora of colorful leaves and the canopy wasn't so thick it blocked the sky. Not that the sky in Faery was any more orienting.

When Cary looked up, the sky was a yellowish-cream color, solid, almost like a painted ceiling, except that it glowed and glittered slightly and made her head hurt if she looked at it too long. There was the impression of daytime with that sky. But day and night in Faery weren't the same things as they were in the human realm, so it didn't mean much.

The trees were thick trunked with long branches and thick roots that wove up to the edge of the path. Their leaves were almost entirely gold and blue, and the blue ones had little white spots that resembled stars. The golden drips of light that turned to red flowers when they hit the ground had stopped. No more ground cover of dying flowers. Just the path, which felt like brick underfoot now, and the trees.

Cary watched for vines with carnivorous flowers, or sneaky little glowing lights that were the tiny faeries that liked to bite, or the telltale signs of an impending dragon or other mythical creature stepping into their path. But none of that jumped out at them.

It was probably the most uneventful walk through Faery she'd ever experienced.

Until they stepped into a block of glittering darkness so thick it was as if the sun had been snatched from the sky. So sudden, Cary stopped in her tracks.

There had been no warning. No fading light. No darkness ahead that she could *see* she was walking into. Just suddenly night dropped onto them.

But when she glanced back, the glowing pseudo-daylight remained just behind Deacon. The line between light and dark was so distinct it was weird. The line was sharp! There was no fading one into the other. Just this very straight divide.

And even though looking back she could see that line and the different light and dark areas, she hadn't seen that break from the other side. She hadn't seen the point of cross into the darkness the way she could see the point in space where she'd step back out into the light.

"Okay," she murmured.

"Getting close," Deacon said, tightening his hold on her hand.

She didn't object. Her heartbeat had started to hammer harder the instant they stepped into the darkness. She squeezed his hand back and started forward again, but fear was making a mess of her gut, the churning anxiety crawling through her, tightening each muscle in preparation for… Well, probably running away, but her instincts were not usually to run away. She was a most excellent freezer. She froze in place—fawning they called it—and, at least for a Protector, that was the thing to do. Bad if she hadn't been a Protector, though. Sometimes running away was very important.

The darkness around them seemed to close in, a living thing trying to wrap around their minds as well as their bodies. Despite her shield, she had the sense of the darkness tugging at her, trying to pull her under.

"Falling asleep in Faery would be bad, huh?" she said.

Deacon grunted agreement. She glanced back to make sure he was okay. His eyes were glowing a little more now, but it was that sort of reflective glow that happened in the dark, when his shifter eyesight allowed him to see in a way that was more leopard than human. She could see just fine as well, thanks to the magic she was channeling, but she realized she probably wouldn't be able to see in this growing blackness if not for having to protect Deacon.

At the edge of her vision the trees were changing, too. The branches and trunks thickening and stretching in strange ways. The leaves went from gold and blue to purple and ebony, with the faintest hints of red, like flickering droplets of blood in the branches. Vines grew up over the trees now too, and here, finally, things with thorns on. She'd been waiting for the damned thorns since Belle had first tossed her into Faery. Thorns just seemed to belong here. These thorns weren't as thick as some she'd seen, but needle sharp and glistening in the blackness, reflecting light that wasn't there.

The path of dead flowers that looked like bricks changed and darkened as well. A very strange sort of greenish hue rose from the bricks. Not red or even brick-colored anymore. Black with that bruised-green glow. And harder now. Like they were on actual stone instead of pretend bricks.

Cary kept flicking her gaze between her feet and the landscape ahead, trying to see whatever dangers came at them at the same time as trying not to trip. She knew Deacon would catch her if she fell. But it would be embarrassing since she was the Protector here.

And strictly speaking, she didn't need to see the danger coming. Her shield was up, she was safe. Deacon was safe. But she hated when dangerous scary things just popped up in front of her without warning. She'd scream, or worse squeak in shock, and that was embarrassing, too.

But nothing came out at them from the distorted forest, nothing dropped from the black and purple tree branches, no thorns from the vines shot out at them. The stones beneath their feet didn't start undulating in an attempt to trip them. And the urge to sleep that had been just at the very edge of her awareness faded.

She blinked and glanced back at Deacon. Yup. That's what she'd been afraid of.

"You're doing the golden glow thing," she commented as she faced forward again. "And your clothes have changed." But at least he was dry now. Lucky bastard.

He came to an abrupt stop, and since they were still holding hands, so did she. She looked back, eyebrows raised. He was staring down at his outfit.

She frowned. "You can see the change this time? Or do you still feel like you're in your wet clothes?"

What she could see was Deacon in another golden-tan kilt with faint lines of purple through it. But this time, instead of just the material over his shoulder, he was wearing a full purple cloak, the corner held in place with an elaborate silver Celtic brooch. The animal heads at the curved ends were very obviously leopards now. The brooch itself was larger and more elaborate than any he'd had before, with jewels incrusted in the woven knot pattern of silver. And now he had a small diadem on his head, a crown that flickered with purple stones and diamonds.

This was Faery recognizing him as a king again. And despite the fact that she knew *why* it was happening now—sort of—it was still an impressive and slightly shocking sight. Because like this, Deacon looked like he belonged here. He looked as ethereal as Jaxer and Eriana had when they entered the Irish court and they all came face-to-face with Danu. His tan skin glowed, his black hair looked like silk, and he looked taller and stronger and just...more.

And Cary was never going to get over the fact that her leopard shifter mate *could* look like he belonged in Faery. Not just belong. He looked like a king of *this* place.

But he never seemed to see it. Sometimes the different clothes —obviously, he'd seen the kilt last time, but he'd shifted into that on accident—but not the whole, impressive...impact of it. And if it was glamour this time, instead of clothes he'd shifted onto his own body, then he might not even see the kilt and jewelry.

"I see the cloak," he said. "The brooch. Pretty similar to what your bosses gave me that first time."

"But...?"

"But I can't see any other changes. I didn't shift clothes. I'm not seeing the kilt this time. Or anything else."

"That is so weird," she muttered. Everything about Faery was always so weird. And nonsensical. There was no consistent logic. Which was very irritating.

And maybe that was the point?

"Very." Deacon looked up at her. Then blinked. "Uhm, you look different, too."

Her eyebrows rose sharply and she glanced down at herself. She still had on her leather jacket, covered by the raincoat that she had unzipped because it was too warm. And because it was warm, she pulled off the now-dry raincoat, but kept her leather jacket on because of the pockets. Beneath that, she got this impression of a dress if she looked out the corner of her eye and squinted a little. Without the effort, she still looked and felt like she was wearing damp jeans and hiking boots. But…yeah, there seemed to be some sort of glamour overlay with a fancy, shimmery dress she couldn't quite see.

"How's this getting through your shield?" Deacon asked.

"Probably not dangerous? Maybe something given to us by a friend? Jaxer's glamour didn't fritz out that first time, even though my shield was up."

"But Jaxer was *with* us and inside your shield as well. Someone or something from the outside is doing this. If it's not Faery itself doing it."

"Must be friendly or helpful then. Not something the Protector magic sees as a threat."

"Mmm." Deacon's noncommittal noise carried a lot of meaning.

"What do I look like?" she asked. "I can't see it."

"The dress is… Fitted and shimmery. And blue."

"Helpful." She laughed. "Anything else? Is it see-through? I hate when I'm wearing see-through glamour." If she chose to wear something see-through that was her business, but when this sort of magic put her into something see-through against her wishes, that just felt rude.

"Not see-through," Deacon confirmed. "At least not now. It was before you asked."

"Really?" Whoa. Weird. "What's it like now?" She looked down at herself again, trying to squint enough to actually see the dress.

"Diaphanous but with enough layers to preserve your modesty."

She snort-laughed at that.

"But it's still low cut and pretty sexy." He scowled. "The weird thing is that I can still see your leather jacket over it and the combination is kind of…"

"Unfashionable?" she asked and waggled her eyebrows.

His chuckle made her grin. "Little bit. It's like someone from a different era time-traveled and was given a coat that doesn't fit with the era of clothing they're wearing."

"It's weird the jacket is still in place." She fingered the butter-soft leather. "When Jaxer glamours me, he doesn't leave anything behind of my normal clothes." Not that she could usually see what outfits Jaxer put her into. He found it amusing to ensure the world saw what he wanted them to, but the person wearing whatever he'd glamoured up didn't. They just saw their ordinary clothes.

"Weird," Deacon agreed. "You also have a crown on."

She blinked and automatically put her free hand to her head. All she felt was damp hair, which probably had tufts sticking out at odd angles as it dried and the small hairs escaped her ever-present ponytail.

"What kind of crown?" she asked. "And what does my hair look like?"

"Dry and loose and fluffy," he said. Which she hoped referred to her hair and not the crown. He confirmed with his next sentence. "The crown is the sort that sits low and it's got a lot of diamonds and purple and green stones in it. Very sparkly."

"Your powers of description are amazing," she said. "Also, you're wearing a very similar crown. We have matching crowns. That's…"

"Strange?"

She nodded. "And feels like it's significant. Like whatever is glamouring us up for what's ahead is making a point."

Deacon glanced past her, to the path ahead. "My grandmother?" he murmured.

"Belle," Cary agreed, looking over her shoulder to follow his gaze.

Nothing in the weird, dark, twisted-tree forest had changed. The path was still faintly illuminated in that bruised-green color, the vines still had needle sharp thorns, and the leaves were still purple and black.

But there was this odd air of anticipation now. Unlike the earlier feeling like Faery was trying to put them to sleep. Now she got a vague sense of…hurry. Of needing to get to where they were going. Not because something bad might happen but simply because they were running a little late.

But late to what?

"Okay," she muttered. "I guess we'd better get to…whatever it is we're supposed to get to." She hoped all this meant that Belle was okay. That they'd been worrying about her for no reason.

But the moment she thought that, her gut filled with the crawling anxiety again, the *knowing* that things were not right and her particular brand of help was needed.

"Yeah," she said, tugging Deacon's hand. "Yeah. We need to get there."

"Where?" he asked, but he didn't hesitate to follow her.

"Got me. But wherever it is, I'm needed."

"Fuck," Deacon muttered, with feeling.

"Yup."

They both knew her instincts were tugging her toward trouble.

23

*C*ary had seen exactly two Fae courts in her lifetime—two too many as far as she was concerned. The Irish court… Well, actually, she wasn't sure it had been the court. She and her companions had been in the middle of a lush forest when they met with Danu. So maybe that wasn't the Irish court. The only other two times she'd encountered Danu had been once in Cary's (messy!) bedroom after she'd recovered from dying, and once in an Irish field when Cary had first met Rory the dragon and his hero Joan.

So. Actually, Cary had only probably seen one Fae court in her lifetime. Tatiana and Oberon's court. And it had been a splendid cacophony of light and color and beautiful, weird Fae creatures. An outdoor space under a solid blue, cloudless sky, with the queen and her king sitting on thrones with so much light surrounding them they'd had to dim themselves just so Cary's poor human eyes could perceive them.

Belle's court—or really Nicneven's court—was not like this at all.

No. Belle's court was not in an open clearing surrounded by trees and light. Belle's court was inside an actual building.

The dead flower-brick path led them out of the woods and to the edge of a hill on top of which rose a stone structure like a castle. But as they neared it was clear this "castle" was just one big, open building. A Great Hall. No other outer buildings and no curtain walls surrounding the structure. It was tall, and long, and fronted by a wooden door that was large enough Cary had to drop her head back to see the top of it. Scroll work and knotted designs in silver and gold flowed over the surface of the door, the patterns changing and rearranging as Cary watched—which made her dizzy, so she didn't watch for long.

The scent of pine smoke overwhelmed any other scent here, a lovely, campfire smell, that nevertheless made Cary very anxious for reasons she couldn't entirely explain. Like, because this was the realm of the Fae, that smell probably meant something besides a homy campfire lay just on the other side of this door.

When the door swung open of its own accord, the Great Hall beyond stretched before them like a cheery gothic haven. A lot of gold and silver glittered among the wall hangings of black velvet and silk. The "roof" above them gave the impression of sky and stars, with the stars dropping closer into the hall before rising high above again. There were heavy black and gold marble columns lining the walls, with vines crawling over them, covered in red and black roses, the vines and leaves all swirls of silver.

The center of the hall was one massive fire pit, the flames leaping around like they were alive, and some of the Fae happily dancing around and through those flames. Which made Cary wince. But at least she knew where the pine campfire scent was coming from.

Haunting, eerie flute music, occasionally punctuated by a drum boom, wafted through the huge hall, rising and falling and winding around the conversations and laughter and general chatter. Everywhere inside the Great Hall, Fae moved past, ignoring Cary and Deacon where they stood just inside the large door.

In Tatiana's court, she, Deacon, and Jaxer had brought all other proceedings to a halt with their presence. In hindsight, that was likely more to do with Jaxer than with having a human and a shapeshifter in their midst. But still. Having strangers walk into the middle of the court had at least drawn attention. Here, the other Fae ignored them. Almost as if they didn't see them.

Except that Cary and Deacon were acknowledged with head nods of greeting. As if the reason no one paid them much attention was that they appeared to belong here.

The glamour, whoever had created it, was apparently doing its job.

The fact that Cary had felt drawn here because trouble was brewing and her brand of help was needed sort of…baffled her, though. No one seemed in distress. No chaos or drama seemed to be breaking out. Just a lot of High Fae wandering around, drinking and dancing and chatting, a few of them were fucking in the darker corners. Just a big old party without any worries.

So why the hell had Belle been forced to come here? Why was *Cary* feeling that anxious crawl along her spine that her help was needed here?

She studied the surrounding Fae, looking for clues, as she and Deacon silently made their way down the length of the Great Hall, skirting around the central bonfire, heading toward the back of the room where, if she squinted, Cary could just make out a raised dais and throne. Maybe. The distance kept expanding as she moved so it was hard to tell, and trying to see the distant dais as it receded made her head spin. Instead, she focused on the Fae closer to her, watching for trouble, Deacon walking carefully just behind her.

The Unseelie faction of the Scottish Fae were, like all Fae, a mixture of different creatures with different strengths and weaknesses. Of all the Fae, the High Fae, the faeries, were the top of the hierarchical heap. The queens were always High Fae—except of course in Belle's case. Their king consorts may or may not be High Fae, but typically were. The High Fae rarely mixed and mingled with any other species in Faery for long matings or for having babies—when they had babies, which was so rare as to have become an actual issue in the last few centuries. For the most part, the actual courts in Faery were made up of mostly High Fae, with a few of the other species moving around the edges.

In fact, a lot of the other species that populated Faery liked to avoid the High Fae because they were dangerous and capricious and you never knew when one might take your head off for a laugh.

But High Fae also came in different sizes and shapes and colors and strengths and weaknesses.

Belle's court was no different in that respect. Almost all the Fae around them were what Cary assumed were High Fae, but they were a mixture of shapes and sizes, some so large, she had to look up, some more diminutive, some with mostly ordinary human shapes—two arms, two legs, head at the top, feet at the ground level—but some had extra limbs or tentacles or the occasional set of wings. Long hair, short hair, no hair. Black skin, brown skin, pink skin, white skin, and a few with green or gold skin. Some of the passing beings were so stunning it made Cary wince, some were so ordinary she nearly stopped to stare in fascination, and some were unlike anything she'd encountered before. She couldn't decide if she thought they were ugly or beautiful. Probably a little of both.

One thing she'd learned early in her time as Protector, when she'd read about the Scottish court for the first time—and probably the only time she'd read about the court before coming to Scotland for this trip because she had way too much to learn and didn't have time to go back over things again and again—was that the break in the Seelie and Unseelie courts wasn't down to anything visually obvious. It wasn't like the Seelie were the "beautiful" creatures and the Unseelie were the "grotesque" ones, even though that was a breakdown often put forward by humans. The assumption that the Seelie were the "good" fairies and the Unseelie were the "evil" fairies was a myth.

Both courts were chockablock full of evil faeries. And good faeries. Because most faeries were chaos machines, and their idea of good and evil swung wildly different to what humans considered good and evil.

The real divide had more to do with ancient clans and political breaks from back in a time when Faery was still a young realm. The divide had existed since, which to a human might as well have been forever, and there was a *lot* of animosity between the two factions. Being Seelie, or Unseelie, meant something to the Scottish Fae, even if it wasn't something represented in appearance or moral standing.

Seeing the Unseelie court up close only confirmed what she'd read. Because the beings here were not really any different to the plethora of beings she'd seen inside Tatiana's court. Though, the creatures in Tatiana's court had presented themselves more toward the stunning end of the appearance spectrum. But since no one was allowed to out-stunning Tatiana, there'd still been a range of bearable-to-look-at faeries there, too.

Deacon leaned in close to whisper, "They're ignoring us. And I can't see a problem anywhere. What's happening?"

"Got me," she whispered back, then smiled and nodded her

head in what she hoped passed for a regal manner, when a small group of tall, willowy Fae strolled by and acknowledged her and Deacon. "My instincts are still telling me I'm needed somewhere close," she said once the group had moved on.

"Does it seem like it's taking us a long time to reach the other end of the hall?" he asked.

"Yup."

In fact, every time she looked up, the distant dais remained at the same distance, fuzzy and indistinct. Yet, they weren't walking past the same bonfire again and again. There were just more groups of people in front of them and the distance forward never seemed to shorten. When she looked behind her, though, the distance from the entrance was growing. They were getting farther away from their escape route with every step, but no closer to their destination.

There was probably some philosophical truth or lesson in that. Or maybe it was just the weirdness of Faery.

"Keep walking?" Deacon asked. "Or stand still and wait for the trouble to come to us?"

Huh. That might not be a bad idea. Trouble did have a knack for finding Cary no matter what she was doing. But she still had to do a lot of running and jumping to get in its way, so…

"Let's walk on a little farther."

The idea of standing still made her limbs jittery and her anxiety crawl. She had no idea, now that she thought about it, if that was her own instinct or some weird part of Faery affecting her. But since she was protecting Deacon, and couldn't feel herself absorbing any magic—no excess of tingles along her skin —she *thought* it might be her instincts pushing her to keep moving.

They hadn't gone more than another five steps before someone swung around to block their path. Cary blinked and looked up. For a split second, she thought it was Wee Doug, but a beat later, she realized the being she was looking at was not a troll.

They were long and willowy and tall and actually looked more like dark tree bark than dark rock. In fact, as Cary looked, the tree comparison seemed more and more apt. There were even leaves on the Fae's head instead of hair or nothing at all. Leaves that were black and gold and interspersed with winking diamonds and rubies like little sprites peeking out from between the leaves. The leaves were also cut and shaped, almost like a topiary, into an elaborately tall shape that may or may not have been an animal.

Beneath that impressive mass was a long face, with features that were sharp but exaggerated. The eyes were wide apart. The nose was narrow and too small for the other features. There were no visible ears, but the mouth was extremely wide and the lips large. The entire collection of features felt off-kilter and without symmetry. And somehow still reminded Cary of a tree.

The tree theme was strong with this one.

A dryad, Cary realized. She'd never seen or met a dryad in person before, though.

The Fae wore something that could be called clothes. Gossamer veils in multiple shades of black and gold and red draped across long, thin limbs that may or may not have been arms and legs—there were more than four but Cary wasn't quite sure how many altogether because one would appear and then disappear back into the thicker frame of the body.

The dryad bowed low, its leafy hair rustling with the movement. When it rose again, it said, "Welcome to the Unseelie court, Your Majesties. Please follow me. The queen requests your presence."

Cary and Deacon exchanged a look. Majesties?

Deacon nodded and the dryad turned and started toward the throne again, cutting through the whirling, twirling mass of beings. The flute music took on a more frantic rhythm now, turning the dancing into a cascade of flowing creatures moving too fast for Cary to see. When she tried it made her dizzy, so she kept her gaze focused on the dryad and tried to ignore all the spinning in her peripheral vision.

Deacon squeezed her hand, tight this time. She glanced back. He was staring ahead, toward the throne, his attention so focused he didn't even glance down at her. But his eyes were ever-so-slightly more yellow. Cary frowned and looked at the throne again.

To realize it was only a few feet away now.

And there was someone sitting on it. Someone who was *not* Belle.

This Fae had the general appearance of a woman, though a woman unlike anyone seen in Cary's realm. Her hair was long, and straight, and as black as midnight but there were streaks of red through it, red that curled like Belle's hair. Twinned with that were chains of gold that formed a veil over the Fae's head, and in the center of her brow, a low diadem of gold and rubies and diamonds.

Her gown was also an elaborate twist of black and red veils, not dissimilar to the dryad's, but on this Fae, there were fewer of the veils and they were thin enough to reveal more of the body beneath. On her long, pale arms, she wore a series of gold bands, some with writing that glimmered with purple Fae magic, some that were encrusted with more rubies and diamonds, others that were just solid gold. None had the Celtic knot work Cary might have expected to see in the Scottish court, but she supposed that didn't mean much in the Fae realm.

The Fae woman's face was that sort of glowing beauty that was hard to describe because taken in parts, her features were ordinary. A sharp nose. Thin lips on a heart-shaped mouth. High cheekbones. Uptilted green eyes with long lashes and sharp slashes of eyebrows over. The features combined into something that could be called quite stunning, but still the sort of stunning that wasn't obvious when taken apart.

She had the sort of long, pointed ears that Cary thought of as classically elf—or Vulcan—and the lobes all around were decorated in gold and ruby ear clips and rings, with twining thin lines of silver throughout to add depth.

Everything in this place seemed to be black and gold and silver and red, Cary realized. Which meant hers and Deacon's outfits really stood out in this court. While they had on silvers and golds, there was a lot more blue and purple and tan in their clothing. Light, soft colors with blurry edges. Where everything inside the Unseelie court was dark and sharp and bright.

Since someone had glamoured them up to look like this—be it Faery or Belle or someone else—Cary had assumed the appearance was designed for them to blend into the Unseelie court. But as Cary finally let all of the surroundings and clothing of others sink in, she realized she and Deacon had no hope of blending in.

Maybe that was the actual point?

"You notice…" She leaned into Deacon, keeping her voice low. "You notice the color scheme?"

"Yup," he said. His voice was very deep and guttural.

"You doing okay?"

"Will be better when we find my grandmother."

The Fae on the throne chuckled. So… They hadn't been as quiet as they'd thought. Fair enough.

"You come from the Seelie court," the Fae woman who was not Belle said. "To petition me for lenience?"

"Uh…" Cary glanced around. "Not entirely sure what to say to that. We're actually just here looking for someone. Not *technically* part of any court." Unless she counted what Tatiana said about

Danu claiming Cary for her court, but that was another story and probably best not to mention here.

The Fae narrowed her eyes. "You're dressed of the Seelie court."

"We are?" Huh. Weird. Belle wouldn't have done that, would she? So…someone or something else had glamoured them up? Could it have been someone from the Seelie court? "Yeah, about that—"

"Where is my grandmother?" Deacon said. The power of his voice echoed in the huge hall.

The flute music died. The whirling dance Cary had kept track of in her peripheral vision stopped. Silence descended over the hall.

Every eye in the place turned. Staring. Then as one, the entire court took several steps backward, toward the walls.

Leaving Cary and Deacon in a bubble of isolation in the middle of the hall.

Well. That couldn't be good.

Oh boy.

24

Cary held her breath for a moment, waiting for some sort of magical retribution to fall on her and Deacon, some wrath from the Fae on the throne at Deacon's demanding tone. The hall around them was so quiet she could hear the settling of stones in the walls, a very faint crackling from the huge bonfire in the middle of the hall, somewhere behind them. Not even the air bothered to move. And the dryad who'd brought them to the throne had gone so still, it actually looked like a tree now, planted at the edge of the hall.

The scent of pine smoke from the fire still managed to permeate the surroundings, but now Cary started to pick up a hint of something else she couldn't place. Something a little spicy-sweet creeping through the stillness.

A breathless few moments passed, Deacon's demand hovering in the air.

And yet nothing happened. No spells or magic or weapons or even angry words got thrown at them. Just that eerie silence and the staring.

So much staring.

Cary risked a glance back at Deacon.

Oh. Wow. No wonder everyone had shut the fuck up.

He looked larger than normal, which was an impressive degree of large already. That golden glow that surrounded him in Faery was not just a subtle overlay anymore. He was literally glowing, so bright he was a little hard to look at. The crown on his head winked and glittered. And now there was a sword strapped to his hip that hadn't been there before. Though there was no air movement, his purple cloak seemed to flutter.

And his eyes were bright shifter yellow.

She blinked a few times because the mixing of obvious shapeshifter traits with that Faery glow made her brain rebel.

She kept her hand in his, squeezing tight, but he didn't look down at her. His full attention was on the Fae sitting on a throne where they'd expected to find his grandmother. And while they had most assuredly not come from the Seelie court, Cary understood the mistaken identity. Because Deacon looked more like a Fae king in that moment than he ever had before.

A pissed off Fae king.

Pissed off Fae were usually scary dangerous.

Except, Cary reminded herself, Deacon was *not* Fae. He was a leopard shifter.

Whose grandmother had been secretly functioning as a Fae queen for four decades. But still…

She backed closer to him but still kept him just behind her. She was in that awkward position of not knowing if she was protecting him in that moment or if she was protecting the others *from* him. But either way, she needed to be between him and the rest of the Unseelie court or someone might get hurt.

When the silence stretched past Cary's ability to tolerate it, and no magical mayhem or angry shifter attacks happened, she said, "Yes, that's why we're here. Just looking for his grandmother. Once we have her, we'll get out of your hair. You can go back to dancing or...whatever it is Fae do to while away eternity."

The Fae on the throne—who had still not given them a name and wasn't that irritating—turned her gaze just a little to stare at Cary. Her eyes were a dark and fathomless green that reminded Cary of a still pond covered in algae and tree pollen. They were not comfortable eyes to look into.

"You seek the usurper, then," the Fae said.

Ah. Usurper didn't sound like a good word.

"My mate's grandmother," Cary said since *usurper* seemed a bit harsh. "Yeah. We're here for her. Mind bringing her out?"

"I do mind. She took my throne."

Okay. So. Was this Nicneven then? Cary narrowed her eyes. "Haven't been introduced. This is Deacon. I'm Cary."

There was a little ripple of movement through the hall behind her, and a quite murmuring that didn't bode well. By the time the whispers reached Cary, her gut was tight wondering what she'd said. Had giving their names given some sort of magical key to destroying them? Names carried power in magical spheres. She couldn't remember in her panic if the same thing went in Faery.

Except everyone here gave her their names, so maybe not.

And when the whispers reached her finally, she realized what the sudden commotion was about.

"The king and his Protector..."

"Here. The king."

"The Protector."

"They're here. They've come."

"The Protector is here."

"The king..."

Cary scowled. So Deacon didn't just look like a king,

they were calling him a king as if he'd always been a king here, and that was something that needed clarification. But also, the fact that they knew *her* made her wince. Of course they did. She knew most of Faery had heard about her exploits in the English court. But... Well, for a few minutes there, she'd forgotten they all might recognize who she was. She'd sort of been hoping to get in and out without anyone being the wiser.

She had no idea how she thought she'd pull that off.

"This good or bad?" she murmured to Deacon. "That you're 'the king' and they know who I am now?"

"If we get my grandmother back in the next few minutes, it's good."

"And if not?"

He didn't answer. She glanced at him again. Still very yellow eyes. Still golden glow.

She glanced down at herself out of curiosity. But to her, she was wearing her finally-dry jeans and her leather jacket. She could just see the overlay of the gown in her peripheral vision still, but otherwise, she couldn't tell what those in the hall were seeing when they looked at her. Was she glowing like Deacon? Or was that fancy Fae look reserved for royalty.

Except the dryad had called them "majesties." Plural. As if she was also a queen of some kind. Which, strictly speaking, she supposed she was sort of a queen-consort-like thing among the leopard shifters even if she tried really hard not to think about that. So maybe that's what that was all about.

She'd have loved to ask all these questions aloud. Normally, she would have because while she was protecting someone, it didn't really matter if she annoyed or pissed off the bad guys. In fact, sometimes she did that on purpose to make them go away. And she was infinitely curious and hated not knowing things, so the questions tended to bubble out whether she *should* ask questions or not.

She didn't always get answers, but she almost always asked the questions.

Only, in that moment, she thought maybe revealing too much of their ignorance would be bad. Given where they were, having the other Fae a little… She wasn't sure if she'd call it fear, but at least the level of awe she'd heard in the whispers could serve as a buffer to attacks.

She hoped.

The Fae on the throne tilted her head to one side as the whispers washed over her like an echo. Her expression didn't change, but there was a sort of stillness that swept through her. An eerie quiet. She didn't even blink as she stared at them.

"I've heard of you," she said after another long moment. "The shifter king who is also Fae and yet not. The Protector who both saved and destroyed Faery."

"Uh, yeah, no. Didn't destroy anything." Cary gestured to the surrounding hall and the fact that it still existed. "See. Plenty of Faery still standing."

"You inserted…fresh magic."

"Understood that was good. Kept the place from rotting away. Like it had been doing. For a long time."

"You're of the Fae now, though. And we did not invite you."

"Royal we or just the Unseelie court in general we?"

The Fae blinked. "You show no deference."

"Waiting on an introduction still. But also…yeah, probably won't show much then either." She shrugged.

The Fae's gaze slid back to Deacon. "You are a king."

Deacon didn't so much as grunt at that.

"And will rule your people. Do you also seek my throne? As your grandmother did?"

"I need no one else's throne," Deacon said.

And wow was his voice deep and loud and booming in the hall. And there was a slight hiss under it all, the sound of his leopard near the surface. His hand, where he still gripped hers, flexed and tightened.

"And if you're Nicneven," Deacon continued, "you will return my grandmother out of gratitude for her service to your court. Now."

Another ripple of sound waved through the crowd, though this time it remained too quiet for Cary to catch even hints of actual words. But Deacon's command had definitely set off a ripple of unease and concern.

"You threaten me?" the Fae said.

"Doesn't have to be," Cary said. "But if we need to…"

She glanced around at all those Fae, in a land made of magic that was extremely dangerous for her to come into contact with. And sighed. They were here to get Belle. Whatever worked to get her out safely, they'd do it. Being outnumbered and walking through the middle of Cary's nightmare scenario didn't matter.

They were here for Belle. And they weren't leaving without her.

25

Another long silence followed Cary's confirmation that they'd threaten if needs be to get Belle back. Deacon's hold on her hand was tightening to the point of near pain now, but since she knew that link was the one thing anchoring his control, she didn't even wince—at least not in a way he could see.

Around them, the silent Fae watched, the flickering fire behind them crackling. The Fae on the throne stared down at Cary directly now, her green eyes narrowed.

And then, she broke the silence in the last way Cary expected.

She laughed. Loud. A sound so weirdly harsh and toneless, Cary winced. It was like the Fae didn't know what laughter was and was simulating it. But also there was something strangely compelling about the sound. Something that almost *almost* made Cary want to lean closer to hear more.

It was the strangest set of sensations. When Tatiana did her tinkling laughter, it was an obvious lure, an obvious lullaby, an obvious sweet-song. An obvious trap. At least, the trap part was obvious for Cary thanks to Protector shields. Without that, the trap would catch Cary just as quickly as any other human and Tatiana wielded that power using the sweetest of sounds.

The Fae on this throne did not bother with the sweet or tinkling or musical laughter. Hell, she didn't even bother with a sound that hit a human ear right. Just brayed out a rough approximation of a laugh. And *still* there was power in it. Still there was that trap.

Impressive. And made Cary extremely grateful for her shield.

"I can see why Tatiana and Danu are fighting over you," the Fae said. "You are amusing. For an ordinary human. We like ordinary humans. Did they tell you that? They keep the court fresh. Fresh…blood. So to speak."

"Sure sure." Cary didn't shiver at the reference to blood. She'd dealt with enough vampires to have heard that sort of thing before. It was still gross. "But we're just here for Belle."

"The Traitor."

The moment the Fae called Belle that—the capital T obvious, like she'd given Belle a new name—the entire hall filled with the quiet murmuration of that word over and over again. All of them whispering "Traitor" at the exact same time in the exact same tone. A sort of flat tone, saying the word but it didn't carry any meaning for them.

At a raised finger from the Fae on the throne, the murmuring stopped. "She tried to steal my court."

"Can we just…" Cary sighed. "Are you Nicneven or not?"

"I am the queen here."

"Yeah, that's not an answer." Cary glanced around. "Anyone else? Anyone want to tell me who I'm talking to? Makes life easier. Know that's not the point here, but you know. Still."

None of the surrounding Fae answered. And when her gaze glanced over the dryad who had brought them forward, the tree's big brown-eyed gaze shifted to the stone floor.

Okay. So no answers there.

"Do I get *any* name at all to use here?" Cary said. "Something other than 'queen,'" she said when the Fae opened her mouth. "Got that part already. But, you know, this is Faery and there a lot of you queens hanging around the place." And not the fun drag queen kind of queens, which would have been infinitely preferable in that moment.

"I am queen here, in the Unseelie court. And your kind are not welcome."

"My kind which? Because I have a lot of 'your kind's associated with me."

"*Human,*" she hissed.

"Ah. Wait, you just said you liked having humans around for fresh blood. So contradictory. Not a good place from which to start a negotiation," she said primly, mostly just to push the Fae into losing her temper.

When the Fae lost her temper, they learned things. Like the fact that she considered Belle a traitor but that the court at large did not. They'd repeat the phrase because it was expected, but there was no feeling, so sense of support for the label.

"This is not a negotiation, human. You may be Tatiana and Danu's pet. The Seelie court may claim your leopard as their own king—"

"No," Cary interrupted.

The Fae ignored her. "—but you have no standing here. You are of the Traitor and will be treated as such."

"We just want to take her home. At that point, we'll be out of your hair, and you can bad mouth us all you want and try to win your court back after abandoning them for all these years and leaving them vulnerable to the Seelie court and all the chaos that caused. We'll leave and you can *try* to re-establish yourself as an actual queen and not just a dilettante Fae who left her people to suffer while she went out into the human world to play at being a priestess of witches. Whatever you like. I'm sure they'll forgive you. I'm sure they'll even forgive you trying to label Belle a traitor. But they don't believe it. You don't believe it. And I don't have time to wait around while you figure out that you're the asshole here. We're taking Belle home. And that's that."

The stillness in the room grew so profound during Cary's little speech, that even the fire seemed to have stopped crackling. Deacon stepped closer to her back, rising over her in a way that assured her he'd just puffed himself up to his full and impressive height. She knew already his eyes were glowing, but the presence of his leopard would be obvious now even to the faeries around them.

And he finally released her hand. She risked a glance down. Yup. There were claws there now. He had actually done a partial shift, letting the claws out of his fingertips. He rarely did those, because they were a part of his magic, something other leopards couldn't do. But then again, he was learning to control and use that magic better now. Maybe the partial shifts came more naturally. Something she'd have to get used to as well.

In the ringing silence, the Fae's green eyes began to glow and a crackling of energy around her, swirling in purple, spoke to her temper. Whipping up the magic around her, maybe to prove she was worthy of the office of witches' patron saint.

Cary waited patiently for the explosion. She'd hit a nerve. That was good. That meant they really were facing Nicneven. The long missing Fae queen. Back, and annoyed she had a mess to clean up. Well, shouldn't make a mess if you didn't want to clean a mess.

"You dare…" Nicneven said, her voice low and quiet, almost a hiss. "This is *my* court!"

"Then you shouldn't have abandoned it."

The dryad made a move of some kind. A step. A gesture with

one long limb. Whatever it was, it drew the queen's attention, and in the next instant, a flash of that swirling purple magic whipped out and surrounded the dryad, encircling it until it looked like it was on fire. The being's scream rose, the only sound in the huge hall, echoing off the high ceilings.

"Oh no, we're *not* doing this while I'm here," Cary muttered. She hadn't only been practicing raising her shield. She'd been practicing *where* she raised it.

She flung her hand out and focused, using some of what Angie had taught her with real magic to focus the Protector magic flowing through her. She winced at the awkwardness of it, the effort she had to exert. And for a moment, she wasn't sure her efforts had worked. But then the purple fire encompassing the dryad flickered and went out. Leaving the Fae standing in a bubble of Protector shield, breathing hard, leaning over so that its leaf-like hair fell forward over the top of its head, the topiary style less precise.

Cary glanced back at Nicneven. "No. I'm not standing here watching you torture or kill one of your own."

Nicneven rose from her throne. "You challenge my throne!"

"I challenge your mood. I don't want your throne. My mate doesn't need your throne. And Belle would have gladly given it back without a fight. We're here for Belle. That's it. But I'm not letting you hurt anyone while I'm standing right here." She let some of her righteous steam out in a huff. "It's my job! I have to do it."

There was a brush of movement behind her, a shuffling. Cary didn't even turn to look. Her shield fully encompassed her and Deacon, keeping Deacon safe as well as her. Couldn't just sneak up on her when she was in full Protector mode. And now that mode included protecting someone who wasn't even behind her. That was a super cool new aspect to having "full control of her powers" after passing her Seventh Year. She could get used to that part.

One of the things she'd hated most in the intervening seven years was the fact that she often needed to be in two places at once to protect people, and she physically couldn't be in two places at once to protect people. Now she could! Metaphorically, of course.

She kept her gaze on Nicneven, waiting for the inevitable attack from behind to come, smiling faintly. But Nicneven didn't look smug. In fact, her attention was on the hall behind Cary and her expression was...outraged? Yeah, those raised brows and that tight jaw and the way her mouth worked... That looked a lot like outrage.

Deacon's hand carefully gripped her forearm. "Look," he murmured.

She turned to see the entire Unseelie court had bunched up together. Behind Cary. Just standing there. Behind her. In a tight bunch.

Letting her protect them.

She blinked.

That was...unexpected.

And apparently not going down well with Nicneven.

Oh boy.

26

A rain of purple magic slammed down around the Great Hall. Bolts of lightning that looked like arrows tipped in flames pierced the stone floor, dropped into the bonfire and made it sizzle, shattered some of the overhead metal-ring chandeliers.

Missed ever single Fae in the room because they'd all moved behind Cary in a clump and were now fully within Cary's protection.

Even the dryad who'd had its own personal bubble of protection rushed to stand with the others. Behind Cary. Where she was keeping them safe from their own queen's temper tantrum. Which the queen was having because Cary was keeping them safe. From their own queen.

Lot going on in that moment.

"Uhm," she murmured.

"Probably this will have consequences," Deacon muttered back.

"Shit."

"Yup."

"We need Belle," Cary said. "She's used to navigating all this." She gestured at the hall in general in a way that took in the flying flame arrows and screeching queen and cowering Fae court.

To be fair to the Unseelie Fae, they'd probably been through a lot in the period after Nicneven abandoned them, before Belle took over. Forty years wasn't a long time for an immortal being. It was really just a blink. Which meant the trauma of having a court with no queen was probably still fresh in their memories. Cary really couldn't blame them for hiding behind her shield and letting her protect them. All of this had to be hard.

Not that anything in Faery was every really easy. The machinations and court intrigue always made Cary's head hurt. But maybe it did the same thing to some of the Fae too? That was surprising to consider.

The flying arrows finally stopped dropping around the hall, though their damage remained. Flickering purple-white flames caused small, contained fires all throughout the long room. The fire didn't spread, which was good. And there was no smoke, like an ordinary fire. In fact, the smell inside the hall had shifted to something even sweeter than before. A sort of vanilla-flavored pine smoke scent. It was a strange but nice sort of combination. And that was weird given it had followed a magical attack.

Nicneven took several long, obvious, deep breaths as she glared down from her dais at Cary. She'd risen to her feet, towering over the hall, larger now than she'd seemed sitting. Her black veil robes fluttered around her in a breeze Cary couldn't feel, and her plethora of gold jewelry tinkled. Underneath that, a very faint sound, like a bagpipe starting up. Not the flutes that had previously floated through the hall as the Fae whirled and danced. This was the haunting sound of a single bagpipe, like a harbinger, warning of danger to come.

Even with that warning, what happened next took Cary's

breath away. The Great Hall vanished. Suddenly. Completely. The bonfire, the stone walls and black décor. The throne and dais. All of it. Just vanished.

Along with Nicneven.

Leaving the court who all crowded safely behind Cary, Cary herself, and Deacon all standing in the middle of a forest. But not the lush if strange forest she and Deacon had walked through to reach the Great Hall. This was a burnt and twisted forest, with stalks of looming tree trunks, bare branches, all blackened and charred. The ground crackled like breaking glass. The air danced with little spots of twinkling light. The sky above was dark purplish-green. And here and there, little red flowers with petals like marigolds popped out of the black stone ground.

Where the hell where they? What had happened?

How the hell were they going to get out of Faery from here? Where was even here? And where had the Great Hall gone? Where had Nicneven gone?

"Well this is…"

"Bad?" Deacon said.

"Bad," Cary agreed.

She turned to look at him. His eyes were still glowing yellow. He was still sparkling like a Fae king. And his voice had been very deep and growling. "How are you doing?" she asked quietly.

"Be better if we could find my grandmother."

Cary agreed. "Can you get us out of here…wherever here is? Once we do find her?"

"If I can't, she'll be able to."

Cary heard the unspoken "hopefully" at the end of that sentence.

She took in the crowd of Fae standing behind her, still in a tight cluster, a few quiet wails went up. The dryad stood close enough Cary could see its leaves shivering, like the dryad was trembling.

That couldn't be good.

"Uh," she gave a little wave to the dryad. "Where are we?"

"The cursed land," the dryad said in a small voice. Nothing like the grand and confident voice in the Great Hall.

"Cursed land sounds bad," Cary said, mostly to Deacon.

The dryad answered. "It is the broken land between the Seelie and Unseelie courts." More trembling. "The place of the dead."

Dead? That...was definitely bad. Fae were essentially immortal. They could die. She'd seen one die in her lifetime—or well, she'd known them before they died and knew they'd died afterward, but in the dying moment, she'd also been dying so she hadn't actually witnessed their passing—and she'd heard a story of one Fae having her immortality taken so she died a human death. Those were Jaxer's parents and those were also unusual circumstances.

Apparently, according to the books, there'd been a time when the Fae fought a lot of wars with each other and their people did die during those battles. But the denizens of Faery didn't die naturally. And they weren't the sort of beings a human could kill without special implements. So... Yeah, pretty much immortal to a human way of thinking.

A place of the dead, a place of *Fae* dead, was not something Cary expected to encounter in Faery. Ever.

She really hated this realm.

"So...what's this place of the dead all about?" she asked. "Cursed, you said. What does that mean?"

The dryad started to tremble so hard the sounds of its shaking leaves nearly overwhelmed the quiet moans from some of the other Fae. The dryad didn't answer Cary's question, though. It just pointed.

Cary turned, dread welling up even as she let out a long, pained sigh.

"Ghosts. It just had to be ghosts."

Deacon turned with her. And from the corner of her eye, she watched him debate his instinct to get in front of her with his better instinct to get behind her. The one thing Cary was terrified of, above almost everything else, in an almost irrational way, was ghosts. And Deacon knew that.

But…

She blinked. Something was…different.

She placed a hand on Deacon's arm, the muscles under her palm bunching and releasing, and eased him behind her. "It's okay."

The usual terror wasn't welling up. The gut churning, freeze-in-place, mind blank, heartrate-through-the-roof panic wasn't… there. She didn't *like* the ghosts moving through the trees. So many of them. Like an army of ghosts. Wispy beings of luminous green-white floating over the black ground, in between the dead trees, moaning softly, so softly it was more something she felt in her ears than heard. The sound sent a shiver over her spine, a foreboding. And there was fear. Because…well, ghosts were approaching and the immortal Fae behind her were afraid of those ghosts, but…

Yeah, none of the usual terror. Just a normal level of fear. The sort she'd have no matter what was walking through the dead trees at them.

"Weird," she murmured.

"What?" Deacon leaned into her back, wrapping an arm around her waist.

She allowed herself to settle into him for just a brief moment. "I'm not terrified of the ghosts," she said. "Maybe because of that thing with Death?"

She felt his nod, his hair brushing her cheek. "Maybe. This still isn't a good situation. But I'm…glad, I guess, that you're not terrified."

He sounded so uncertain how to feel, she chuckled. She was a little weirded out that she wasn't terrified, too. "We can analyze my lack of terror when we get home," she said, patting his arm. "For the moment, we have to figure out what kind of mess we're in and how to get out of it. And why the hell did Nicneven send us here."

"You challenged her," the dryad answered. "She is…uncertain. Of us all. Of her court. And that makes her…"

"Dangerous. Unpredictable. Vicious. Nasty."

"Insecure," the dryad finished. "Insecurity is bad in a queen."

"Noticing that," Cary said. "What's your name?"

"Da-a-nieru-drei. Drei is easier for humans to pronounce."

"If you don't mind, I'll go with that, then." There'd been a rhythm and accent to the various "a"s in Drei's name that Cary knew she was going to pronounce wrong under pressure. She needed more time than they had at present to get those syllables right. Deceptively simple. But she'd come back to it. She hated not being able to pronounce someone's proper name correctly.

The ghosts were groaning louder now, the sound raising the hairs on Cary's arms. And a scent like damp mold proceeded them. "Drei, are those ghosts Fae or humans who've been trapped here?"

It only occurred to her that they might be human ghosts since the Fae were kind of notorious for luring humans into Faery and then making them go mad and letting them waste away here until dead. So maybe this wasn't a Fae army of ghosts. Maybe these were all the humans?

If so, there'd been a lot of them over the centuries. Like… a lot.

The green-white glow filled in all the space between the dead trees now. And the ghosts were close enough, Cary could see their outlines better. Mainly human-ish shaped. Though the limbs were a bit ephemeral. Legs seemed to be optional. But there were heads and the heads were moaning. Loudly.

"They are all the dead," Drei said. "Those who died when the courts split. They remain here on the field of their demise, and any they touch will wither and rot."

"Pleasant," Cary muttered as the entities got so close she could see the black holes of their eyes now. The scent of mold grew strong enough to make her nose twitch. "So…mostly Fae, then?"

"Mostly Fae," Drei agreed. "But also some humans. The ones who've been sent here. Their withering killed them. Eventually."

Something about that… Cary frowned back at Drei. "What happens to a Fae who's touched by the ghosts?"

"Withering and rot go on…forever."

"Ew. And Nicneven sent her whole court here? What a bitch." Cary faced the approaching army again and more firmly placed herself in front of the others. No withering or rotting on her watch. Not today. But this was going to make finding Belle harder.

A horrible thought caught around her throat as the first ghost hit up against her shield and came to a confused halt.

What if Nicneven had sent Belle here? Without Cary to protect her, had she been taken by the ghosts? Was she even now dying? *Would* she die? She wasn't Fae, but also, now, she wasn't quite *not* Fae. And while leopard shifters were long-lived, they were far from immortal.

Shit. "Did Nicneven send Belle here?" Cary asked Drei as the ghosts piled up against her shield, their moaning continuing to grow louder.

For a long moment, no one said anything, and the dread in her gut tightened.

"Answer," Deacon commanded in a voice that sounded suspiciously regal.

"She did," Drei said immediately, its voice very small. When Cary glanced back, Drei pointed again.

Cary frowned and gazed in the direction of the dryad's long, branch-like finger.

To a small, round-top metal cage hanging from a black branch high above the dead tree forest. And inside, curled onto the floor with her knees up by her chin…

Belle.

"Oh hell," Cary muttered.

The ghosts had surrounded them now, their mold stench permeating the air. The Fae behind her gasped and cried out and there was a lot of noise.

Cary took a moment away from her fear for Belle to say, "All of you stay behind me. Let me keep protecting you and you'll be safe. Do *not* try to run away."

She could practically sense the hesitation, the desire to run. And she sympathized. Even without the overwhelming fear that usually took her around ghosts, she was having a hard time being surrounded by so many of them. Piles and piles of translucent, moaning, mold-scented entities scratching at her shield, trying to get past. Withering and rotting a scant touch away.

Cary chose not to look at the individual ghosts too closely. She had a feeling that would tip her over the edge of fear into that old familiar terror.

When no one bolted and Cary could be reasonably certain their fear would keep them bunched up behind her, she faced Deacon. Ghosts at her back, the low moaning, made the hairs on her nap stand up. Wow was this not something she could have done a few months ago, turning her back on all those ghosts…

"So, how do we get your grandmother out of the cage? What

kind of cage is that? And then we need to get everyone else out of this dead forest and back…I guess to their court? I don't want the queen to just send them all here again. But that's a second problem. We have first problems to deal with first. Like getting your grandmother out of that cage."

She was rambling a little. That happened when she was scared, or when she was nervous. Right now, she was scared and nervous. But mostly, she was scared for Belle. And terrified she wouldn't be able to save Deacon's grandmother.

From this distance, she couldn't tell if the ghosts had gotten to Belle yet. She had no idea if the older shifter was even still alive. But she couldn't consider that. Not now. Back to firsts—getting to Belle and getting her out of that cage.

Deacon considered the cage for a long moment. Then, "I'm going to do something that you won't like."

"Oh good."

He glanced down at her and his mouth twitched, the faintest hint of humor at her sarcasm. "I've been practicing with my grandmother. I can do this. But I have to do it alone. You need to keep the others safe."

"What *exactly* are you going to do?" He was right. She didn't like this at all and she hadn't even heard the plan yet. "Wait, you're talking about doing that porting thing, right? The one that you've only once managed to do without knocking your grandmother over?"

"That's the thing. And I'll aim for the base of the tree. Once close, I can jump up to the branches, assess the cage. Get her out. Then I'll get us back here. Even if I have to just run normally."

His normal speed was pretty impressive. And the ghosts weren't exactly moving at speed—they were significantly creepier moving in that slow, moaning way. But she wasn't positive they *couldn't* move fast. Which meant they were counting on Deacon's ability to move faster than a ghost.

"Yup. Hate the idea," she said. "But since you're always going along with my bad ideas, and since this isn't a bad idea, just a dangerous one, I won't argue. But I'm going to dance around worrying until you get back, so don't take too long. And also, if you need me, I will push my way through the ghosts to reach you so just keep that in mind."

He cupped her cheek. "You'd wade through ghosts to reach me?"

"I'd wade through hell and death and, yes, even ghosts to reach you. Always."

His expression softened, and he leaned down for a gentle kiss. "Same," he murmured against her mouth. Then took a few steps back.

He looked around at all the circling ghosts and sighed. "I apologize in advance if I knock anyone over."

"Wait!" Cary grabbed his arm. "Remember to ignore the lure of Faery. You won't have my shield keeping you safe. It's going to come for you. Ignore the call. Focus on Belle."

He nodded. Kissed her again, hard this time. Then stepped back once more.

This time, Cary gave him some space. The bubble of her protection wasn't a small thing at the moment because she was keeping so many beings safe. But there was only so much room the ghosts were giving them. Still, he had a small circle of open area around him.

He glanced at Cary once, then focused on his grandmother in the distance.

Pulled in a deep breath.

And the next thing Cary knew, she was on the ground,

scrambling quickly back to her feet in case the fall had disrupted her shield.

Her heart pounded, but her shield held. A few of the Fae, those who'd been closest to Deacon, were pulling themselves back up as well, or being helped by the others near them. And a few muttered curses—or at least Cary thought they were curses. She didn't speak whatever Fae language they were using to cuss—filtered through the group.

"Anyone hurt? Everyone still safe inside my protection?"

Murmured affirmatives around the group. Good. Now she just had to worry about her mate. And his grandmother.

And the fact that they were very far away now.

And some of the ghosts had turned to head in their direction.

Deacon landed at the base of the tree he'd been aiming for. Suddenly there, and without knocking the tree over. That had to count as a success. He glanced hurriedly back to his mate. He couldn't see her through all the encircling ghosts, but no one was screaming in pain so he assumed her shield still held.

Gods, he hoped so.

He looked up at the cage swinging from the dead tree above him. From this angle, all he could really see was the circular metal base. It looked thick, and worn. Mostly black metal. But if he looked at it from the corner of his eye, he spotted the glowing purple of Fae magic.

Fuck, shit, damn. He had no idea how to break through that. Cary's Protector magic could probably just brute force through that if it meant protecting someone. But he wasn't sure he could do the same.

There was no sound coming from the cage above him, which terrified him, but he sank all his emotions under the control he'd spent his lifetime perfecting. That control over his emotions kept slipping lately. He couldn't afford to allow that now. Magic use or not, this was a time for logic and action.

A tickling at his ear, the warning sign that Faery was calling…

He couldn't explain the lure to Cary clearly. Or even Jaxer. It was so subtle, so… Instinctive. A drive that *felt* like his own instincts calling him to go…somewhere. To give chase. A call that started out so quietly he could ignore it.

But the fact that it was already there, already tickling his ears, meant he didn't have much time.

He glanced back one more time toward Cary. And realized some of those ghosts were heading his way. Shit. Even less time.

One quick study of the blackened tree, and he leapt up to a branch that looked thick enough to hold his weight and also brought him close to Belle's cage.

At that height, he could see Cary and the Fae court safely inside the bubble of Cary's shield. He could also she her attention was on him and she was literally shifting from foot to foot, "dancing" as she waited for him. If he hadn't had to shut down most of his emotions to do this, that would have made him laugh.

A soft moan drew his attention to the cage. Inside, his grandmother was curled into a tight ball, touching the base of the small cage but not leaning against the outer bars. He couldn't see her face, she had it tucked against her knees, and her hair hung in long red curls around her shoulders. She was dressed in a shimmering gown that was a combination of whites and blacks and some purple woven through. Not the gown she'd had on when she left her cottage. And not a match to the rest of the Unseelie court. At least…not the court as Nicneven had arranged it. Had the court favored different colors under his grandmother's reign?

Something for later. It was clear she wasn't dressed as whatever glamour had dressed him and Cary in Seelie court colors. And if her clothing was glamour, it was a glamour that held through the magic around the cage.

"Nan?" he murmured, inching closer to the cage, along a branch that cracked beneath his weight as he crawled forward. He pushed claws out through his fingertips in a partial shift that gave him better purchase on the delicate limb.

His grandmother groaned and finally raised her head. "Ye shouldna be here," she murmured. "Go. This place will kill you."

"We're getting you out. Going home. We'll deal with the rest there."

"The cage is bespelled. Nicneven's having a tantrum." Belle tsked. "After all these years, this is her answer. Bitch."

"Cary said the same thing."

"I knew I liked yer mate." Belle's eyes widened. "Is she here? That's…"

"She's protecting the entire Unseelie court from the ghosts, so she's fine."

That sentence, and every sentence like it, would never cease to hit Deacon in his instincts. He both loved that Cary was so much *herself*, so willing to get between danger and innocent people, and he hated that she so often had to be in danger to protect people. The oxymoron of his love's life.

"How do I get you out?" he asked his grandmother. "I can see the magic. Without Cary to brute force through it, how do I break it?"

"Yer mate couldna brute force this," Belle said. Then, "Could she?"

"She could. She's done it before. Makes a lot of noise apparently. But if it means protecting someone, she can." She had. With him. When they'd first met and she'd broken the binding ring keeping him from escaping a demented wizard. He could hardly believe that was only a year ago. "But she can't be in two places at once. We need to do this."

"Nicneven spelled it to keep a shifter in. It's not magic I can break." Belle shook her head, her gray-threaded red hair dancing with the gesture. For all she must have been in the cage for a while, she didn't look too bad. There were circles under her eyes, and her skin looked tight. Her jaw muscles flexed if she got to close to the cage bars, a wince she was trying to hide.

"Does it hurt you? Touching the bars?" He heard the growl in his voice, but he didn't have time to regulate that now.

She waved his question away. "Can you touch them without getting a shock? That'll tell us what we have to work with."

Deacon could clearly hear the approaching ghosts that had broken off from surrounding Cary's group and were heading his way. He wasn't sure ghosts could climb trees, or Belle would probably have not survived this long, but he wasn't sure they *couldn't* climb trees either. So he didn't want to take any chances.

"We don't have a lot of time," he murmured.

He ensured his balance on the tree branch, his position a crouch that resembled his leopard crouch, but in a way that suited his human body. Once he had a firm grip on the branch, he stretched one clawed finger toward the cage lock, touching it with just his claw.

The jolt of sizzling electricity shocked through his body. He blinked.

And he was looking at the world through his leopard's eyes.

Sight heightened and sharp, every line more distinct. Everything a little brighter. The colors slightly different. His sense of smell stronger now too, the mold of the approaching ghosts, the slightly burnt flavor of the forest air, the fried ozone stench of magic on the cage. Under it, he could even detect the scent of his mate, even though she was far away. That scent helped settle him into this unexpected shift.

He growled, his lip lifting in a snarl. Paws were not as handy as hands when breaking a lock. But had it been the magic on the cage that had caused the shift or just the shock of getting hit with it that had thrown him into this shape?

His leopard wasn't the logical one. His leopard wanted to tear through the bars to get at Belle and then return to his mate as fast as he could move. Deacon needed more logic than instinct then, as much as he needed hands.

The shift back to his human form happened as fast as the shift to his leopard had, in a blink. He'd always been fast at shifting, no need for the process that most shifters went through. But this one left him a little breathless and dizzy with the speed. That was… new. And maybe not welcome.

"So, that'll be a problem," he said, nodding to the cage. "If I can't touch it without shifting."

"Now that you know what to expect, try again," Belle said, her eyes narrowed and a sort of hungry expression on her face.

Something in that look nagged at Deacon's instincts. But his instincts were also occasionally telling him he needed to chase something through the dead forest so he ignored this too.

"This time," Belle said, "let yer magic out a little more. Concentrate on the power in the lock. See if you can feel yer way through it."

"We're talking about this in a way I haven't worked with magic before."

"You can do it. It's in yer blood."

That was the terrifying part.

He stretched out his claw again—the one part of his form he hadn't shifted back to human—but this time, just before touching the lock, he tried to *see* the magic there, sense it, feel it. He tried to remember the things Angie had been teaching Cary during the demon fight, but most of his memories of that night were just nightmare images of his mate in trouble now. So he focused on what his grandmother had been teaching him. How to access his own magic, channeling his emotions into the core of that part of him he rarely reached for. He'd made the leap to her using that magic. It answered his call this time easily.

Maybe too easily.

And there… He could sense the spell inside the magic around the lock. A sort of knot of intentions. Like so much of his shifter nature, he didn't have the words to describe what he sensed, but he *could* pick up the spell, the intricacy of it.

"This is beyond anything I've dealt with before," he murmured, and only then realized he'd half closed his eyes.

"There's a point inside the spell," Belle said. "There is in all Fae magic. A tiny dot of light that will unravel it all. But it'll be hard to find. The spell on the cage…muddles my thinking. I havna been able to concentrate enough to find that point. You need to. Find it. And hit it with a jolt of yer power. It'll crumble the spell."

"That sounds…" Too easy? Impossible?

He wasn't sure, so he didn't waste time with words.

Ghostly moans and the stench of rot and mold neared. Below him he could sense the ghosts getting closer, moving with a sort of inevitable deliberateness designed to make a person's dread increase. He ignored his dread just as he ignored all his other instincts and emotions to concentrate on the magic around the lock.

And finding the key to breaking his grandmother out.

28

Cary quite literally danced in place while waiting for Deacon. Seeing him suddenly at the tree was both exhilarating—he'd made it and didn't knock the tree down!—and terrifying—he was no longer in the safety of her protection and that meant Faery could lure him.

The wonderful dumbass had gone through Faery once without her—coming to try and help her when he thought she was in danger—but had had the good sense at least to bring a couple of faeries with him that time—Jaxer and Eriana, who he'd needed just to get into Faery at that point—and even then, he'd been caught by Faery and Eriana had to save him. The longer he was outside Cary's shield, the more chance Faery's song would call to him.

Shifters were not safe here.

But…

Belle came in and out all the time. She was currently trapped inside a cage, but still, she knew how to be here without the song taking her mind. Which meant she could help Deacon even as Deacon tried to break her out.

Which appeared to be taking…time.

Shit shit shit.

If she were there, she could just brute force open the cage. Because Protector. It's what she did. But she wasn't there. Because she had a gaggle of Fae to protect from moaning, creepy ghosts who were surrounding them and would make them wither and rot for eternity if she left them. So, yeah, no, couldn't do that.

And worst of all, there were ghosts heading toward Deacon and Belle. They moved at a snail's pace, thankfully. Just floating and moaning and easing their way closer and closer. That was probably by design. The *most* creepy way to approach a victim. Slow, and inexorably, giving you time to think you could just run away except then suddenly you can't and…

No. Not going to think about that right now.

Okay, so ghosts on the way, but not moving too fast. And the shifters were fast. That helped.

Belle was also high up in a tree and maybe that had kept the ghosts from reaching her? So they were safe in the tree? Maybe. Hard to tell. But Belle did seem to be awake and talking to Deacon, which meant she wasn't dead or rotting and withering. Hopefully.

Lot of hopefully going on here. With Cary trapped by ghosts so she couldn't help.

She really really wanted to be in two places at once. *Needed* to be in two places at once.

She technically *could* be in two places at once. Right?

She'd managed it in the Great Hall, hadn't she? Thrown that bubble of protection around Drei. Could she do that for Deacon? He and Belle were pretty far away. But they were definitely in danger. That counted—even if that wasn't a technical requirement anymore because supposedly *control*—and there were ghosts heading toward them.

Could she extend a shield over them? That wouldn't help with breaking open the cage. Deacon would just have to figure that part out. But it would keep the ghosts and Faery itself from slowing him down and interfering.

Maybe.

She could also, maybe leave the group inside a shield, shield herself, and walk all the way over to Deacon. Through ghosts. But...she hadn't practiced that. If she walked away and she couldn't keep the shield around the Fae court, the ghosts would get to them before she could figure out how to make the shield around them work.

Damn it. She really did need more practice doing this and figuring out all the ways she could control her powers now.

But she did know she could send a shield to someone not right next to her. She'd done it in the Great Hall. She could do it here.

She opened herself to the sense of the Protector magic flowing through her. She still couldn't feel it. Even here in Faery where she was essentially on the doorstep of the source of the power. But really, she'd never needed to feel it to make it work, to channel it through her. So she focused on what Angie had taught her about visualization. She focused on what she'd learned about visualizing her shield over the years. What Jaxer had taught her. What she'd done inside the Great Hall...

The hand gesture, throwing her hand open and out toward Deacon and Belle, may or may not be necessary, but it certainly helped with all the visualizing.

Unlike with Drei, who'd been on fire and had gone out when Cary's shield came up, there was no fire or obvious signs that Cary's shield encircled Deacon now. She squinted at the distance, trying to see him better, hoping for some indication he was protected.

Instead of Deacon, though, Belle was the one to turn toward Cary. Deacon's head remained bent over something on the cage—Cary assumed lock but couldn't see from here. But Belle turned in her cage to face Cary. Cary couldn't see her face clearly, couldn't read her expression, but Belle raised a hand, a sort of solute.

Was that…good? Or was she just waving?

Cary raised her hand back. Then put her thumb up and wobbled her hand back and forth, hoping that series of hand gestures made even a little sense to a Scottish shapeshifter. Since Belle could see at that distance better, maybe she'd even see the question in Cary's expression. Protector enhanced eyesight was not doing a thing for her ability to see Belle's expression.

After a beat, the shifter raised her thumb and nodded. A thumbs up and a nod. Could mean the shield was in place. Could definitely mean that.

Could also mean things were going just fine, no worries, they had this. Which…maybe they did. But it was taking a shit load of time.

Or maybe not. Maybe it just felt like it was taking forever because she was scared. That was a definite possibility.

She nodded back at Belle, tried to focus on keeping two distanced shields up, tried not to think about the moaning ghosts encircling her and the Fae court, or the ghosts walking toward Deacon and Belle.

And tried very hard to stop dancing in place with nerves.

She failed at the dancing part spectacularly.

29

In the back of his mind, at the edge of his senses, Deacon felt the change. Felt when the call to run away into Faery cut off abruptly. Felt when the lure of the chase dropped. He even felt a sort of fresh-air-head-clearing he hadn't known he needed.

He was too focused on finding the key to break into his grandmother's cage to look up, to deep into the knot of magic, looking for the spark that would unravel things. But a part of him definitely felt the change.

Quietly, in a tone that wove through his brain without breaking his concentration, he heard his grandmother's voice.

"Yer mate is strong. She's sent us a shield. Dinna know she could do that."

He couldn't answer yet, but knowing Cary had managed to send him a shield was…more than he had words for at that moment.

It definitely helped his concentration. Big time. Because finally, finally! There…

The spark Belle had talked about. The key.

"Found it," he muttered. "Now what?"

"Hit it with a jolt of yer power," his grandmother commanded. "Just as I said."

The sound of her strong voice, the power in it that hadn't been there moments ago, was so reassuring he did what she said. He'd never sent the magic he had into anything or anyone—except for Cary. So he tried to do what he'd done during the demon god fight. Throw some of what made him *him* at that little spark of light in the middle of the writhing purple magic.

The blast knocked him backward, nearly sent him flying from the tree.

He caught the branch in his claws, clinging to the black wood as angry magic washed past him, shaking the tree.

When the lights cleared, he blinked away spots, his gaze going right to his grandmother.

The door to the narrow, cylindrical cage wasn't just open now. It had been blown off completely.

"Oops," he said, feeling like Cary would understand this moment better than anyone else he knew.

"Bit excessive, there, love." Belle snorted and stepped out of the cage onto the branch. She didn't shift, but she stood at her full height on the limb with perfect balance.

After all that time in a cage, and how exhausted she'd looked a moment ago, he was more than a little impressed by her bounce back. And surprised.

She noticed his frown and shrugged. "Yer mate's shield cut through the magic that was draining me. Cut off the call of Faery, too. My leopard nature is more…comfortable now. Never realized it could be this easy being inside Faery."

Deacon started to rise, but the branch shivered under him, his weight significantly greater than Belle's, so he stayed in a crouch and studied the approaching ghosts, the distance back to Cary.

"We need to get out of here," he said. "Back to Cary. And then we'll need to get everyone out of this place."

Now that Belle was out of the cage, everything in him yearned back to his mate. He knew she was fine. She was shielding him and Belle at a distance. If something was wrong, she wouldn't be able to do that. Still. Staying away now that his grandmother was free was like keeping a rubber band stretched too tight. He needed to bounce back to Cary.

"Ah. Yes. About that."

The ghosts that had come for him moaned, closer now, nearly to the tree. He didn't have Cary's terror—or her former terror—of ghosts, but that sound still made the hair on his nape and arms stand up. His leopard growled and the need to shift so he could move faster itched under his skin.

"Back to Cary first," he said. "Then we can talk about leaving." He nodded down to the ghosts. Then frowned up at his grandmother. "Can you do the porting thing you've been teaching me?" It hadn't occurred to him she might not be able to until just this moment. She hadn't during the training sessions, but he'd been so focused on doing it himself, he hadn't thought about it.

"I can't," she admitted. "At least not in our realm. But here in Faery, I've been a queen long enough to have some tricks up my sleeve."

"Are you a queen anymore, though? Now that Nicneven is back, doesn't that... I don't know. I don't know how all this works. Aren't you just...you again?"

"I'll never be *just* me again," Belle said with a sigh. "Havna been since the affair, really. But forty years of keeping the Unseelie court in line has changed me irrevocably." She raised a hand. "I'm good with it. I'm not bemoaning the fact. I can do things I wasn't able to do as a shifter. But…" She made a face and glanced out over the dead forests, her eyes glittering.

Deacon's nose twitched as the ghosts gathered beneath the tree. The moldy stench crawled along his skin, that scent of death. But ghosts shouldn't smell like…anything, should they. They weren't corporeal bodies that were decaying. Why the hell Fae dead had to smell like death, he had no idea.

"We have to leave now," he said. "You can explain more when we're safe. Can you move fast enough to get around the ghosts? Or should I carry you?"

Could he carry her and port? Probably not yet. He'd be able to eventually. She'd said he could—he'd of course been thinking of Cary at the time and how useful it would be to be able to just whip her out of trouble—but he hadn't practiced taking someone with him as he bent space, so he was reluctant to try it for the first time like this. Especially with his grandmother.

"You flash back," Belle said. "I'll meet ye there."

"How?"

"Well, I canna bend space the way you do, but in Faery, I can…run between the raindrops, so to speak. Distances aren't as… solid for me here."

"I have no idea what that means, but if it'll get us back to Cary without coming into contact with the ghosts, I'm all for it. I'll trust you to get there."

"Might even beat ye," Belle said with a wink.

He was very tempted to take up that challenge, mostly to ensure *she* got back quickly. She wouldn't hang back if this was some kind of a race. Even to let her grandson win. But…

"Just get there," he said. "Go now. I'll follow."

"We'll be outside yer mate's shield for a bit," Belle warned. "Unless she can keep it moving with us."

Since Cary was only just learning how to hold shields in two different places, he doubted that. Especially at a shifter's speed. But they just had to get back to the space behind her to be safe.

"Faster we move, the better," he said. "Go. I'll be right behind you. Unless I beat you there, of course."

Belle's smile widened, her eyes sparkled. And for a brief instant, Deacon recognized the woman he'd known in his childhood. Mischievous and sweet and challenging and…a shifter.

She winked and then she was gone. Deacon blinked. He hadn't seen her move and he usually saw shifters move when they did. Better than other shifters!

With a snort that might have been a laugh if he wasn't so worried about Cary now, he focused on the area just inside her shield, that bubble of safety around her and the court. If he landed there, he was probably going to knock people over. Better that than getting caught by ghosts.

He concentrated on doing exactly what he'd been practicing, bending the space, taking hold of those two distant points and squashing them together so he could just leap off the branch…

And land next to Cary.

30

Cary found herself on her ass again suddenly, but this time she was delighted. She hopped back to her feet and wrapped her arms around Deacon before she'd even really *seen* him appear next to her. She didn't have to see him to know it was him and that he was back and safe and she could keep everyone safe now.

"Okay, we need to not do that too often," she said into his neck, "that being separated part. Do. Not. Like."

"Me neither." His arms tightened around her, carefully so he didn't squash her—which she appreciated—but tight enough she felt all secure and safe and happy.

Not that she could wallow in that feeling for long. She leaned away reluctantly and looked around for Belle. The Fae was standing just beyond the circling ghosts, in a position that left her vulnerable to touching those ghosts.

Shit! Cary was about to throw up a shield around her again, opened her mouth to shout…something. She wasn't sure what. *Get over here. Look out.* Something anyway.

But she never got a chance.

She blinked and Belle was standing right next to her. There was a breeze that sort of caught up after Belle had moved. And the ghosts that surrounded them did a wavering thing, like the breeze had blown them in one direction and they were moving back.

Whatever Belle had just done, she'd gotten through the ghosts, though. And now Cary could protect her without any trouble at all and that was the important part.

Still. She was curious. "How?" she asked.

Belle gave a little shrug and didn't bother to explain. "We've a wee problem with getting out of here," she said, her gaze on Cary and pointedly not looking at the other Fae all gathered around.

"What problem?" Cary glanced between Deacon and Belle. "We can't take all the other Fae back into our realm? We don't have to keep them there long. Just long enough to get them back to someplace less…withering and rotting."

One of the court behind her moaned quietly and Drei's leaf hair shivered.

"Aye, it's not so much that we canna bring some of them into the human realm, which is true, it's more that only a queen can access this part of Faery."

"Uh… What?" Cary glanced at Deacon. He was scowling at his grandmother.

"Only a Fae queen or king can access this section of Faery. It isna part of any one court. It's as close to neutral as any territory in Faery gets. And outside of the dead themselves, no one can move into or out of this land. Except the queens. And a few of the kings, though not all."

"And you're telling us you're not a queen anymore, so you can't get us out." Cary closed her eyes and shook her head. This was bad. Very very bad.

Very very bad.

"So you're telling us we're stuck here," Deacon said. And that low growl in his voice did not bode well for anyone.

"Until Nicneven decides to free us, or one of the other queens takes pity on us… I've no way to get us out."

"Not even back to the human realm?" Cary tried, though she knew she couldn't leave any of the Unseelie court behind and some of them couldn't travel into the human realm—there were just some Fae that could not take the human realm full of iron and…well, humans she guessed. Mostly, it was the iron though. The human realm wouldn't take long to kill those Fae. And Cary wasn't sure she could protect them from that. She wasn't sure they'd risk it. So even if the human realm was an option for some, that wouldn't solve the problem completely.

"Not even," Belle said. "There's no access to the human realm from here. And be glad that's as it is. You do'na want these ghosts in that realm."

Cary shivered. No she did not. "So what, we just…wait here? That's…"

"Not a good plan," Deacon finished for her. Even as one of the ghosts moaned loudly to remind them all of its presence.

Like Cary could forget being surrounded by ghosts. "I was going to say bad. But also, yeah, it's not a good plan. It's very bad plan. A plan like something I'd come up with. Which is bad. I always have very bad plans. This ranks up there with one of my plans. That's bad. This is all bad."

Deacon's arms tightened around her, stilling her rambling. In her head, though, she was still repeating the phrase, *This is very bad. Very very bad.*

What the hell were they going to do? Waiting around in Faery with a human mind and two shifter minds was *not* good. Even with her Protector magic keeping them relatively safe, the call of Faery was still *there*. And then there was all that surrounding magic just waiting to creep in and sink into her cells and kill her.

She really hated Faery.

The only good thing about the ghosts was they were absolutely a threat to everyone here so at least her shield wasn't going to drop without her realizing.

"Okay. Okay," she said after a minute. "We have to do something. I mean, the others might be okay here indefinitely so long as my shield holds, but you and Deacon and I are going to need food. None-Fae food that won't trap us here. More than we're already trapped." She winced. "And I don't want to add my ghost to all the surrounding ghosts, please and thank you. So there has to be something we can do. Can we…can we get a message out to someone. Let Nicneven know we've all learned our lesson, punishment meted, time to bring us back… Or something. Maybe one of the other queens can help? Even if only to piss off Nicneven?"

Belle rubbed her jaw and looked at all the ghosts, still not looking at any of the other Fae. "We might be able to contact another queen. But there's no telling who will show up and they might be more inclined to punish us for the fun of it as they are to release us to annoy Nicneven. Hard to say."

"I hate this place," Cary muttered. "Where's Wee Doug, by the way? He didn't get punished for helping you, did he?"

"He's…safe. For now." Belle didn't meet Cary's gaze when she said that, which made Cary very nervous.

Lot of *very* emotions going on here. Bad ones, not good ones.

Very very bad ones.

"What about this Strix being that was trying to kill Deacon and I in Edinburgh?" Cary asked. "Any help there?"

Belle snorted. "Who do you think finally got Nicneven to return to her court? That one's been playing behind the scenes for years and when his attempts to break me dinna work, he went for the one thing that would dethrone me. The real queen."

"But that means he can't take over the Unseelie court now, right? Or…whatever he was trying to do. It means things will stabilize and he's lost any hope of…whatever he was trying to do." Cary still wasn't entirely clear on what the Strix had been attempting, but honestly, the machinations of a Fae court were beyond her, and she really didn't care to understand them so long as none of this spilled into her world.

Except some of this affected their ability to get out of the cursed lands.

"Given that Nicneven was mad enough to send her entire court here?" Belle said, her brows raised. "I'd say he's achieved instability. Nicneven is alone now. Whether she likes it or no, punishing all of us left her as vulnerable as she was with a court she couldna trust. None of this is good. And while we're trapped here, the Strix could be whispering in Elphame's ear that now would be a good time to try Nicneven. A fight between the two leaves both courts vulnerable. Leaves room for him to sweep in and take power."

"I really really hate it here," Cary said, again, her gaze steady on Belle. "I have no idea how you've deal with all these people for the last forty years. The politics is…"

"Complicated," Belle allowed. "But the stability was worth the effort." She sighed and looked around. "Until just now."

"Okay, so no Strix, no Elphame." Cary winced. "Tatiana? She hates when I'm in Faery. Maybe she'll show up and get us out just to have me gone?"

"That'd be worse," Belle said with a snort. "She'll definitely challenge Nicneven's seat. War with the English court would be inevitable."

"So…what then? What are we going to do? We have to get out of here."

Belle glanced away, not meeting her gaze again. "Might be one shot. If Wee Doug can get an audience with Danu."

"Why Danu?"

"Because she's claimed you," Belle said. "And when I sent him to get her, I might have implied you'd be in danger if she dinna help me."

"Did you know we'd end up here?" Cary said, belatedly remembering that Belle did have a touch of future vision. Predicting the future could be difficult because there were so many moving parts. But Belle might well have seen them all in this cursed land before Cary and Deacon even left the human realm to find her.

"I worried," Belle allowed. "Neither your or my grandson were the types to let me disappear without word and… Well, I dinna think Nicneven would take kindly to yer visit."

"She did not," Cary said with a sigh. "But will Danu help? And won't that be just as bad as Tatiana showing up?"

"The Irish court and the Scottish court are less…at odds," Belle said. "The understandings between them are stronger. Danu's presence would be less likely to set Elphame off. Though in thwarting Nicneven, there will be tension." Belle sighed. "But Danu hasna responded yet. So it's possible she willna bother. It's possible Wee Doug hasna even been allowed to see her yet. Or that he's been taken captive by the Irish court and is being held as a political prisoner."

"I thought you *just* said the Irish and Scottish courts had an understanding!" Cary could not believe all this shit. Really.

"Doesna prevent prisoner taking if it suits the whims of the queen."

Cary couldn't hate Faery more if she tried.

"But now that you're here," Belle said, "Danu may show up."

"And if she doesn't?" Cary could not just wait around on the whims of a queen who had, apparently, claimed Cary as one of her own but who didn't really like Cary much.

She looked hard at Deacon who was scowling so fiercely she was a little worried he might shift to his leopard at any moment. His eyes were glowing, but they'd been doing that since they'd gotten here. But he looked even more angry than she felt.

He was also still glowing, though. That glittery golden glow that had surrounded him every time he'd stepped into Faery. And there were the impressively glamoured clothes that Nicneven had taken as Seelie court attire. And the crowns he and Cary were wearing.

To Belle, she asked, "Did you do the glamour on our clothing? Was that you?"

Belle finally looked back at them and shook her head. "Not me. My magic wouldna reached out of this place for me to do that." She blinked and turned her head a little to one side. "I dinna even see it until you mentioned it."

That was weird. Glamour usually worked the other way around—you saw it until it was mentioned, and then you could see through it.

"Do the rest of you see it?" Cary asked the Fae at her back. "What am I wearing?" she asked Drei.

Drei described the diaphanous blue gown and diadem. And when Cary asked about Deacon, she described his full kilted regalia and crown.

"And this isn't your doing?" Cary confirmed with Belle.

"Couldna have done it. I've been here since you arrived in Faery."

"Then who the hell would dress us up like Seelie royalty and put crowns on our heads?"

"Not necessarily Seelie," Belle said. "That was just Nicneven's assumption from the lighter colors. Elphame prefers light, wispy things because she thinks she's all light and sunshine. But…these are not the colors of the Seelie court. They're more neutral, to be honest. But with the purples and blues of royalty here. The golds and silvers to mark you both as…" Belle blinked and looked at Deacon. "To mark ye as a king and queen."

"Wait. What?" Cary glanced between them both.

Deacon being recognized by Faery as a king was one thing. There was Belle and his position with the leopards that gave that idea some weight. But Faery shouldn't be recognizing Cary as anything close to a queen. And no one else in Faery would *ever* consider Cary a queen. Of anything.

Except maybe chaos.

But even then…

"We've already established that Faery recognizes Deacon as a king of some kind," Belle said. "The realm keeps doing this to him."

"But I thought that was because of you, and you're not a queen anymore." Cary swiveled her gaze between Deacon and Belle, who were staring at each other.

"I thought it was too," Belle said. "I dinna think Faery would continue to recognize him after Nicneven reclaimed her throne."

"You're saying it still does, though? That Deacon is…a king here?" That was weird and probably wrong, but also what they really needed right now was a king or queen who could get them out of the cursed lands, and if Faery thought Deacon was a king… "Can he get us out?"

Deacon's fierce scowl softened to confusion. "How? How could I do that when you can't?" he asked his grandmother.

"I'm not sure," Belle said. "Not all the kings are capable. Even if Faery does recognize him, that doesna mean he can access the outer realm." She shrugged. "But it willna hurt to try."

"If it doesn't work, what happens?" Deacon asked.

"Ye canna open the way." Belle shrugged. "We'll be no worse off than we are now."

"I won't accidentally kill anyone or knock people over or trigger some sort of catastrophic event?"

Belle's eyes narrowed. "I do'na think so. It's never happened before."

"Oh good." Deacon put his hands on his hips and glared at the crinkling black ground at his feet.

Cary bumped his shoulder. "Now you know how I feel."

He snorted an almost laugh but didn't look up. He remained that way for a long minute.

The ghosts around them continued to moan and scratch at Cary's shield. But none showed any signs of breaching the barrier. Cary would have been astounded two months ago to hear she could stand in the middle of all these ghosts and not be a pile of freaked out goo. Yay for growth!

Sort of.

A distant wind blew through the dead trees, making the branches creak and moan in ways that rivaled the ghosts. A shiver traveled down the length of Cary's back. That…probably wasn't good.

Belle looked up at the breeze and moved to stand a little closer to Cary and Deacon, putting herself in front of them as she did.

"What's happening? What's coming?" Cary asked, her voice hushed. As if they needed any other problems.

From behind her, Drei leaned close, the brush of leaf hair surprisingly soft against the top of Cary's head. "He approaches," the dryad murmured.

"Who? Who?"

"*Him.*"

Okay. Yeah, that didn't help at all.

Cary motioned everyone into a tighter clump behind her, including Deacon and Belle. Belle hesitated before joining Deacon at Cary's back. Cary faced the circling ghosts, trying not to look too closely at them—less freaked out but not entirely fine with ghosts still—and focused on the direction of the breeze. A breeze that didn't feel normal. The haunting sounds of creaking and moaning above the ghosts too eerie to ignore.

The sky darkened from its purple-green bruise to something almost like night. No stars though. No real light. Cary's night vision kicked in—thanks Protector magic—so she could still see, but the darkening around her felt almost claustrophobic. Like walls closing in.

"Belle?" she asked as the ghosts started to sway and swivel, no longer scratching at Cary's shield, but moving in a sort of circular dance around her group now.

A howl went up. A loan, piercing sound of sorrow and intent. The hairs on Cary's arms rose.

"He shouldna be here," Belle murmured. "How could he get here?"

"Who?" Cary took a single step backward, for reasons she couldn't entirely understand. She was the Protector and her shields were working fine because no ghosts had gotten through to wither and rot any of the attendant Fae. She shouldn't be stepping back. She should be moving forward to ensure everyone was safe.

Yet some primal part of her started to worry, to tremble. To fear.

What the hell?

"It's him," Belle said, her voice quiet and confused—which was *not* reassuring. "It's the Strix."

31

A fog rolled in from the surrounding deadlands, thick white clouds piling up across the black ground and through the dead and blackened trees. The ghosts just outside Cary's Protector shield picked up speed, their swirling dance blending with the fog so that it was hard to tell which was what. The darkness that had fallen suddenly, closed in tighter, only the fog to provide any light at all—and it weirdly did, from an internal glow that would not have been normal in the human realm. Beyond that fog, even the shapes of the trees were nothing but fuzzy shadows.

"The last time there was unexpected fog, it was poisoned and trying to kill us," Cary commented as she watched it pile up against the edge of her shield again.

"Less poison this time," Belle said. "More dramatics."

"Always with the dramatics in Faery." Cary sighed. Though, honestly, after all this, she was insanely curious about this Strix person and what he was and what he intended.

And also the fact that he could get to the cursed lands when he wasn't a Fae queen or king and so shouldn't have been able to get here.

But if he was here, when he shouldn't have been, either someone was mad at him and sent him here, or…

He would know a way out.

Cary was hoping for that last. Someone—maybe even Faery?—might have dressed her and Deacon up like a queen and king. And Faery might consider Deacon a king of some kind. But none of those things meant this cursed land would let Deacon open a way for them to get out. This new development, someone being here who shouldn't have been, meant they had another possible option.

Yes, yes, the Strix wanted her and Deacon and Belle dead, but that was beside the point. Cary could *prevent* the death thing. It was the getting out thing they needed help with.

Through the fog, a silhouette emerged. A darker line of gray against the white glowing mist. A shape roughly human with no added wings or obvious tails, or anything to stand out. Just a generally human-shaped entity moving toward them.

But when that entity walked out of the fog and swirling ghosts enough to be visible, Cary gasped. Blinking hard. She must be seeing things. Or…or this was some weird illusion pulled from her imagination because…

"Why does he looked like the goblin king?" she whispered.

"He doesn't," Deacon said, with a growl in his voice.

"Not the real ones," Cary said, still blinking. "He looks like the goblin king from *Labyrinth*. Like…David Bowie's goblin king." Complete with the tight pants and big white hair and sharp, handsome features, and vaguely steampunk-ish overcoat. There was even a fucking white owl on his shoulder!

If this man started spinning crystal balls around his gloved fingers, she was absolutely definitely going to know this was a joke and he was doing this on purpose. But…

"Why?" she muttered, looking the being up and down. Just… Why?

"Same question," Deacon said, his voice very deep and the snarl very obvious. "Why is an enemy showing up in a form that you've had a crush on for years."

"Right? It's…weird."

It took her a moment to realize the deep snarling hiss in Deacon's voice could mean more than just his leopard was on guard. She glanced up and he was glaring holes in the newcomer. His eyes were glowing so brightly yellow they were very nearly a light of their own in the darkness. Which was, outside of the white fog lighting things up, pretty absolute now.

"Whoa, big guy," she said putting a hand on his arm. "Don't let the illusion give you ideas. I'm not seeing this like I would be if I met the real David Bowie dressed as the goblin king. And even then, that wouldn't be so much…crush as awe and inability to speak and he'd just laugh at me and then I'd ask for an autograph like a silly fangirl. So yeah, you can roll back that jealousy. Not needed. This isn't giving me movie and rock-star crush reactions. I'm just weirded out."

She said all this while the Jareth Goblin King lookalike stepped up close to her shield, and his quiet laugh made the hairs on the back of her neck prickle. No. This was not her getting to meet a rock-star crush and melting into a puddle of starstruck bemusement. This was a weird coincidence or a purposeful attempt at swaying her. And she was not happy about it. Especially not happy about what it was doing to Deacon.

They'd had to work their way through some of the instinctive jealousy that had cropped up for both of them as a result of the mate bond—jealousy that was chemical and neither of them could control and it had really sucked for both of them. She *loved* that they'd gotten past that, to a point where their bond was tight enough those weird jealousy instincts didn't hit anymore. Having this enemy cause Deacon's to flare again just pissed her off.

"So…" the Jareth lookalike said, and his voice was deep and rolling but most definitely not the dulcet tones of David Bowie, "you are the infamous Cary Redmond?" His gaze flicked over her, a quick, mostly disdainful glance. "I don't see what all the fuss is about."

"Ha! You're so funny. You should do standup."

The Strix blinked.

She grinned. "Why the Jareth get up? Or is that how you really look? In which case, I like your owl." And now that she was looking at the owl, the name Strix finally made sense. Strix was a genus of owls. She probably should have realized that.

What was the howling about, though?

"I am the Strix," the Strix announced in a booming voice.

"That wasn't what I…" She sighed. "Okay. Anyway. How did you get here when you're not supposed to be here?" *And also how can we all get out*? But she kept that question to herself because she knew this asshole wouldn't tell her willingly.

"I can be anywhere. I am the Strix."

Oh boy. One of these guys. Looking less and less like the sexy goblin king by the moment. "I got that part. About your name. You can drop that. I know you're not supposed to be here. Did Nicneven banish you? Or maybe Elphame?"

"I cannot be banished. I am the—"

"Yeah, yeah, if you say that again, I'm going to scream. And the court behind me are freaked out enough. Can't blame them. How are you standing with the ghosts and not withering and rotting?" Cary raised a hand. "And don't say I am the Strix again. Really. That's just not an answer."

His gaze flicked to Belle finally, and he gave her another of those disdainful smirks. That kind of made Cary want to punch him in the face. Definitely nothing Deacon had to worry about here. There was nothing about this Fae that wasn't irritating to her.

"She finally rid us of you," the Strix said. "Finally."

"I don't know what yer talking about," Belle said. "But it seems she's also gotten rid of you."

"I'm not banished here."

"Then you're here to gloat?"

"I'm here to end you once and for all. If Nicneven doesn't have the stomach for it, I do. Usurper."

"Still don't know what yer talking about. Got something wrong in the head, this one does," Belle said as an aside to Cary. "Never could understand why the two courts kept him around."

"Starting to see what you mean," Cary said back, scowling at the Fae. "But also, no one is 'ending' anyone here." She grinned again, just to irritate the Strix since he was so fucking irritating to her. "Would love to know how you're here, though."

He turned his attention back to Cary, his neck moving not unlike an owl. She vaguely wondered if he could spin his head around to look behind him the way an owl could. That'd be both cool and freaky to see. He also had weirdly black eyes. No pupils or anything. Just solid black points in his head. They were not comfortable eyes.

The fog surrounding him piled higher against Cary's shield. Behind the Strix, the ghosts continued to whirl in the fog, their moans getting louder.

And it occurred to her that the whirling and spinning maybe weren't voluntary. That the Strix was somehow doing that to them and that was what was keeping him safe from all the withering and rotting. If so, good trick. Spooky. But also impressive.

She really didn't feel like being impressed by him, though, so she raised her brows at his stare, giving him impatience and her own sort of disdain. Not that she did disdain well. She was more sarcasm and irreverence if she were being completely honest.

From the fog, two more entities moved close, coming up beside the Strix's legs. Two very large, gray and white wolves. They weren't shaped like normal wolves, though. Not even like werewolves. They were huge, coming up to the Fae's waist, and he was as tall as Deacon. And the wolves had heads and tails that were longer compared to their hunch shouldered bodies. Almost the shape of a hyena but with definite wolf around their faces. Their ears were sharply pointed, their snouts hung open and dripped saliva. Their teeth were very very sharp. And their eyes were a solid black that matched their master's. They snarled as they pawed the ground next to the Strix.

Guess that explained the howling.

The Strix poked at Cary's shield, his finger hitting the invisible barrier as if he'd poked at a solid wall. He gave it a little push. Then nodded.

"It is as it is rumored to be. I do not like this move to embrace Protectors. You are an abomination to the realm. Like a shifter as a queen is an abomination."

"I really wish you didn't have Jareth's look," Cary said with a sigh. "You better not ruin the goblin king for me. I will be really ticked off if you do."

"Human woman. Faery will take you."

"Weird Fae creature. No, it won't."

At least, she hoped it wouldn't. No guarantees. But as long as her shield was working as well as it was at that moment, she was confident enough she wouldn't go charging off to her own death any time soon. Not that she *liked* being here. She'd really prefer to get out.

"What's the end game here?" she asked the Strix. "Just here to gloat or what? Cause you're not getting through me." She considered him. "You know. I think you were banished here. I think you're trapped here too and you're pretending not to be but are actually really freaked out. I bet you want me to protect you, too, don't you? You're here looking for help."

His snarl confirmed she'd hit a soft spot. Wonderful. She loved finding a bad guy's soft spot.

"I could protect your dogs," she went on. "Would you like that, puppies? Do you want Cary to protect you from the mean ghosts."

The wolves snarled and snapped at her, one launching against her shield only to be tossed backward a few feet.

"Guess not," she murmured. Then grinned at the Strix. This would be fun if they weren't in so much danger here. "So, what...? Political machinations finally bite you in the ass?"

"Danu had no right!" the Strix shouted and then clamped his mouth shut and snarled at Cary.

Well. That was...interesting. "So it wasn't Nicneven who sent you here? Danu did? Didn't know she could do that with a member of another court. How? Why? Yeah, answer that last first. Why would Danu do that?"

"You..." He snarled again and stretched the word *you* out like it contained twelve syllables.

"Gonna need to explain that more," she said, trying to maintain her outward calm. But Danu being involved anywhere in all this was kind of terrifying. What the hell did Danu want with her now?

"You should have stayed away," the Strix said, stepping as close to her as her shield would allow. Which, as it happened, was exactly two feet away. "It was all working out. I would have been given the Unseelie court. And then *you* arrived."

Something white and sparkly hit the shield, scattering over it like luminous salt. Cary blinked at the substance as it filtered to the ground. And ate through the black rock.

Yeah, that would have hurt.

"I'm just here to get Belle back," Cary said. "Then you all can do whatever Faery politics amongst yourself. I just need to get me and my mate and his grandmother home." She shrugged. "And make sure no one kills the entire Unseelie court because that would be rude."

"Thank you, majesty," Drei said, leaning close enough for its leaf hair to flutter over Cary's head.

"No problem," Cary said. "But also, not a majesty. Cary is fine."

"Oh, I don't think I could do that," Drei said, straightening away.

Cary would have sighed but she didn't have time. Because if Danu had sent the Strix here, it was either to kill Cary or he was trapped here too. And given his mood and the fact that he'd just thrown salt that ate rock at her, she was going for him being trapped here too.

Which was unfortunate. Because it meant he *didn't* in fact have a way for them to get out of here.

She faced Deacon, ignoring the Strix now. "No help from that direction," she murmured. "Looks like you're still our only hope of getting out."

"He can't help," the Strix snarled. "He's just a human."

"Shifter," Cary corrected. "And the fact that you tossed human around like an insult? I didn't miss that." She focused on Deacon again. "You can try. If it fails, we'll come up with something else. But I think you need to try."

Deacon looked past her to Belle. "It's possible?"

Belle shrugged. "It's Faery. Depends on its mood."

Cary rolled her lips into her mouth so she didn't reiterate how much she hated this place. But really. She hated this place.

"You will all die!" the Strix snarled.

The owl on his shoulder launched into the air and circled overhead, screeching out a noise that would probably have hurt Cary's ears if not for the shield. The wolves launched at the shield again, clawing and scrambling at its edges.

Beyond the Strix, the ghosts still swirled around in the fog, moaning and whining, the noise a nails-on-chalkboard sort of creepiness that raised goosebumps along Cary's arms. The fact that the Strix could hold off the ghosts with his fog was pretty impressive, even if she didn't like him. Being able to do something about ghosts felt like a really handy skill. She was a little jealous.

"How did ye get here?" Belle asked Deacon, ignoring the Strix and his animals and the ghosts and the fog.

"We went to the stone circle."

Belle nodded. "No handy trolls to amplify things, but you've opened a way into Faery once without the stones, so you can do it again. To save yer mate, you can do it again."

"And everyone else," Cary added. "We need something that gets us all out of here."

"Even the Strix?" Deacon asked, though his gaze was on his grandmother.

"Eh. Not really worried about him. If he gets back with us, fine. If not…" Cary shrugged.

The Strix snarled and his beasts howled.

"I would be sad if the death wolves and owl got stuck here, though," she said. "Even if they are trying to eat me and break my brain. If we can get them out, that'd be good."

Deacon pulled in a deep breath. "Just as I did before?" he asked his grandmother.

"We'll start there. If that doesn't work, we'll try something else."

Deacon nodded. Straightened his shoulders.

And the regal golden glow around him sparked brighter. The glamoured crown on his head seemed to solidify until it was as real as Cary's leather jacket. The brooch at his shoulder flashed with silver-purple light.

"No!" the Strix snarled. "It's not possible!"

Everyone ignored him as Deacon's glow filled the interior of Cary's shield.

Thunder cracked. The ghosts moaned louder. The wolves whined.

And in the distance, a sound like a snap.

Then everything around them went black.

Oh boy.

32

The darkness was absolute. Cary couldn't see through it, despite her vision being enhanced by her Protector magic. There simply wasn't any light to see by. Or maybe something had happened to her eyes? Hard to tell. But the silence was absolute, too. She couldn't even hear a shiver of Drei's leaf hair. She couldn't hear her own breathing.

Oh shit. Maybe she was dead?

She didn't remember being dead the last time she died. For a while, she remembered the pain and the blackness after. But within a month, the visceral feel of the pain had started to fade. And now more than two months later, she didn't even remember the last moments before she died very well. Certainly didn't remember the moment of death.

There was still this vague memory of blackness, of blankness, before waking up in her bed with her whole body aching. But she wasn't sure if that was something real or just a trick of her brain. And when she'd channeled the powers of Death, that hadn't been like dying. She wasn't *dead* in those moments. She was *Death*. Very different feeling.

All this sped through her head as she was trying to decide if Deacon had accidentally killed them. Poor man. He'd be so upset if he did!

Then sound crept back in. Dripping. The brush of air against her cheek. A faint crackling sound.

Slowly, slowly, her vision brightened. She blinked hard a few times. Realized she could blink. And let out a low breath. Not dead. She was pretty sure dead people didn't blink—at least not regular dead people. Vampires had to blink occasionally. She wasn't sure about zombies. But anyway, a human who was dead and not rising again for some preternatural reason wouldn't be able to blink. And she'd just blinked.

As the light came up around her, and her vision cleared, and all the sounds filled in again, she looked around.

Stone walls and floor, drapes of blacks, silver, gold and pops of red, dark chandeliers overhead. The dais. The throne.

They were back in the Great Hall.

He'd done it!

She spun in a circle, looking for Deacon. He stood beside her, his head bowed. She wrapped her arms around him and gave him a big hug.

"You did it!" She pulled back. "Are you okay? Did you hurt yourself? Are you going to pass out?"

She tended to pass out after doing something she wasn't supposed to be able to do—like that time she leveled an army of supernatural creatures. Deacon had just done something no one had thought he could do. Passing out was a definite possibility. And in Faery that was dangerous.

"Not going to pass out," he murmured. His arms came up

around her then and his hug was fierce and almost a little too hard. "Thought I'd killed us for a moment there."

"I know, right! I was so worried you'd feel bad about that. But we're fine. See. No one is dead." Oh wait. She looked around to make sure that was actually true.

Belle, alive and fine. Drei, alive and fine, looking a little awed. The rest of the Unseelie court, alive and fine, also looking around the Great Hall in awe.

No ghosts had come with them. That was good. And the Strix was standing to one side of the Hall looking…appalled? Maybe. That expression was hard to read. But it did make him look less like David Bowie and she was grateful for that. She didn't like that this asshole Strix looked even a little like the outstanding human who was David Bowie.

She looked back up at Deacon. "Yup. No one dead." She grinned. But he was looking down at her with a furrow between his brows. "What?"

"You were *worried* I'd feel bad about killing us?"

"Well. Yeah. I know you'd be upset about that. If, you know, you could know anything after being dead. You'd beat yourself up if you'd accidentally killed anyone. I didn't want you to feel bad. We were in a tough place and this was one of our only chances of getting away from the—"

She didn't get to finish her rambling explanation. Deacon's mouth dropped onto hers, his kiss so gentle and so fierce at the same time she sighed. Yeah. Definitely not dead.

When he lifted his mouth, he set his forehead against hers and shook his head. "I love you."

She grinned. "Love you, too. Wish we could do more of this. But we do have a *situation* here."

"Still in Faery."

"Yup. And Nicneven is gonna be pissed."

"Nicneven is…impressed," the Fae queen in question intoned.

She hadn't been on the throne when Cary had glanced around the hall, but when she leaned back from Deacon to check again, there she was. Nicneven. Sitting on her throne. Her expression inscrutable.

"He really is a king," Nicneven murmured. Quietly so Cary wasn't sure she was supposed to have heard those words. But the queen would know both shifters could hear her.

"Looks like," Belle said, a little louder. "One Faery recognizes. One Faery has given the…keys to the realm, so to speak."

Nicneven's expression tightened. Her only show of emotions.

"This is not possible!" the Strix declared, stomping toward the queen. "It is a trick. They have deceived you, my queen."

Cary raised her brows at that. But the queen and the Strix ignored her.

"How were you with them?" Nicneven asked, the full weight of her gaze now on the Strix.

"I banished him," another voice in the room.

Cary's eyes widened as she turned to face the giant white deer standing opposite the throne. Putting the entire Unseelie court in the middle of two queens.

This was the Danu Cary had first met. A giant, enormous white deer with glowing green eyes, the softest white fur, and a twining bit of gold like vines circling her head as a crown. The deer's "voice" entered the head without it looking like the deer was actually speaking. And there was an inner glow that surrounded the creature so brightly she was hard to look at.

The brightness dimmed a little, as if the queen—who was seen more as a goddess among those of the Irish court—had noticed

Cary's discomfort and turned her illumination down. Or maybe that was just part of the show. Appear as a brightly glowing white deer and then dim a little so the rest of her magnificence was obvious.

Yeah, probably that last.

Danu turned a little so her green eyes were focused on Cary. And Cary got the distinct impression of amusement even though there was nothing in the deer's expression she could technically read—not like deer smiled or anything.

Danu's attention returned to Nicneven. "The Strix has been… engaging in the usual deceptions. Attempting to take your court while you were away."

Cary's eyes widened. Oh shit. Danu had known Nicneven was away. That meant she probably knew Belle had been more than just a liaison for the Unseelie court.

That was probably a very bad thing.

"You think I was unaware of everything that was happening here?" Nicneven said.

A chuckle that a deer probably shouldn't have been able to make. The sound was deep and echoing. Not the light, high, tinkling sound that Tatiana affected—and that hit Cary's ears like nails on a chalkboard—but a throaty, almost sexy laugh.

"I think," Danu said, "you were having too much fun to notice. I do not blame you. Entirely. And I wouldn't have interfered. But your servant endangered one of *mine*. And that I will not have."

"She is not yours," a third voice stepping into the conversation. This one high and sweet… And *not* familiar.

Cary looked to her left to see… Well, the most fairy faery she'd ever seen.

Tiny, though not like butterfly small, but really only about the size of Cary's forearm. Iridescent wings that glowed with rainbow colors, fluttering in the still hall air. The being on the other side of those wings had a glowing, green skin tone, looked vaguely human woman shaped, but with four arms instead of two, and legs that seemed a little short for the length of her body. Her face was exquisitely pixie-like, heart-shaped and sharp chinned, with a cupid's bow mouth. Her blond hair was stacked up into a high bun with little curly tendrils cascading over her cheeks. She wore a soft, flowing, iridescent gown in a pale pink. And the crown on her head was gold encrusted with pink and white diamonds.

Everything sparkled around her.

"Elphame," Nicneven greeted in a tone that was aggressively neutral. "You were not invited into my court."

Oh, that sounded like a threat. Cary moved out of Deacon's arms and motioned the Unseelie Fae closer. She couldn't exactly get between them and the three queens because of the way the three queens were spread out in a loose triangle formation, but she could make it clear to her own powers that she was protecting the court, and then she didn't have to worry about things like direction.

The Fae crowded close to her without question, so close, they were bunched up in a tight knot.

When Cary looked back at Nicneven, her eyes were narrowed and her mouth tight as she stared at Cary. And the entire Unseelie court gathered close to Cary.

Gathering them close like that was probably an oops.

But really, Nicneven couldn't blame them! Cary was the Protector, and there were three queens standing around about to get into a fight. Anyone with any sense in their head would let Cary protect them from the impending...whatever was about to happen. They all knew it was going to be bad.

Once before, Cary had gotten into trouble with a queen—Tatiana—when that queen's court had listened to a command from

Cary. She had a feeling she'd just done the same thing here, with Nicneven. Again.

Oh well. Not like there was any hope of Nicneven not hating her at this stage.

Deacon stood at Cary's side, and just behind her shoulder, his gaze on Nicneven too. He was still doing the kingly glow thing, and his crown looked a lot more solid now, like it had just before he'd done…whatever he'd done to get them out of the cursed lands and back here. Like she could reach up and touch it and take it off his head if she wanted to.

Which, given their company, she did not want to. Faery viewing him as a king was probably, maybe a good thing in their current circumstance.

She hoped.

"None of you have been invited into my realm," Nicneven said, her gaze slowly moving back to the other queens. "This could be considered an act of…aggression."

"I am just checking on my co-ruler," Elphame said, her voice wispy and high and soft. Almost gentle. "We have heard… disturbing things in the Seelie court. It is good to see those things may have been an exaggeration." Elphame glanced at Cary, then back at Nicneven. "Or maybe not."

"All is perfectly in control in my court."

A snort like laugh that was neither delicate nor wispy erupted into the hall. Cary blinked and turned with a sense of inevitability to see Tatiana standing to her right. Because of course she was here too. Looking as glowingly queenly as she had when she'd approached Cary a few days ago. Her pale skin luminous, her hair decorated with winking diamonds, her gown a series of transparent silver and gold veils wrapped around her in a way that was both sexy and revealing.

And now Cary and her charges were circled by Fae queens, none of whom were happy with the others.

Oh good.

She wanted to ask if she and Deacon and Belle could just go while they worked this out, but that would leave the Unseelie court vulnerable. So she stood there silently.

Waiting for the fireworks.

33

*I*n the quiet that followed Tatiana's appearance, Cary finally realized that the crackling she'd heard when first getting her senses back was the fire in the center of the Great Hall. It was behind Danu now, snapping and creaking, filling the huge hall with a lovely scent of pine smoke. The lights inside the hall were probably dimmer than it seemed now with three of the four queens present literally glowing with white light. But that crackling fire made clear they were in Nicneven's court.

And the other three queens hadn't been invited.

Not that she or Deacon had been either. But they weren't technically a threat to Nicneven's power. Or, well, maybe she considered them to be since she'd banished them to the cursed lands. Hard to say. Right now, however, the other queens were *definitely* the bigger threat.

"Why are you here, Tatiana?" Nicneven asked, her voice very quiet and deliberate.

"You tried to banish my favorite to the cursed lands," Tatiana said. Her voice bright, and sweet—unlike her snort of a laugh—and grating. "Have you missed me, Cary?"

"No," Cary said. Because it was best not to humor Tatiana in this one thing. And since Cary was safe in that moment from death consequences, she was able to be blunt.

"You wouldn't have been so rude if I'd come to rescue you."

Tatiana's pout was so disingenuous Cary almost, *almost*, rolled her eyes. She wasn't prepared to go *quite* that far. Blunt was fine. Insulting was maybe a step too far. But it was a close thing.

"Didn't need rescuing in the end," Cary said. "Thanks."

"The King of No Land has been given the key," Danu said. Her deer head swiveled to face Cary and Deacon. "I would not have let you linger there much longer. After your troll found me, I had to punish the usurper first. I knew you would be safe until I got there."

"Usurper?" Cary avoided glancing at the Strix. He'd said Danu banished him there because of Cary. But had Danu also done it because of his threat to Nicneven's court? Or did she care enough for that?

The deer blinked at Cary, slow and deliberately. And said no more.

Fair enough. Guess the usurper part was for Nicneven and Elphame to worry about. Danu wasn't going to admit to anything else out loud.

So Cary switched tacks. "Who's the King of No Land?"

Tatiana laughed. "She doesn't know. They don't know. They should not know."

Cary did wince this time. That sing-songy thing Tatiana did was really grating. "Not know what?"

Belle's hand curled around Cary's arm. "Best we talk about this when we get out of here," she murmured. Then louder, "We were just on our way out, majesties. Nothing to see here."

Cary leaned in to Belle and whispered in her ear, "I can't leave the Unseelie Fae. Nicneven might send them back to the cursed land again. How do we make sure they'll be safe?"

"Aye. That's going to be tricky." Belle straightened. Then faced Nicneven and dropped to her knees. A move so sudden—and unexpected from someone Belle's age—Cary blinked.

Belle folded forward, forehead to the ground, prostrate before Nicneven. "My queen," she said from that position, and her voice still managed to carry throughout the hall, "I would beg your leave as your humble servant. And that the court may resume their revelry at your…celebration."

The pause wasn't long. But Cary heard it. And from the narrowing of Nicneven's eyes, she'd heard the near slip too. That Belle had almost said "return" at the end of that sentence. That would have made it impossible to pretend Nicneven hadn't been missing for the last forty years even though it was obvious from Danu's earlier comment, she at least had been aware of the absence.

But Belle had covered the near slip well. Elphame's eyebrows were raised but she didn't seem to find Belle's actions or little speech anything unusual. Tatiana was still staring at Cary with a sort of vicious smile that made Cary's shoulders tight. Danu's gaze was impossible to read because Cary couldn't read a deer's expression.

"She's lying!" the Strix shouted. "The shifter stole the Unseelie throne. She must be punished."

"How could a shapeshifter steal the throne of a Fae queen?" Elphame asked. "Why?"

The Strix spun on Elphame. "You said if I got proof, you would allow me the court, allow me the throne."

"Why would I say such a thing about another queen's throne?" Elphame said, but there was a small hiss in her voice.

"An absent queen," the Strix declared. "The shifter has been serving this court as their queen. It is an abomination that should never have been allowed! You poison our realm by letting this happen." This last he turned on Nicneven.

"You go too far in your ambitions," Nicneven said, her tone quiet. "Do you wish a return to the cursed lands so soon?"

The Strix straightened. His wolves and owl—who'd come out of the cursed land with him—gathered around him, the wolves snarling. The owl landed on his shoulder.

"Enough," he said, his voice deep. "I have had enough. You, Nicneven, left this court to fester. Left us all at risk. And allowed an outsider to take over. You are unfit for this position."

"Are you declaring a war against me?" Nicneven said. Her voice was extremely neutral but the sound of it was loud and booming in the high-ceiling hall. "You have no army."

"You think I don't? You think there have not been those dissatisfied with your absence, those who want a *real* ruler on this throne?"

"None of this is good," Cary murmured to Deacon.

"Nope."

"Would be better if we weren't here as witnesses," she said.

"Yup."

"But I can't leave the rest of the court without protection."

"I know."

She took his hand when he reached for hers and squeezed. Maybe if they just snuck out of the hall while the queens and the Strix sorted all this out...

"You must stay," a voice in her head.

Cary jolted at the sound. She knew she hadn't heard that voice out loud. And that the voice was Danu's.

Danu. In her head. Telling her to stay.

Shit. That probably meant Danu could read all her thoughts and that was horrifying.

"Only because you are mine," Danu said gently. "But I fear I will not be able to claim you much longer." There was a sigh in this last.

And it sparked a whole *host* of questions. None of which Cary could ask right now.

She didn't know why she needed to stay, though, outside of keeping the Unseelie court safe. This was mostly nothing to do with her, or Deacon. They were just here to get Belle out. The rest was for the queens to fight about.

"You must bear witness, or it will not be complete," Danu murmured.

Again, raising more questions than answers. But Cary kept her mouth shut, squeezed Deacon's hand again, and tried not to think too much now that she knew Danu was reading her thoughts.

Wow was that intrusive. How did she *not* think things? How could she avoid thinking things that would definitely get her into trouble here?

The quiet chuckle of Danu's laughter in her head did not help.

Cary winced.

Meanwhile, the Strix and Nicneven continued to exchange threats and accusations. Tatiana danced in a little circle, weaving closer to Cary and then dancing away. Elphame fluttered in place, most of her attention on Nicneven and the Strix, her mouth turned up in a small smile that Cary did not like the look of.

Belle remained prostrate, which was starting to bother Cary. Nicneven hadn't even acknowledged Belle's request.

Cary leaned over Belle. "You might as well get back up. Nicneven isn't paying attention to us."

"She is," Belle murmured. "If I do'na want to make things worse, I need to stay as I am." There was a soft snarl in Belle's voice. As if she didn't really want to remain bowing before Nicneven.

Cary couldn't blame her. If nothing else, the position didn't look comfortable.

But before she could say as much aloud, a thunder clap echoed through the hall, making Cary wince and many of the Fae behind her scream.

And then the hall filled with more and more bodies. More and more Fae popping up all around the huge room.

"What's happening?" Cary asked as she straightened.

"A reckoning," Danu murmured in her head.

More Fae appeared in the Great Hall. So many the only available space seemed to be around Cary's group where her shield kept them safe, and around the queens—probably because no one dared get too close to them.

Among the Fae popping into the hall, Cary realized Oberon had shown up. He moved up behind Tatiana, a dark contrast to her light. Black hair and skin, dark green eyes, thick sharp features, shoulders to rival Deacon's. As spookily handsome and eerily ethereal as his queen.

The first time Cary had met Oberon, she'd had a hard time even looking at him, or Tatiana. They were both so beautiful and ethereal, she would have been hard pressed to describe them. Now, they both appeared more...solid maybe? Tatiana showed Cary a more solid beauty every meeting since that first. And now Oberon appeared more...describable, too. She could *see* him in a way that she really hadn't been able to that last time.

And what she saw was yet another outrageously beautiful Fae.

Unlike last time, though, he'd appeared in the Great Hall wearing a suit of armor, gold and illuminated by soft purple light. The Fae, with their allergy to iron, didn't wear steel armor.

Weapons like swords and knives were made of softer material here in Faery and strengthened by magic.

Oberon dressed for battle, appearing with all the other Fae filling the Great Hall, was more worrying than the sudden appearance of so many more magical beings. Because that meant some of these Fae were probably from the other courts and not just the Scottish courts.

Tatiana leaned into Oberon, her smile still focused entirely too much on Cary. In addition to her crown, now she also held her golden scepter, the diamond at the top winking in the glow from her and Oberon. That completed her queenly regalia. And with her king here…

What was this?

"What is this?" Nicneven demanded. She finally rose from her throne and purple magic like lightning danced around her, turning her green eyes purple. The magic lightning gathered in her hands, coiling around her forearms almost like rope.

"You are not fit to rule," the Strix announced. "They are here to pay witness to the new king!"

More thunder sounded. And a wind kicked up, blowing hard enough through the hall, Elphame had to flutter her wings faster to stay in place. So hard some of the surrounding Fae who'd just arrived gasped. The Fae taking cover behind Cary whimpered and a few moaned.

More thunder.

Now Nicneven looked nervous. She held up her hands with their coils of purple magic, as if she'd cast that magic out any moment.

Cary braced, ensuring the Unseelie court and Belle were safely behind her. Not that she needed to worry about the court. They moved even closer to her so that she was practically being hugged by scared Fae.

More thunder boomed.

"The realm has spoken!" the Strix said. "A new king rises and I will have this throne. This court is now mine."

The wolves howled. The owl on the Strix's shoulder screeched and flapped its wings. More wind whirled faster and faster around the hall, almost like a tornado building up.

Cary glanced nervously back. She couldn't see the open fire pit in the center of the hall for all the Fae in the way, but she sure hoped that wasn't being spread around by this wind. Last thing they needed was for the Great Hall to go up in flames with all these Fae inside.

Would that even hurt them? Could Faery fire hurt faeries?

Weird she'd never thought to ask that before.

She should have kept from thinking the thought too. Because, as if called by her thoughts, in the next instant, a whooshing sound.

And a column of fire rose to the ceiling from the middle of all those gathered Fae.

34

The wind collected around the column of fire, swirling it faster and faster until it was a blur of red and orange, a faint hint of purple at the edges, like the fire was inside a clear glass tube that only showed itself in faint reflected light. But purple light like Faery magic.

Cary's breath caught at the fire tornado. But she gasped when the towering column began to move.

"Everyone stay close," she shouted. Had to shout, because the hall had filled with chatter.

Not the screams Cary had expected, though. A lot of…cheering.

Cheering?

What the hell where they all rooting for?

Drei pushed close enough to Cary to lean over and shout down at her, "This is the reckoning. A new ruler will be revealed."

"A new ruler for the Unseelie court?"

Drei was silent a moment. Then, "Not necessarily. The king or queen must be revealed first. Then the battle over the court can commence. The Strix has called the reckoning to prove he's a king. Once that happens, he can challenge Nicneven formally. He can overthrow her without having to do all the…machinations he's been engaged in to steal the throne from Belle."

"Who wasn't technically supposed to be sitting on it anyway?" Cary asked.

Drei's leaf hair shimmering in the wind, a pause before saying, "Belle was revealed a queen when she took the throne."

"Wait." Cary turned to face Drei more fully. Ignoring the column of fire as it inched through the parting crowd toward the throne. And the Strix. "What are you talking about? I thought Belle was just…pretending. Filling in. She's a shapeshifter. How can she be recognized a queen of Faery for real?"

The column swirled faster the closer it got to the front of the Hall. As it neared, in her peripheral vision, Cary watched the crowds moving aside, opening a path for the flames.

"It was not a formal reckoning as this one is, with all the queens and courts of the isles present."

"All? The Welsh queen is here now?"

Drei nodded and gestured with one long, branch-like arm toward a being Cary hadn't noticed in all the appearing Fae. A very tall being who'd taken the form of a red dragon wearing a golden crown. The dragon was similar enough to the dragon on the Welsh flag Cary had to wonder if that was actually not the queen's usual form. But she didn't have time to dig into the Welsh court at the moment. More on that one later—especially since Deacon's father was Welsh. That seemed like something that might come up later.

For now, though, she turned back to Drei. "What happened with Belle's reckoning?"

"We were in turmoil without a queen to stabilize the court. In Faery, that means the magic that holds our part of the realm together goes…awry. Those here will start to get sick. The land will start to go bad. It requires the strength of a queen to stabilize those magics."

"A king will work?" Cary asked, thinking of the Strix and his attempt to take over Nicneven's court. He was claiming king not queen status. Cary had no idea if the "queen" and "king" part of all this actually referred to genders as she understood them. A "queen" here probably didn't have to appear or identify as female because there were a lot of Fae who weren't either male or female. (Drei was a case in point.) But the Strix hadn't called this reckoning claiming a new *queen* would be revealed. He'd said king.

"A king is…less reliable, but in a court like the Scottish court, which already has a queen in the Seelie faction, a king in the Unseelie faction would be sufficient. A king with a queen is a very stable combination to head a court."

Cary flicked a glance at Tatiana. Who was smiling. At Cary.

So weird.

Cary turned back to Drei, trying to ignore Tatiana. "So… technically, the Strix could take control as a king, and maybe later bring on a queen?"

"He would not. The queen would have equal power in the court. He is…not inclined to share. Any more than he already must with the Seelie court and Elphame."

"But because of the Seelie court, if he takes over Unseelie, that would still stabilize everything?"

"It would be enough. Not good. But enough."

"Okay. So…then what happened with Belle?"

"It takes a great deal of power to call a reckoning," Drei said.

The side of the dryad's face glowed brighter now. Cary started as she realized the column of fire was close enough she could feel the heat. Shit.

Drei also glanced at the column, but then faced Cary again. "We were in turmoil. We needed a queen. Belle had been a favorite of Nicneven and had been blessed with magic from their union. We thought she could help us to identify a new queen to take over. But… Things didn't go as we anticipated."

"Belle was revealed a queen?"

"It was actually not conclusive. The fire waivered. None seemed to be revealed as usually happens. But a lick of the flame jumped out to dance around Belle. Not a full acknowledgement of a queen. But it was enough to give her control of the court. To allow her to stabilize the magics. Once she'd done that…" Drei's leaf hair shivered. "I'm afraid she was stuck as our queen. It was not any of our intent. But she was able to bridge the gap left by Nicneven's absence. In a way even Faery recognized as temporary."

"What happened when Nicneven showed up again?" Because Belle had said she wasn't a queen anymore.

"The bridge was broken. The true queen returned. The bond that had held Belle in her place as temporary queen broke. She returned to the blessed shifter she'd been before taking control of the court. It would have been fine. For everyone. But Nicneven felt the sting of her entire court choosing an outsider to hold her realm instead of…"

"Of what? Letting it all fall apart?"

Drei gave a shrug. "Instead of wooing her back."

"She left. Was out in the human realm having a grand time. And thought it was your responsibility to get her back when things started to go to shit instead of just returning to her responsibilities? Is that right?"

Drei nodded. "Her assumptions were not without precedence. Wooing and worshipping a queen are often part of court life."

"Like the way Danu's court see her as more of a goddess than a queen?"

"Exactly," Danu said in Cary's head.

Cary scowled at the deer, hoping her gaze said, "Stay out of this." Because she couldn't shout it at the deer over the now incredibly loud roaring column of fire that was within a few feet of them, moving past on the way to the throne.

"Why didn't you seek out Nicneven, then?" Cary asked. "Why go to Belle instead and try to find a new queen?"

Drei glanced at the column of fire, then back at Cary. "If a new queen had been revealed, we would not have to worry about Nicneven again. We were…convinced this was a better option than trying to get her back."

"Convinced?" Cary shook her head. "By the Strix, right?"

"He did not expect us to go to Belle when he made the insinuation that we could find a new ruler. In fact, he counselled that we should not reveal our vulnerability to the other queens by even approaching Elphame. A reckoning without all the queens and courts present is… less formal, but possible. The Strix expected us to ask him to help, to call the reckoning. And, based on what's happening now, I can only guess he assumed he would be revealed a king during that ceremony."

Well shit. So…Faery had given Belle a sort of half-acknowledgement of queenship to stabilize the realm, thwarting the Strix's plan to bloodlessly overthrown Nicneven. And that probably would have worked if the court had turned to him instead of Belle. No wonder he was so pissed off. All that manipulation only to have it go the wrong way.

She faced the column of swirling fire again, close enough now she could have walked over and touched it—not that she would!— but she wasn't worried about it hurting her or the court. Her shield was up. Everyone was protected. The rest of this…

Well, she felt sorry for the Unseelie court. There was no telling who'd come out winner in a challenge between Nicneven and the Strix but the end result would probably be some years of instability for the Unseelie faction. All because Nicneven wanted to take a forty year holiday and the Strix was power hungry.

But at least once this was done, she'd be able to get Belle and Deacon and herself out of here without lingering issues. This was definitely Faery court stuff that had nothing to do with them and now that Belle's link to the throne had been severed by Faery—or Nicneven? Drei hadn't clarified that part—there was nothing keeping them here after the reckoning revealed the king in their midst.

As she waited on the big reveal, though, she realized the column had stopped moving. It just waivered in the open space between Cary's protective shield and Nicneven's throne. It continued to swirl fast, the flames almost solid like lava they moved so rapidly. The wind whipped around the column. Cary could smell the fire this close, though it was no longer a pleasant pine scent. This one was something sharper like burnt metal. And there was just a touch of something weirdly sweet in the smell. Almost like melting sugar.

The gathered Fae seemed to be holding their breath as the column continued to remain in place. Everyone waiting for a reveal.

That Cary realized…might not happen? The Strix wasn't able to get them out of the cursed lands. Which meant, even if Faery acknowledged him as a king, he wouldn't have all the powers of a queen. Right? Or maybe he needed the acknowledgement in the reckoning first, before he could do kingly things?

But then why had Deacon been able to get them out of the cursed lands?

Before Cary could turn to Drei to ask, the Strix made a noise halfway between a screech and a howl. Cary wasn't even sure how that sound was possible. The owl on his shoulder lifted into the air and circled the column of fire.

"Why do you hesitate?" the Strix demanded, stalking toward the flame column. His wolves whined and followed, their legs stiff, the hair on their backs raised. The owl let out an ear-piercing screech. "Why do you not reveal what we all know? I am the new Unseelie king. This will be my court!"

"What's happening?" Cary asked Drei.

"There is…question."

"Question? Just one?"

Drei didn't get a chance to answer.

"I am destined to rule this court!" the Strix shouted. "You require my proof? I give you the proof. Then you will bow to me and love me and I will be your king."

Before Cary had a clue what the Fae intended, before she could so much as gasp, the Strix laughed.

And stepped into the column of fire.

35

 ary took an involuntary step toward the flames, and the Strix standing in the center of that tornado of fire. A knee-jerk Protector instinct she had to check. She had others to keep safe in that moment. And the Strix seemed to know what he was doing. Her job wasn't to rescue him from himself—though sometimes that was her job with bad guys, and she didn't like it. Right now, though, her job was to stand in front of Belle, Deacon, the Unseelie court and keep them safe.

From what, she wasn't entirely sure anymore.

According to Danu, she was also here to witness this big reveal. So one way or another, she needed to just stand here.

Nicneven stood before her throne, the purple ropes of magic circling her hands and arms crackling but not doing much else. Around the Great Hall, the gathered Fae from all the courts of the British and Irish Islands watched the proceedings. Breathless and waiting for Faery to reveal a new king.

And the Strix, stepping directly into the column of fire to prove he was the destined king.

All very dramatic.

And despite herself, Cary was fascinated. What happened if the Strix was revealed to be a king? What happened if he wasn't?

What felt like minutes passed as the Strix stood inside the fire tornado, the fire swirling around him so fast it made his blond, spiky hair lift and dance in the currents, some of it dropping across his face. His long coat snapped in that breeze. His pale skin seemed to glow.

But as the minutes ticked past—or maybe only seconds, Cary could never tell in Faery—nothing seemed to be happening.

Cary finally gave in to her curiosity and leaned into Drei again. "Is this it? Is he revealed to be a king now or something?"

"This is…" Drei shook its head, leaf hair shivering. "Not what we would expect."

"What happens when a king is revealed?"

The fire column chose that moment to finally move again. It moved away from the Strix.

Was that good or bad?

Oh, Cary wished someone would just tell her what was *supposed* to be happening. Because this didn't look very…reveal-y to her.

The fire tornado spun away from the Strix, inching away from the throne, too. In fact, it edged so close to Cary's protective barrier, she could practically reach out and stick her fingers into the flames. Not that she intended on doing that. Still. The fire was very close.

The Strix gasped as the fire tornado left him standing where he'd been. He wasn't burnt or on fire. So that answered one of Cary's questions. Maybe. Or maybe this was the reveal?

Except the Strix didn't look happy when the fire moved away. He scowled and scurried to catch up with it. Walking into the middle of the column again.

The column moved away again.

The Strix stepped into it again. And again, it flowed away.

This might have been funny if it wasn't so weird.

"This isn't working, is it?" she whispered to Drei.

"It…doesn't seem to be."

"What is supposed to happen?" she asked again as she watched the Strix chase the column of fire again.

"There should be…signs. The reveal is normally very dramatic."

"How so?" Cary was feeling a sort of secondhand embarrassment for the Strix as he chased the fire tornado, a few feet at a time, ignoring the fact that he was obviously being rejected. Or whatever. What did you call it when a column of fire refused to reveal you as a king? Not good for the wannabe king, that was for sure.

"It's different for every reveal," Drei said, sounding a little bemused.

Cary couldn't read the dryad's expression very well, but Drei also looked bemused watching the Strix.

"Is this a… I don't know. A test?"

"The test isn't usually…this. The test is normally letting the fire choose you."

"This is weird, right?"

"Yes, majesty." Drei nodded.

Cary scowled at the honorific. She really wished Drei wouldn't do that.

She opened her mouth to repeat that request, but before any sound got out, the fire tornado shifted positions again, abruptly, moving in a way that wasn't normal for fire and was absolutely a sign that the tornado was magical—if the fact that it wasn't burning anything up wasn't proof enough.

The fire swirled away from the Strix again, moving even

closer to Cary's shield. It paused at the barrier. She could see the way its flames sort of flattened as it came up against her shield.

And then, to her absolute astonished horror, it moved past the barrier. Coming *inside* Cary's protective shield.

Cary panicked. How? How was that possible? Once she was protecting people, the shield stayed up.

But the fire was definitely inside her shield now. And before she could even accept that reality, the flames had moved over the top of…

Deacon.

Oh shit.

He scowled at the fire tornado, which was not burning him thankfully, then looked at her through the flames. His eyes glowed yellow, definitely his shifter right there. But the sort of golden aura he had in Farey also brightened around him. Sparkling with little pinpoints of light. The tan kilt glamoured over his jeans and t-shirt shimmered, fading away so that his jeans were obvious again. The crown on his head, however, did not fade. Neither did the purple cloak and silver brooch at his shoulder.

Deacon glanced down, lifting the edges of the cloak as if it was a real thing he wore now and not just glamour. He looked up at her, mouth open to say something.

And the column of fire exploded.

"Deacon!"

She lunged forward, only to have Drei bring her to a stop with a gentle but firm hand on her shoulder. Cary was momentarily surprised by the feel of the dryad's tree-limb hand and how soft it was. Then she tried to lunge toward Deacon again.

Except…

He wasn't burning or on fire. And the column of flames had coalesced around him again. Only this time, the flames were…

Purple. Solid, unmistakable shades of purple.

And he was once again dressed in a kilt. But this one far exceeded the previous tan version. This was…regalia. The knee-length wool was a deep, rich purple color, the tartan pattern subtly wove of golds and browns. Fur of some kind draped around his waist and over his shoulder, the shoulder pelts a soft downy white. The crown on his head was larger now too, with a center of purple velvet surrounded by diamond and sapphire encrusted gold.

There was also a lot of other jewelry. More than she'd ever seen on Deacon before, even in these glamour guises. All of it with a Celtic flare, knotwork and scrolling patterns with hints of animal shapes popping up. The cloak over his shoulders was still the deep purple, but now the material was edged in white fur. And the brooch at his left shoulder was huge, and gold, the pin through the circular shape the size of a knitting needle, but a lot thicker. There was also no mistaking the leopard heads at the ends where the brooch came together.

Each leopard head boasted jewel encrusted eyes—golden eyes.

Okay. So. Cary let out a long breath. There was no mistaking…

"Deacon's just been revealed a Faery king, hasn't he?" she murmured to no one in particular.

She felt someone move up close to her shoulder. Belle. "The realm has been treating him as royalty since his first trip here. This is just the formal acknowledgement."

"This is so weird," Deacon said from inside the column of purple fire.

"How do you feel? Can you see all the…clothing and jewels and stuff?" She winced at the flames but since they weren't hurting him, she held her place.

"I can see everything. I think I may really be wearing all this stuff now. It's heavy. Especially the crown." He ran a finger over the brooch, frowning. "Do those leopards have my eye color?"

"Yup." He was right. The whole thing was really weird.

"No! It's not possible!"

The Strix. Having a tantrum. Because that's what bad guys did when they didn't get their way.

Cary didn't want to deal with him, but he charged the column of purple flames, and since he was not a good guy and she couldn't tell what he intended on doing, she took a few steps forward to protect Deacon.

And a small bit of the fire jumped from the column onto Cary. She blinked at the little purple flame dancing over her hand, circling around her arm, up to her shoulders. There was warmth, like a small animal was winding around her, but one without claws, because there was no pain in the process. Just a waving streak of fire winding around her neck, her head. It raced around her body a few times as she watched wide-eyed. Then jumped back to the column still encasing Deacon.

"That was weird, right? You all saw that? What the hell was that?"

"You're not hurt?" Deacon asked. He stepped out of the column of fire to check on her, bringing all his regalia with him.

Yup, probably not glamour this time. Although, it still could be. Jaxer's glamour was so good, people could literally see and feel the things he glamoured up and feel like they were real. If Jaxer could do it, an entire realm of magic could probably create illusions that felt real, too.

Once Deacon had moved out of the purple flames, the column collapsed. Leaving nothing behind to show it had even been there.

Deacon and Cary both frowned at the spot where the column had been, then faced each other again.

"This is…" she started.

"Weird," he finished.

"Very."

He ran his hands over her arms and up to her face, cupping her cheeks. "You're okay, though? Not hurt?"

She shrugged. "I'm fine. You?"

"Fine."

"Except you're apparently a king of Faery now."

"Impossible!" the Strix again.

Cary sighed, but didn't glance at the enraged Fae when she said, "He got us out of the cursed lands. This wasn't *that* unexpected." Although, she hadn't actually been precisely *expecting* it either. Mostly because Deacon was a shapeshifter and not Fae and wasn't looking to be acknowledged as a Fae king.

"I'm just going to keep repeating that this is weird," she muttered. "I don't have any other words for it."

She glanced at Belle to ask more questions but spotted Nicneven past her shoulder and paused. The queen had collapsed back onto her throne, her eyes wide. The purple magic that had been wrapped like rope around her forearms and hands had vanished. She looked pale and somehow smaller than she had a few moments ago.

Cary took a moment to study the other queens present. The Welsh queen didn't look much different, although reading anything in the expression of a small, red dragon wasn't Cary's strong suit—even after months of working with a dragon mentor. Ditto Danu who was still in deer form and that form was excellent for hiding facial expressions.

Tatiana and Oberon were staring at Cary and Deacon, but their expressions were closed and the glow around Tatiana was brighter now, making her harder to see.

Elphame had fluttered closer to Cary's shield, which Cary was only sure was still there because she wasn't absorbing magic—and because when the Strix threw himself against it, he bounced back a step. The Seelie queen's expression was…hard to describe. Her green skin seemed a little paler than it had been when she'd first arrived, but she was also glowing more strongly now, the way Tatiana was. Her rainbow wings cast dancing light around the hall as she hovered above the ground, on a level with Cary and Deacon's faces. Her eyes were narrowed, her cupid's bow mouth pinched. But she wasn't frowning. And Cary would have called her expression speculative, except she didn't know Elphame well enough to be certain.

After a moment of fluttering contemplation, Elphame said, "Will you claim the Unseelie court now, majesty? It is yours, should you so wish it."

Wait. What?

"What?" Cary and Deacon asked at the same time. Deacon even took a step back from Elphame.

Belle explained, "The reckoning was…designed to show who should, or rather, *could* lead the Unseelie court. It was the same as happened to me. But I wasn't given the full queen glow-up."

Cary raised her eyebrows at Belle. Was she laughing? This wasn't a funny moment. Deacon couldn't be a Fae king. Or well, obviously, Faery considered him one. But not one that would have a whole court here in Faery! That was…

Well, the Strix had that part right. That was impossible. Even if Belle had served as queen for forty years. Deacon was not getting stuck as a Fae king like that.

"I'm not going to be stuck as a Fae king," he said, echoing Cary's thoughts perfectly. He waved at Nicneven. "The queen is back and sitting on her throne. They do not need a new leader. And I'm a shapeshifter. With my own responsibilities. That are not here. In Faery. Where I'm not a Fae."

The last few points were made with a growl in his voice. Like his leopard was rising. But his eyes weren't glowing so Cary wasn't too worried. About that anyway.

He leaned in closer to his grandmother. "I'm not going to do what you've done. I can't."

She patted his shoulder, holding his gaze. "Aye, I'd never ask it of you either. As ye said, Nicneven is back. It's not the same situation I was put in. You do'na need to take up the position because there's no vacancy to be filled." She gave the Strix a side glance. "If he hadna pushed the reckoning, this wouldna even have happened."

"What was with that little flame that danced over Cary?" Deacon asked. "That was what happened to you, and it got you stuck as a queen here, or queen surrogate."

"It was." Belle gave Cary an assessing look. "Not entirely sure why the flames leapt to Cary without surrounding her. I guess yer not a queen."

"Oh, thank god," Cary said before she could think better of it. Then winced. "Sorry," she said to Deacon. "But honestly, the whole leopard thing is overwhelming me when I think about it too much. I'm not sure I could take that sort of thing with Faery."

"I think the fire was just acknowledging yer relationship with the king," Belle said quietly, frowning. "That you'd be his queen if he chose to take up this court, but that you aren't, technically a queen here."

"Yet," Danu said into her mind.

Cary faced the giant white deer. "Yet?" she mouthed. What the hell did that mean?

Danu didn't deign to answer. Cary scowled at her. Danu let out a delicate snort that might have been a laugh.

Not helpful.

"How could you be a queen with only that acknowledgement, then?" Deacon asked, taking Cary's hand in his.

She wove her fingers with his without conscious thought, still frowning at Danu.

"There was the hole left by Nicneven's absence," Belle said. "I was the best the court could get at the time." She waved at the other gathered queens. "But I was never meant for this forever. I was a stopgap. To prevent disaster."

"I'm not going to be a Fae stopgap either," Cary muttered, as much to Danu as to Belle.

"Ye do'na need to be," Belle said.

"But what about me?" Deacon said, gesturing at the crown on his head. "I'm not taking over the Unseelie court."

"Are you sure?" Elphame asked, fluttering into view again, right up to the edge of Cary's shield. "You would make a strong co-ruler."

Cary narrowed her eyes at the queen's sultry tone and thought, *Hands off, sister. He's mated. He's mine.* But she didn't say that out loud because the surge of jealousy was a tiny bit embarrassing given everything else that was going on.

"A challenge!" the Strix shouted suddenly. "There must be a challenge for the new king to take the throne."

"I. Don't. Want. The. Throne," Deacon said, slowly. Carefully. His voice very deep and growly.

Cary shivered. Not fear. She just liked the way his voice sounded when it went that deep.

"He has spoken," Danu said, aloud this time, for the entire court to hear. Her voice didn't seem to be raised, but it somehow wove around the entire hall so that her pronouncement was clear to everyone. "There will be no king of the Unseelie court. Nicneven has retained her seat." Danu turned huge green deer eyes on Deacon. "You will remain the King of No Land, then, majesty."

Remain? Cary wanted to ask aloud, but Danu didn't pause long enough to give her an opening to.

"And all in Faery shall know the King of No Land."

A cheer went up suddenly around the Great Hall. So suddenly, Cary jumped and took a step closer to Deacon. He squeezed her hand and pulled her close at the exact same moment. Standing sort of half back-to-back, they slowly turned in a circle as the hall cheered for the King of No Land.

Weird. It was the only word. Just…weird.

Nicneven rose from her throne again and the cheers died down. Elphame turned to face the Unseelie queen, fluttering closer to her now.

"I will brook no challenges to my court," Nicneven said. "I am the Unseelie queen. And all mine will bow before me."

The Unseelie Fae Cary was protecting all dropped to their knees or into deep bows instantly, without any hesitance.

Which was probably the best possible thing that could have happened this entire time. Because Nicneven straightened at the sign of felty, her presence growing again. The dark purple ropes of magic circled her forearms and hands once more, but she didn't raise her arms to cast that magic. Just looked regally at her subjects, with a small approving smile on her face.

Okay. Cary whispered to Belle, "Does this mean they're… forgiven or whatever, and she won't send them back to the cursed lands or try to kill them?"

Belle nodded. "She needs them now. With challenges to her throne, and a new king revealed, she canna afford to banish her entire court anymore. By showing her felty in this moment, they're also allowing her to…save face. She willna need to fight a challenge if the court is with her and Deacon doesn't want her throne."

"So…we're good here? Everything is fixed and okay? We can go knowing the Unseelie court will be fine?"

If so, that was…

Well, she wasn't sure easy was the word. Getting stuck in the cursed lands and currently being surrounded by all these Fae queens with their weird tempers and mercurial moods wasn't exactly *easy*. But it would be good to get out of Faery without Deacon being forced into a fight and without any of them dying.

That'd be really super extra good getting out without anyone dying.

"There's one more thing we must attend to today," Elphame said, her light voice a cold breeze over the crowd. "The usurper." Her gaze turned to Belle. "The one who tried to take the Unseelie court from its rightful ruler. That cannot be allowed."

Cary stepped in front of Belle before Elphame had even finished speaking.

Afraid she'd spoken too soon thinking they could just leave without anyone dying.

The tension in the Great Hall ratcheted right back up again with Elphame's pronouncement. All those Fae behind Cary who'd begun to relax and move back from crowding her moved in a little closer again. Since Elphame was really just threatening Belle, the move struck Cary as a sort of solidarity with their former acting-queen rather than a move to protect themselves. She liked that.

She still intended on protecting everyone. But it was nice to know more than Deacon had her back in that moment.

The Strix strode forward from his place too close to Nicneven's throne, moving past a fluttering Elphame where she hovered almost level with a sitting Nicneven, not quite next to her, but close—a demonstration to all in the Great Hall that they were both still co-rulers of the Scottish court. The Strix had been so thoroughly thwarted in his efforts to take Nicneven's throne, he looked panicked. He marched right up to the edge of Cary's shield.

"Hand her over for judgment," he snarled at Cary.

Yeah, he didn't reminder her even a little bit of David Bowie's Jareth anymore—thankfully! Now when she looked at him, all she saw was an asshole.

"No," she said, staring him right in his beady black eyes.

"And you'll need to get out of my mate's face," Deacon said. "Now."

The Strix snarled at Deacon. "You and I will meet again. False king."

"False?" Cary snorted. "Tell that to the magic fire tornado you called. But whether Deacon is a weird hybrid Fae-shifter king or not has nothing to do with anything. You can't have Belle."

"Weird?" Deacon murmured against her ear.

"Tell me you don't think this is all weird without choking on that lie?"

He grunted but didn't answer. And Cary thought, *mmm huh.*

"Elphame, queen of the Seelie, has spoken," the Strix snarled. "Belle must be brought forward for justice. She usurped Nicneven's throne."

"Pot. Kettle. Black." Cary was almost certain the Strix would not know the old saying. It was something Cary's dad loved to say so she'd picked it up. But she doubted the Strix had spent enough time in human society to *get* it.

Nicneven's mouth twitched from her position on the throne. But it was the only movement she made, and if the twitch had been the start of a smile or smirk, it never formed.

The Strix frowned at Cary, proving he hadn't gotten her reference, and opened his mouth, but snapped it shut when the door to the Great Hall banged open hard. The echo bounced off the high ceiling, trembling through the gathered Fae.

With the door open, a fresh wash of pine and heather-scented air moved through the hall, the breeze cooling a room Cary hadn't noticed had gotten pretty stuffy with all the bodies. She turned to see what fresh hell had walked into the giant building, but with all the various Fae courts in the way, she could barely see the top of the door…a very very long way away.

The way space worked in this place was so disorienting. Time too. She felt like they'd been in Faery for a few hours—and she had managed to be here this long without absorbing any magic which was a fucking miracle thanks to always having someone to protect!—but there was no telling how much time was passing in her realm.

She really hoped her mother hadn't been trying to call. She'd freak out if she couldn't reach Cary all the way in Scotland. Or Marianne—who would also freak out but also would only be calling at an unplanned time if there was an emergency. What if something was wrong with the dogs? Shit.

The momentary panic about things outside Faery passed quickly, though, as she watched the mass of Fae standing between the front of the hall and the door started to move quickly aside, parting way to allow…someone through.

Or, as it turned out, someones. A whole phalanx of someones.

A whole phalanx of trolls.

Well, probably only about six trolls, Cary realized as they got closer. But six was enough. The creatures were so huge, six might as well have been a whole platoon.

The trolls marched right past Cary and her charges, including Belle. Which surprised Cary because Wee Doug was leading the group. He didn't even glance at Belle or Cary when he marched by, though he did pause to give Danu a brief head nod. The deer-goddess nodded back. And if a deer could preen, Danu preened.

"I do not preen," Danu said in Cary's head.

Cary rolled her eyes mentally, wondering if Danu would pick that up, too.

The six trolls marched up to the throne, to face Nicneven and

Elphame. The sounds of their passing almost as loud and echoing as the Great Hall door banging open. Rock on rock, rolling across the ground like an earthquake. The floor even shook a little as they passed.

Wide as three Deacon's and taller than most of the beings in the room by at last a foot, the trolls were an impressive sight as they formed up in front of the queens. And then, sharply, turned to face the crowds.

That was some precision military coordination. Little spooky, too.

Cary very much wanted to ask what Wee Doug and the others were doing there. But she also really didn't want to be the first one to break the silence that had descended around the Great Hall. The tension wrapped around her muscles, holding tight.

The Strix looked at the gathered trolls, at the wall of rocky muscle they formed in front of the Scottish queens, and smirked. Tatiana's mildly insane, high-pitched giggle wove through the silent Fae. Not helping. Tatiana amused was bad for everyone here. The Strix being happy about the trolls' appearance was also not good.

Nicneven stood from her throne, and Elphame fluttered higher so the two queens' heads were level.

"Bring the usurper forward," they said in unison, their completely different voices blending together into a single voice. And not just they matched tones and styles and cadence and all that. Their voices literally came out sounding like only a single person was speaking.

Cary found that fascinating in the split second it took her to realize what they'd said.

Then she moved farther in front of Belle.

The trolls might have served Belle faithfully, but that didn't mean they would—or even could—defy the true Scottish queens.

Two of the six detached from the line and moved forward, the hall echoing with the sounds of their big rock feet hitting the solid stone floor. Wee Doug was one of the two. Cary had never seen the other standing stone trolls in their troll form, but she had to assume all six were from that circle.

Wee Doug and the other paused a foot away from Cary's barrier, and the Strix started to laugh again. His owl circled overhead while his two wolves had moved back to his side and were snarling at the trolls.

"No one may sit on the throne who does not belong there," the Strix snarled at Belle. "You must face justice."

Wee Doug moved then, a lot faster than a being that size, made of rocks, really should move. Cary stepped directly between him and Belle in the same instant, determined to protect her.

And Wee Doug scooped the Strix up off the ground before anyone could so much as gasp.

With the Strix firmly in his grip, his arms wrapped around the Strix like he was carrying an oversized cat in front of him, Wee Doug and the other troll marched smartly back to the throne.

It took a moment for even the Strix to figure out what had happened. Like the big rocky arms of a troll wrapped around him didn't mean what they really meant. But when he was set down before Nicneven and Elphame, the Strix finally recognized what was happening.

And so did everyone else in the hall.

A low chanting chorus of "Usurper, usurper, usurper…" Started rising through the open space. Even some of the Unseelie Fae took up the chant. Cary turned a questioning look on Belle, who shrugged. Then looked past her charges to Danu. Who didn't deign to comment or even look at Cary.

Everyone was staring at the Scottish queens and the Strix standing before them.

"I did nothing, majesties," he shouted. "I tried to save your thrones from the shifters. I did nothing wrong."

"The entire hall just watched you try to claim a kingship and the Unseelie throne," Nicneven and Elphame said in that single voice. "There are many witnesses to your crime."

"I didn't steal the throne! The shifter *did*. She sat there for years pretending to be the queen of the Unseelie court. How can you not punish her?"

"Her punishment was meted out and has been served," the queens said. "You will be punished too."

"Shit," Cary said. "I'm not supposed to save or protect him, am I? Cause I don't want to. But I also can't stand by and let them just…kill him or something."

"They willna," Belle said. "Banishment or some other punishment. That'll feel worse to him. He should have prostrated himself when brought forward. The punishment will be worse for not showing the proper deference."

"Did you do that before getting sent to the cursed lands?" Cary asked.

"No. Which is why I know he should do it now."

The gathered Fae stopped chanting, letting the hall fall silent again. Except for the occasional giggle from Tatiana—what the hell was wrong with her? Was she drunk?—no one spoke except the Strix, who pled his case.

Apparently, the queens weren't having it.

The six trolls formed up in a circle around the Strix. A tight circle that gave him no room to escape or run. Not that he seemed to have that sort of self-preservation instinct. He tried to push through the trolls to reach the queens.

"I am being wronged! The shifter should be punished! She sat on the throne!"

The trolls tightened their circle and then…transformed.

Cary had sort of seen Wee Doug do this. In the dark. When she'd been nervous and worried. She was still nervous and worried, but there was enough light in the Great Hall to see the trolls clearly.

And to watch them turn into a small, tight circle of standing stones was pretty amazing.

"No!" the Strix shouted. "No!"

"Your animal familiars are free to leave or to join you," the queens said, "as they deem appropriate. We will not bind them. You, however, Strix, shall be banished from this court. To wander the shadows between courts. If a ruler takes pity on you, we will not prevent you finding another home. But as your crime is attempting to steal a throne, I would not count on the benevolence of another ruler. This punishment will last for one hundred years and one day. You may petition for a return to court at that time."

Since Cary had been fearing some sort of beheading—or something along those lines—the hundred years banishment with a chance to return seemed a pretty mild punishment. A hundred years wasn't all that long to an immortal being. It wasn't unnoticeably short. But it could have been a lot worse.

The Strix got off easy.

Cary was also happy to hear the animals weren't being punished just because of the company they kept. That would have struck her as very unfair. The *owl* hadn't tried to claim a kingship.

"I will not be set aside so easily! Not after all I have done for this court." The Strix spun around inside the circle of standing stones.

The stones made some sort of noise that sounded like a hum, but Cary felt it more than heard it. A vibration that moved through the soles of her feet and up through her bones.

The Strix raised his hands like he might hit one of the trolls, then made a noise that sounded remarkably like his owl's screech, but so loud it made Cary cover her ears.

By the time she dropped her hands from her ears, the Strix was gone. The area inside the circle empty. The standing stones grew and transformed back into six distinct trolls. And the trolls moved to stand in a row in front of Nicneven and Elphame again. A solid barrier between the Scottish queens and the rest of the room.

Wee Doug finally glanced at Cary. His deadpan stare broken only by a wink so quick she might have imagined it. Then he looked forward again, an intractable soldier standing guard.

The owl swooped low over the crowd and then spiraled up to the ceiling and…disappeared through the roof. Just flew right through it and kept going like the roof had never been there and was just an illusion. Which, Cary realized, it might actually be given where they were. The Strix's two wolves did the same thing through a side wall, looping off into the forest that surrounded the Great Hall without paying any attention to the gathered crowds.

Cary half wondered if they were going to join the Strix in exile or if they'd just decided to return to the woods for good. Be interesting to find out. Be even more interesting to find out what had happened to the Strix.

"What just happened?" she asked Belle.

"The trolls sent him into banishment. He'll wander for a hundred years. While he *might* find refuge in another court, that's unlikely given he was banished for attempting to usurp a throne. Most rulers will frown on that and no' want him in their court."

"How will they know why he was banished? He's not going to tell them."

Belle shrugged. "Fae gossip. It'll get about. That's why everyone in Faery knows who you are now."

Ah. And also *ahhh*! She hated being Fae famous. It felt…dangerous.

"What now?" she whispered to Belle, a little afraid of the answer.

"Now… Now I go home for a well-earned rest, Nicneven resumes her throne, thank the goddess, and I resume being solely a shapeshifter for the first time in forty years." She blinked. "Not sure I remember how." She glanced at Deacon. "You've a choice you'll have to make eventually, but as the King of No Land, you've no court to worry about. A technicality, the title. I'd say they'll be happy to let you ignore it. Given…" Belle glanced at Cary, her look speculative. "Given everything else in your life."

"Me. You're talking about me. They don't want me here." Cary couldn't agree with that any more if she tried. She didn't want to be there either.

"It would be better for everyone if you spent as little time as possible inside Faery," Danu said into her head at the same time as Belle said, "Aye. There's a lot of…mixed feelings here about you."

"I don't have mixed feelings," Tatiana put in. "I would still claim her."

"No," Cary and Deacon said at the same time.

And to Cary's surprise, Danu said, "No." The deer turned her green-eyed gaze on Deacon. "She has already been claimed."

"She has," Deacon said. And for reasons Cary couldn't precisely pinpoint but that seemed like they might have something to do with the reckoning thing that had happened earlier, his comment sounded as commanding and…final, as anything the other queens had said that day.

"You'll have to keep her," Oberon said, pulling Tatiana to his side. "My queen wants her." He glanced at Cary. "I would have her, too."

The first words he'd spoken this entire time, and they were a challenge to Deacon. What an ass.

Cary looked Oberon dead in the eyes and said, "That was creepy. No. You've caused enough trouble already." She was thinking of the break between Jaxer and Eriana, which Oberon had had a hand in.

His chuckle was not the response she'd been expecting. "Little human woman. We shall see."

"Little?" She scoffed. She was *not* a little woman. Even if the human part was mostly right.

Mostly. But after all the magic and demon gods and death stuff…even that wasn't entirely true anymore either.

As if on cue, her skin started to tingle. Just a little. But it was there at the edge of her awareness. Shit. The danger here had waned enough that her shield wasn't keeping all the magic out anymore. Damn. She'd managed hours here under threat just fine. *Now* the shield decided she didn't need it as much.

"Raise it yerself," Wee Doug said from his position in front of the queens.

She blinked. Had Wee Doug just read her mind?

"He can see your shield," Danu murmured in her head. "Even if the rest of us cannot."

The fact that the rest of them couldn't see the shield any more than she could was an interesting revelation. Almost as interesting as the fact that a troll *could*.

She focused on her shield, on the very thing she'd been practicing with Wee Doug before this sojourn into Faery. Focused on seeing the shield rise, on setting it into place around her and Deacon and Belle—she had to assume the Scottish Fae were safe now since the shield had started to ebb—focused on mentally seeing it flow back into place.

The tingling on her skin eased and then stopped.

"Good job," Wee Doug said.

Cary grinned. And preened. Unlike Danu, she did preen.

Danu chuckled in her head.

"Think that's our cue to leave," she said to Deacon and Belle. "How do we get out of here?"

"We can send you home," Elphame and Nicneven said in that voice that was a single voice. "It would be our pleasure."

"No!" Belle took a step forward.

Cary had just enough time for her adrenaline to spike.

And then the court around them dissolved and darkness closed around her hard and fast.

$\mathcal{C}$ary held perfectly still as the darkness slowly receded. Or, well, it didn't precisely recede. It was more that enough light rose she could see in the darkness. She blinked hard a few times and looked around, her shoulders relaxing when she spotted Deacon and Belle with her.

Her moment of relaxation did not last long, however.

Around them rose a towering ruin of dark stone. A cold breeze rushed through the open walls, bringing the smell of heather and damp soil and salty ocean. The sound of waves cresting against rocks. And a trail of beautiful stars overhead. The Milky Way.

So...not likely to be Faery. But definitely not the woods outside Belle's cottage.

Where the hell where they?

"Where the hell are we?" she asked Belle.

Belle sighed, hands on her hips, and shook her head. "Dunnottar Castle. All the way up the coast."

"How far from your cottage?"

"More than a hundred miles," Belle said with another sigh.

"We're closer to Aberdeen. But still not within walking distance. At least not in this form and not with you." She cursed under her breath. "A parting shot from Nicneven and Elphame. I held their bloody court together and this is how they treat me?"

She shouted this last up at the air, as if yelling at the queens.

Cary couldn't really blame her. Honestly, Belle deserved a reward not a punishment for the years she'd put in as queen of the Unseelie court. But the High Fae were difficult and a real pain in the ass.

Belle snarled but glanced around and said, "At least they dinna drop us into the well. That's something."

Cary looked in the direction Belle was looking. A big ring of tightly packed stones in the middle of the grassy courtyard, circled by a small metal fence which Cary assumed was to keep tourists away. And inside the ring, dark water glistened in the faint light from the stars. Cary couldn't really see the water very good, but assumed Belle could see it just fine with her super shifter vision.

Getting dropped into that well didn't sound fun. She supposed Belle was right that this could have been worse.

But a hundred miles away from home was not good.

"What now?" She turned to Deacon. He was no longer wearing the regal kilt and cape and Celtic brooch he'd had on in Faery. And when she glanced down, Cary couldn't see any of the glamour that had dressed her anymore either.

But to her surprise, the crown that had appeared on Deacon's head during the reckoning was still there.

She gestured to it. "That's real?"

Belle looked around from scowling at the castle ruins and raised her brows. "Huh. Dinna expect that to follow us out of Faery. It will appear most of the time when you go into Faery now, by the way. Not sure why ye have it still."

Deacon reached up and pulled the crown off, turning it over in his hands and scowling at it. "I have enough responsibilities already," he said. "This better not add to them."

Belle's expression was hard to read in that moment. "They gave you No Land. Ye should be just fine."

Belle sounded less certain now than she had in Faery.

But for the moment at least, they were out of Faery. Belle had finally been released from her responsibilities in the Unseelie court. And no one had died.

Good night actually.

"Now what?" she asked again. "How do we get home?"

"Yer cellphone battery still charged?" Belle asked.

Cary pulled her phone from one of the magic pockets in her leather jacket, and smiled at the battery charge. "Seventy-five percent will do. How long were we in Faery?"

Last time she'd gone in and out had taken a month and this felt like she'd been in a lot longer than that. She loved that her phone battery hadn't died. But she dreaded any messages that would come up. The fact that her phone hadn't immediately erupted with a worried series of texts and voicemails was probably a good sign, though. Maybe, despite how it felt, they hadn't been in Faery as long as she'd feared.

She checked the date herself since she was the one holding a phone and was, despite everything, surprised to see, "It's only been two days. We really weren't in there very long."

Her stomach growled and she winced even as Deacon smiled one of his slow, sexy grins, the ones that made her a little weak-kneed. "Long enough to get hungry I guess," she muttered, and rolled her eyes when Deacon pulled her close with a casual arm over her shoulders.

"If you do'na mind me using yer phone, I'll call Fiona. She'll get a car up here to us sharpish. I'd rather not travel back through Faery to get home."

"No," Cary and Deacon said at the same time.

"No more Faery," Deacon said.

"I'm not going in there again unless I have to," Cary said.

Belle snorted. "I'll not argue with that." She took Cary's phone and made her call.

Cary folded herself against Deacon, letting his naturally high body heat warm her up as the ocean wind picked up and frosted the interior of the ruins. They had a long night ahead of them, waiting and then driving back to Belle's place.

But Cary could handle a little cold and a long drive if it meant they were all safe.

And at least she got to see another castle.

CARY FINALLY GOT TO SEE EDINBURGH CASTLE, TOO.

After another week at Belle's place, with Deacon practicing his magic—which hadn't seemed to get better or worse after his time in Faery, something Cary hoped was a good sign—he declared he needed a break and he took Cary to Edinburgh for a long weekend.

They booked a fancy hotel in the center of the city and spent the entire weekend touristing.

Edinburgh Castle had been worth the wait.

And Cary, despite always declaring she wouldn't do one, let Deacon talk her into a walking ghost tour of the city. That had also been fun. The history was fascinating, the storytelling chops of the guide were excellent, and the ghosts were, for the most part, pretend. Those were her kinds of ghosts.

In a pub after the tour, exhausted, her sore feet wanting nothing more than a soak in a hot bathtub and a long night's sleep, she and Deacon sat around their pints, pretending to watch the highlights of some soccer game that had gone on that day. Well, she was pretending. Deacon seemed genuinely interested.

"It was Celtic versus Rangers," he told her. "Big rivals up here. Always a big deal when they play."

"Cool," she said sleepily and drank the rest of her Guinness.

The pub was one of those lovely, dark places with lots of dark wood, sticky round tables, and a bar the full length of one side of the place. Behind the bar, mirrors back the alcohol wracks, but the beer taps were the most active. The place had a nice hoppy smell from all the beer, and despite the late hour, they were still serving some pub food. The plate of French fries the table next to them ordered had Cary's stomach wondering if she was hungry.

The noise level in the pub was that rumble of sound that made talking possible, but no one at the next table stood a chance of overhearing anyone. She could smell their French fries, but couldn't hear what they were talking about. Which was good if she and Deacon wanted to talk, but Cary was nosey and kind of wanted to know what her French fry eating neighbors were chatting about. The sound was up on the TVs over the bar, and there was some yelling over goals and fouls and whatnot. There was also Celtic music playing quieter in the background, but Cary had a feeling the music was for the tourists more than the locals.

When their second round was delivered, Deacon turned away from the TV over the bar and took hold of one of her hands across the dark wood table, playing with her fingers.

"Oh oh," she said. "Last time you had that expression on your face, we ended up in Scotland. Not that I'm complaining about the Scotland part. But the reason we're here was a little worrying at the time."

"I'm feeling better about the magic now. It'll take more time, of course. Regular training. But I think another two weeks here, and I'll be ready to go home. My mother can help with the other things I need to learn."

"Oh. Okay. That's great. I love it here and all, but I miss the dogs."

"Video chat didn't make you feel better?" he asked with a faint smile.

She rolled her eyes. Not long after they'd gotten back from Faery, she'd arranged a video chat with Marianne so she could see the dogs. And Marianne of course. And catch up on all the gossip back home.

"It did help," she said. "But I still miss my little pack. And home. Mostly."

She'd also had a couple of long phone calls with her mother—who was still worried about her sister's latest pregnancy. Cary had had to promise to be home for Christmas because they'd decided to do a whole family gathering as Valorie's husband had some time off and his parents didn't do much about Hanukkah. But because it was close enough to Christmas that year to ensure a long and fun celebration for the kids, Cary's mom had decided they'd be doing a whole thing, all of them together.

Cary hadn't broken the news to Deacon yet—his presence was expected, so if Cary went, he had to go too—and she still thought Valorie might cancel it all, claiming she was too far along in her pregnancy at that stage. She wouldn't be, she'd still be able to fly until the middle of January. But since Cary's mom and sister were having *conversations* about this fourth pregnancy and what it meant for Valorie's marriage, Valorie might still back out.

At any rate, there was family stuff Cary had to face when she got back—which made staying in Scotland really appealing. But only if she could bring her dogs over. And her best friends.

Since she couldn't do that, she figured she'd be ready to go in another two weeks.

"The Nags will expect you back to work soon," Deacon said. He rubbed his thumb over her fingers, his attention mostly on her hand as he spoke.

"Yeah." She sighed. Then grinned. "But I feel better able for it now. I can raise that shield like nobody's business."

She'd continued practicing with Wee Doug while Deacon worked on his magic, and that had helped a *lot*. She actually felt pretty confident she could raise the shield fast in times of stress. Hopefully. Outside of Faery, there hadn't been any other required emergencies to drive her practice. Still. She was feeling pretty good about her skills now.

"And," she continued, "thanks to being out of town for so long, I'm willing to bet most of the people who hate me have stopped thinking about me." She was mostly thinking of the vampires because her relationship to them and the Master of Portland was still…complicated.

"Vampires have longer memories than a month," Deacon pointed out.

"But there's a truce! And James has bigger things to worry about. And all the demon stuff is settled. At least with Holland. And the wizard who wanted me dead is dead. And Sheldon seems to be handling all the reparations work your mother hands out to him well. I doubt he'll try to kill either one of us again. So…yeah. Should be a good time for a fresh Protector start. Maybe I'll even get to meet more Protectors finally."

She was excited about that. She'd only met one, and that was the result of unique circumstances. She really wanted to meet and talk with other Protectors. See how all this worked for them.

Deacon fell silent, his thumb still caressing over her fingers on the hand he held. She took a long sip of her Guinness, waiting him out. Her foot had started to bounce under the table, though, by the time he finally started talking again—despite her sore feet.

"I've been thinking about our future," he said quietly. "Our technical anniversary coming up at Halloween."

"Oh yeah! We'll still be here. Do they do cool stuff in Scotland for Halloween? I bet they do. Can we do some of it?"

He grinned at her enthusiasm, and the grin made her stomach tumble around in that giddy way that still sometimes surprised her.

"We can look into it, yes."

"Yay!" She squeezed his hand. "Thanks. I almost forgot about Halloween. I love how you call it our 'technical' anniversary."

"It was the night we met. And I realized you were my mate."

"And I had to rescue you from a deranged wizard and had my ribs broken in the process. Good night all around."

His mouth flattened into something like a scowl but it didn't last long against her grin. He relented and said, "I'm not sure I want to count Halloween as our real anniversary because of the broken ribs part."

"Na, I think that's a perfect day to mark our anniversary. True, I wasn't buying into the whole mate thing at that point. But still. You have to admit, our first introduction to each other was pretty epic and is a moment we should celebrate."

"Glad you think so now. I wasn't sure you would for a while there."

"Ha! I wasn't sure I would either. Lucky for you, you turned out to be wonderful, and I couldn't help falling head over heels in love with you."

His smile softened and his grip on her hand tightened. "Glad you think so," he murmured, just loud enough to be heard over the music and TV noise. "And very lucky indeed."

She leaned across the table to give him a light kiss because she couldn't resist that soft smile. Or him really. She never could resist him. Even when she'd thought she might want to try. That had been a ridiculous idea on her part anyway. Resist Deacon? Yeah, no. That was never going to happen.

When she settled back into her seat, he continued to rub his thumb over her fingers, his attention once again on the table and a little crease between his brows.

"What's wrong?" she asked. "You started this conversation with that expression. I'm not sure I like that expression."

After a moment, he pulled in a long, deep breath and looked around the pub. Then shook his head abruptly and blinked a few times. Like he was shaking off his mood. When he faced her again, he was all smiles and casual shrugs.

"Never mind. It's nothing. It can wait. You said you had something to tell me earlier. What's that?"

"Ah. Yes. That." She was still insanely curious what he'd been trying to tell her, but they had another night in Edinburgh and another two weeks in Scotland. She was sure he'd open up about what was worrying him eventually. He usually did without her having to nag too much.

While he continued rubbing his thumb over her fingers, she said, "I figure I'd better warn you and now that you're two pints in and tired from our tour, this seems like a good time."

His shoulders tightened. "Warn me about what?"

"So. My mother wants to do a whole family Christmas thing. With Valerie and her family and…and all of us. She's even talking about inviting your parents down."

Deacon blinked. "Wait, what?"

"Unless Valerie decides to cancel, it looks like we're going to need to spend a week or so with my entire family at Christmas. And maybe yours too. And…" She tightened her hold on his hand. "There is going to be drama."

Deacon's eyes widened and he glanced back at the bar as he

rubbed his free hand over the back of his neck. "Family drama and *both* our families in the same place?"

"Uh huh," she said with a resigned sigh.

He met her gaze again, only this time he looked well and truly trapped. "We have to?"

"We have to."

Deacon let out a loud, hard breath. "Oh boy."

She couldn't have said it better herself.

THANK YOU

Thank you for reading THE TROUBLE WITH SHIFTERS AND FAE COURTS! I hope you enjoyed this continuing adventure of Cary Redmond and Deacon Jones. As you can tell, there's more to come. Taking the two of them down this new direction proved really fun, so I will be writing more of their books.

There is also all kinds of background gossip I haven't had a chance to put on the page yet! Like what's going on with this secret Lucy is keeping? Will Brandon and Marianne ever get together? What's happening with Angie? I have to keep writing. LOL

Also, for those of you wondering what Deacon was on about in that ending…find me. We'll talk.

I need to add a special thank you here. This book got an additional boost from some super wonderful Kickstarter backers, who helped support bringing book 8 to the public. I can't thank all of you enough for your support and enthusiasm for this project! Thank you! You have my eternal gratitude.

If you'd like to know more about my books or keep up on

current releases and news, please consider joining my author newsletter. New subscribers also receive two free stories that aren't available anywhere else—one Cary Redmond novella, and one short story in my Tiger Shifters, paranormal romance series. You can also stop by my fan store, KatSimonsBooks, for all the latest news as well as books and merchandise and all kinds of book related fun!

For those who'd prefer, you can always visit my website for updates, follow my author page at BookBub or your favorite vendor, or find me on social media—I'm mostly on Instagram, though there, I mainly talk about baking experiments, my morning walks in our local cemetery, and sports. Books are mentioned occasionally.

Thanks again for reading The Trouble with Shifters and Fae Courts!

~Kat

Don't miss the latest Kat Simons
news, updates, excerpts, cover reveals, and more!
All new subscribers get two newsletter exclusive stories.

Join Now!
https://bit.ly/KatSimonsNewsletter

BOOKS BY KAT SIMONS

The Cary Redmond Series

* The Trouble Black Cats and Demons * The Trouble with Ghouls and Serial Killers * The Trouble with Leopard Queens and Shifter Wars * The Trouble with Baby Gods and Vampires * The Trouble with Magic and Faery Curses * The Trouble with Wizards and Old Enemies * The Trouble with Death and Demon Gods * The Trouble with Shifters and Fae Courts

The Cary Redmond Series Box Set Books 1-3

Cary Redmond Short Stories

* When Cary Met Jaxer * When Cary Met Pickles * When Cary Met Marianne * When Cary Met Lucy * When Cary Met Angie * Cary and Deacon (Try to) Go on a Date * Date Night Take Two * Third Date's the Charm * Cary vs the Goblin King * Dinner with the Joneses * Cary and the Cursed Jack-O'-Lantern * Cary and the Demon Witch * Cary Goes to Hawaii * Cary Holidays * Cary and Dragons and Goblins * Cary's Galentine's Day * Cary at the Haunt and Howl * Cary's Leprechaun Troubles * Cary's Beltane Night Out

When Cary Met the Good Guys (Collection 1)

Dates, Dinners, and Other Disasters (Collection 2)

Witches and Weavers and Ghosts, Oh Boy (Collection 3)

A Very Cary Holiday (Collection 4)

Romancing the Leopard: A Tiger Shifters-Cary Redmond Crossover Novel

Tiger Shifters Series

* Once Upon a Tiger * Along Came a Tiger * Here There Be Tigers *
Her Tiger To Take * To Tempt a Tiger * Down Will Come Tiger * To
Catch a Tiger * What a Tiger Wants * Taming Her Tiger

Tiger Shifters Series Vol 1 (Books 1 - 3)

Tiger Shifters Series Vol 2 (Books 4 - 6)

Seven Families Series

Wolf Family

Darkness in Stone

Redemption in Stone

Fated in Stone

Wolf in Stone: A Seven Families Box Set, Books 1-3

Demon Witch Series

Howling Dreadful

Moonlit Strange

Bone Lantern Witch

Spiderweb Witch

Storm Shadow Witch

Joan of Kerry Series

Joan of Kerry: Joan and the Abhartach

Joan and the Leprechaun

Joan and the Kraken

Joan and the Selkie

Dragon Thief Series

Dragon Thief

The Chicago Job

The Poisons Book Job

The Vault Job

The Femme Fatale Job

The Scavenger Job

The Crown of Kingship Job

Destiny Cats

Destiny Through the Cats Eyes

Hourglass Through the Cats Eyes

Haunts and Howls Collections

Haunts and Howls and Guardian Spells

Haunts and Howls Where Demons Dwell

Haunts and Howls and Jesters Bells

*Tombstone Wizard * The Unshattered Sword * Going Out of Business: Everything's for Sale * Anger Management * Demonic Dates * Friday's Curious Shop * The Museum of Small Art's Everyman * Burning Inside a Stone Circle * Bored Questless

MORE BOOKS BY KAT SIMONS

Pick Your Genre Collections

Who Steals a Dragon

Contemporary Romances

Designed for You

Poinsettias and Possibilities

Captured by You

Coming Soon in 2024

Mystery and Thrillers

Ross and O'Neill Adventures

Galileo's Pendulum

Percy James Mysteries

Movies May Murder

Cookies Can't Crime

Diamonds Do Damage

Vacation Deadly: A Thriller Vacation Collection

Coming Soon in 2024

ABOUT THE AUTHOR

Kat Simons earned her Ph.D. in animal behavior, working with animals as diverse as dolphins and deer. She brought her experience and knowledge of biology to her paranormal romance and urban fantasy fiction, where she delights in taking nature and turning it on its ear. She writes urban fantasy, contemporary fantasy, and paranormal romance in series which combine action adventure, the otherworldly, and a frequent dose of sexy romance.

The newest book in her bestselling romantic urban fantasy series about Protector Cary Redmond, The Trouble with Shifters and Faery Courts, sees a new direction for the intrepid Protector, her sexy leopard shifter mate, and the entire crew. Kat also launched a new novella length paranormal romance series that follows the adventures of a magical thief and the dragon shifter prince she just can't seem to shake—and really doesn't want to. The first six stories of the Dragon Thief series release throughout 2024, beginning in February with Dragon Thief.

For something a little different, Kat also publishes fantasy, science fiction, and the occasional hockey romance under the name Isabo Kelly (https://www.isabokelly.com).

After traveling the world, living in places like Hawaii, Germany, and Ireland, Kat now lives in New York City with her family and a library's worth of books.

For more on Kat and her future books

Website: https://www.katsimons.com/
Newsletter: https://bit.ly/KatSimonsNewsletter

KatSimonsBooks

https://tanddpublishingbookstore.com/

Social Media

Facebook Page: https://www.facebook.com/KatSimonsAuthor
BookBub: https://www.bookbub.com/authors/kat-simons
Instagram: https://www.instagram.com/isabokelly/
Bluesky: https://bsky.app/profile/katsimons.bsky.social